Pineapple TRIVIA Night

A Pineapple Port Mystery: Book Eighteen

Amy Vansant

©2023 by Amy Vansant. All rights reserved.
No part of this book may be reproduced in any form, by any means, without the permission of the author. All characters appearing in this work are fictitious. Any resemblance to real persons, living or dead, is purely coincidental.

Vansant Creations, LLC / Amy Vansant
Annapolis, MD
http://www.AmyVansant.com
http://www.PineapplePort.com

Editing/Proofreading by Effrosyni Moschoudi & Meg Barnhart

CHAPTER ONE

The old man seemed happy. *Giddy*, even. Well, as giddy as someone with terminal cancer could be, anyway. Breathing had become a full-time job.

I watched him from the doorway to his bedroom until he noticed me.

"Is everything ready?" he asked from behind his oxygen mask, raising a pale hand to catch my eye. His blue veins shone through his thin skin.

"Almost," I said.

There was one thing left to do.

"Tell me the answers," I said, approaching the bed.

His brow knit. "Hm?"

"Tell me the answers. Tell me how to win."

He laughed—a horrible, sputtering sound.

"Nice try," he said, wiping the spittle from his chin. "I couldn't tell you if I wanted to."

My head cocked.

It wasn't the answer I'd expected.

"What do you mean? It's *your* game."

He nodded. "Yes, and I planned most of it. Heck, it took me *years* to put this together, but I had help, including three lawyers. No *one* person on the planet knows the correct path, and the winner will be required to show their work, so to speak."

He chuckled as I shook my head, no doubt amused by my expression of horror.

"Don't look so surprised," he said. "Believe me, if you'd hosted a game show for as many years as I did, you wouldn't trust anyone either. You'd be shocked to know the things people offered to do for me—to do *to* me—over the years."

He winked, and I fought back my revulsion.

"But, how can someone *win*?" I asked.

His boney shoulders bounced. "The way they're supposed to. They'll play the game and either solve the puzzle or not."

"*Or not?* There has to be a winner, right? Or whoever gets closest?"

He shook his head, sending his oxygen line dancing.

"Nope. If no one wins, it's all going to charity."

Again, my jaw fell.

"How could you do that to your family?"

A rattle snapped in his throat—another attempt at laughter. *He* was having a wonderful time.

"If my family were such wonderful people, I would have doled out the money like a normal dying man."

He leaned toward me and lowered his voice to a whisper. He said something. I couldn't hear him.

"I can't hear you," I said.

He pulled down the oxygen mask with a shaking hand to repeat himself.

"I *said*, between you and me, I'm *hoping* no one wins."

I swallowed.

This wasn't how I'd planned it.

When I gamed the possibilities, I'd never considered he was *this* much of a jerk.

Time for plan B.

"So you can't tell me how to win?"

"Nope."

"Not even if you wanted to?"

He grinned, flashing a lower row of yellowed natural teeth and an upper row of shockingly white implants. With his sunken features, those teeth made him look like a horse.

"Nope. Couldn't tell you if I wanted to," he said.

I sighed.

That answers that.

"Then what good are you?" I asked.

Before he could respond, I whipped the pillow from beneath his head. His gray, speckled head bounced on the mattress beneath it.

"Hey, what's wrong with you?" he snapped, his milky eyes glaring at me.

"Sorry," I said.

I don't know why I said it.

I wasn't.

Adrenaline coursing through my veins, I shoved the pillow against his stupid face.

He struggled, but it was like crushing a sparrow. He had no strength. He clawed at the pillow, the air, my arm—all with yellow nails that needed a clipping. When he stopped struggling, I held the pillow a few moments longer, just to be sure.

When it was over, I turned off his oxygen machine. The room fell quiet but for the ticking of the grandfather clock in the corner. The one with the carved monkies on top.

I had no idea how he'd slept for decades with that thing banging away. Once I won the house, the first thing I'd do is throw that thing out the window.

Done.

I flopped into the cushioned chair beside his bed and took a moment to think. My backup plan needed a *little* more work. I glanced at my watch.

I had time.

My attention drifted to the old man.

What to do with him?

No reason anyone should enter his room, but I couldn't chance it. I couldn't leave him in bed.

I had plenty of strength to hold him down, but I didn't relish dragging him around the house.

My gaze pulled to the large, ornate wardrobe in the corner.

For once, the old man's stupid antiques would come in handy.

I stood and steeled myself before rolling him off the bed. I let him drop to the floor with a thud. Next, I dragged his body to the wardrobe.

He was heavier than he looked, and he smelled *terrible*. I realized he'd soiled himself and took a moment to dry heave.

Careful to avoid the messy bits, I stuffed him into the wardrobe, folding his limbs at awkward angles to make him fit. Mission accomplished, I closed the doors, my breathing heavy.

Whew.

Killing the crazy old bastard hadn't been as difficult as I'd feared. I hid any doubts behind closed doors in my heart—just like the old man's lifeless body in the wardrobe.

His death took a minute. Maybe two. I didn't even break a sweat.

After serving as his nurse for months, there wasn't a man on the planet I wanted dead more than the legendary Xander Flummox.

CHAPTER TWO

Charlotte pulled the darts from the dartboard and handed Declan his three.

They'd been sitting in the new Charlock Holmes Detective Agency office, staring at each other. Work had dried up. That was the problem with being a detective—it wasn't like being a doctor or a lawyer. People didn't *have* to hire a detective—usually, they just either did or they didn't.

Everything felt extra slow because Declan had decided to start the agency with her after his pawn shop burned down. Working with him seemed terrific and *fair* since one of her cases caused the fire.

She'd accidentally destroyed his entire career.

Whoops.

Together, they'd fixed up the little office outside her community. She couldn't be more excited to work with her fiancé—but she also felt a lot of pressure to make it work for both of them.

Then work dried up.

Wasn't that the way things always worked?

Not only did no one need a private detective, Sheriff Frank hadn't even asked them to help with an interesting local murder like he sometimes did.

Nobody was murdering *anyone*.

Pfft.

She and Declan had decided to discuss developing a marketing plan, but after ten minutes of hemming, hawing, and staring at each other, they agreed the mindless tossing of sharp objects would make it easier to think.

Luckily, their little office had a dart board.

It only felt a *little* unprofessional to play darts at work if they talked about marketing *while* they played.

"It's good we're getting in some practice since we'll have to start hustling darts for money if business doesn't pick up soon," said Declan, stepping to the line they'd taped on the floor to throw a dart.

The closest to the bullseye would go first for the next game. He hit an inch to the left of the mark.

Good. Not *great*.

Charlotte stepped up and hit the outer ring of the bullseye.

She gave a little whoop of happiness before she could stop herself.

"*Ha.* If I keep playing lights-out like this, we might need to add other games to the office so you don't get a complex."

He scoffed. "Easy, killer. You've beaten me *once* today."

"Sure, but we've only played once, so I'm beating you *one hundred percent.*"

He chuckled. "Look at you, doing *math.*"

She hated math.

She put her hand to her head.

"I know. It *hurt.*"

The entry bell on the office door rang, and they turned, darts in hand. They'd salvaged the door ringer from Declan's pawnshop. Instead of the bright tinkling sound it used to chime when people entered his shop, it had more of a sad *clatter.*

Apropos.

Charlotte glanced at it.

"We might need to take that down," she mumbled.

The new office on the outskirts of the Pineapple Port retirement community was one room of six hundred square feet. They didn't need a bell to know when someone entered. She suspected Declan had hung it during a moment of nostalgia for his old shop.

Maybe he'd saved it as a reminder of how easily things can go up in smoke if you're not careful.

Charlotte refocused on the tall auburn-haired beauty walking through their door. She looked about thirty years old—pretty, with bright blue eyes, a sharp jawline, and high cheekbones.

"Hi," she said, gaze dropping to the darts in their hands.

Charlotte handed hers to Declan, who turned to stick them in the board.

Abby, Charlotte's soft-coated Wheaten terrier and office mascot, wandered over to give the woman a good sniff.

"Hi, don't mind us," said Charlotte. "Taking a little break. How can we help you?"

The woman eyed Charlotte from head to toe and smiled a large, genuine smile.

"You're *perfect,*" she said.

Charlotte laughed. "Thank you?"

The potential client held out her hand to shake. "I'm sorry. My name's Hollie."

"Charlotte. This is Declan."

As Hollie leaned toward Declan to shake his hand, a gold necklace with a large dangling letter H slipped from beneath her crewneck shirt.

"I've got a strange request for you," she said.

"Please, sit down," said Declan, motioning to a chair in their postage-stamp-sized waiting area. Their collection of four chairs and a table served as a waiting room, lounge, and lunch spot.

Having sniffed and cataloged the visitor, Abby curled beneath the dartboard to continue her morning nap.

Charlotte and Declan took seats beside Hollie.

"I can't wait to hear this strange request," said Charlotte.

She didn't bother to mention she'd be happy to hear *any* request at this point, particularly if it paid well.

"I've been told you're smart," said Hollie.

Charlotte laughed. "So far, I'm *perfect* and *smart*. I wish you'd swing by every day."

"Should I ask what people are saying about me?" asked Declan.

The woman glanced at him. "Nothing that I've heard."

He nodded and looked away.

"Good. I guess."

Hollie continued. "Anyway, like I said, I've got a strange problem. My great-uncle is Xander Flummox. He was—"

Charlotte straightened. "The *Tiki Trivia* host?"

"Yes, you know him? I didn't think anyone under sixty knew him."

Charlotte stabbed a thumb over her shoulder toward Pineapple Port.

"I grew up in the retirement community behind us, more or less adopted by the neighborhood. I read and watched what they read and watched—so I have the memories of a much older person."

Hollie covered her mouth with her hand to stifle a giggle. "This keeps getting better and better."

"How so?"

"Uncle Xander is running a trivia competition at his home this weekend for the extended family. How you score determines how much of his fortune you get."

"That's kind of fun, I guess," said Charlotte. She couldn't decide if having a family compete for a fortune was exciting or cruel. If she had to be honest, she was leaning toward *cruel*.

Hollie frowned, leading her to believe she wasn't a big fan of the idea, either.

"Fun if you're good at trivia. I'm *not*," she said.

"I'm not seeing how we can help?" said Declan.

Hollie sighed. "That's why this is an odd request. I want *you* to go to the party as *me*."

"As *you*? Won't Xander or the rest of the family know I'm not *you*?" She chuckled and nodded to Declan. "Assuming you meant *I* would pretend to be you and not *him*."

Hollie smiled. "He would be a stretch, but you're perfect. Xander's never met me. I'm surprised he remembered I existed at all. The families were estranged, and I lost my parents long ago. I'm lucky I got the invite."

Declan crossed his arms against his chest and leaned back in his chair.

"If Charlotte won and the other family members found out—you'd be disqualified, wouldn't you?" he asked.

Hollie reached into her purse to retrieve a sheet of paper.

"No. That's just it. Look at the last line."

Charlotte took the paper. At the top sat Xander Flummox's classic logo, where a question mark replaced the L in Flummox. Below it, she read the official invite to his *Tiki Trivia Inheritance Edition Event*. In bold letters at the bottom, it said, *There Are No Rules. Just Be Clever!*

Charlotte glanced up at her. "And you take this to mean you can swap yourself out?"

Hollie nodded. "Yes. Nothing there says I can't, and look at us—we're practically twins, just in case someone ever did see a photo of me somewhere. There won't be questions. I'm sure I'm not the only one pushing the boundaries."

She nodded at Declan.

"You're allowed to bring a partner, too."

Declan chuckled. "Oh, good. When the family finds out you tricked them, they can try to kill me, too."

Charlotte read the note over a few more times.

"I don't know. Wouldn't it be safer to study up and give it a shot yourself?"

Hollie huffed. "I tried that. There's no *way* I'll ever get smart enough to win. I haven't made this decision lightly, either. I've researched you. I've run it through my lawyer. This is the best plan. I'm *sure* of it."

Charlotte snapped the corner of her mouth. She still didn't love the idea.

"It's not like I'm a *Jeopardy!* champion—if you can send *anyone*, wouldn't someone like that make more sense?"

Hollie turned over the invite and pointed to the small print on the back. "It does say *no professionals* in the fine print."

Pineapple Trivia Night 11

"So *no rules* isn't exactly true," said Declan.

Hollie leaned toward Charlotte. "You've never been a trivia professional, have you? Or won a prize over one thousand dollars?"

Charlotte shrugged. "I won a Thanksgiving turkey once. Around Thanksgiving, they're almost worth that much."

"You said you hired a lawyer. That's never cheap. How much is at stake here?" asked Declan.

Hollie took a deep breath.

"Top prize is twenty million dollars."

Charlotte's eyes popped wide.

"Wow."

"Exactly." Hollie folded the invite and put it back in her purse. She pulled out another rectangular piece of paper, smaller than the first.

Check-shaped.

She held it out for Charlotte to inspect.

"I have a check to cover your time for the weekend. The event is tomorrow night at his mansion near Orlando. It's formal dress, so you might need to buy something. This should cover it."

Charlotte took the check and read the amount for the fifth time.

Ten thousand dollars.

She tilted it to show Declan.

He seemed impressed.

Charlotte bit her lip. "That's more than our hourly rate would have—"

"Thank you," said Declan, taking the check.

Charlotte glanced at him.

"I—"

Hollie held up a hand to silence her.

"Take this," she said, unclasping her H necklace and thrusting it toward her. "It will make you seem like a Hollie, right? And there's an incentive bonus. If you come in the top three, I'll give you a quarter of one percent of the winnings."

Charlotte's jaw slipped open.

"A quarter percent of twenty million dollars?"

"That's fifty thousand dollars," said Declan.

Charlotte looked at him.

He smirked. "You're not the only one on their math game today."

She returned her attention to Hollie.

"I don't know. It's just—"

"—It's just we need the directions to the house," said Declan, standing.

Hollie beamed and stood to shake his hand. She turned to Charlotte to touch her arm.

"I know you can do it. And, if you don't come in first, it's not the end of the world."

"No pressure?" asked Charlotte.

"No," said Hollie. "I'll take second place. That's *fine*."

CHAPTER THREE

Darla knocked and entered Mariska's house without waiting for an answer. She found her friend on the sofa eating ice cream in front of the television. An unfamiliar white dog lay beside her, rolled on its back with its legs curled, looking like a dead albino cockroach. Mariska's own almost identical white mutt, Miss Izzy, lay nearby, one eye closed and one glaring at the other dog.

As Darla entered, one of Izzy's satellite-dish-sized ears rotated in her direction.

"I don't know how to tell you this, but Izzy duplicated herself," said Darla, moving a fake cat to sit in a cushioned chair. "And she regrets it," she added.

Mariska smiled. "This is Buster. Word is getting around about my pet-sitting business. In fact, I just got a call from another woman. She's bringing over *Sir Sleepsalot.*"

Darla chuckled. "Sounds like an easy dog to watch."

Someone knocked on the front door, and Mariska rocked back and forth, working up momentum to fling herself out of the sofa's deep cushions.

Darla frowned. "You have *got* to get a new sofa. That one's a maneater."

"You think? Next time Bob acts up, I'll tell him to have a seat," she said, tittering as she invoked her husband's name.

Mariska escaped the sofa and walked to the door to answer. A middle-aged woman with frizzy blonde hair stood on the small landing behind her screen door, grinning. She held what looked like a fake tree in her hand.

"Hi, I'm Kelly. I called?"

"Yes, come in," said Mariska stepping back to make room.

She watched the ground, expecting a dog to appear, but none did. Instead, the woman entered her narrow foyer, tugging the tall fake tree. The leafless oddity had a stand at the bottom, and Kelly set it down in Mariska's living room before twirling on her heel to head back to the front door.

"I'll get Sir Sleepsalot. Just a second," she said, hustling away.

Mariska and Darla stared at the branch and then looked at each other.

"What is *that*?" asked Darla.

"I was going to ask you the same thing."

Darla clucked her tongue. "If that's what the dog likes to play fetch with, you're in big trouble."

"Do you think it's a cat? Maybe that's a scratching post. I'm not sure how a cat will do with Izzy—"

Izzy stared up at her as if to say, *not well.*

The front door clattered, and Darla and Mariska turned as Kelly entered the kitchen with something large and furry in her arms.

"This is my little man," she said.

A smiling golden face with a large dog-like black nose stared back at them. The similarities between the creature in Kelly's arms and a dog ended with the nose. It had shaggy fur and long arms ending with claws that would give Freddy Kruger nightmares.

It looked like a spider, a cheap wig, and Captain Hook had a baby.

Darla's jaw fell open as if the hinges had given way.

"Holy..."

She looked at Mariska, who stood so still, eyes wide and mouth ajar, that it seemed she'd left her body entirely.

The dog, Izzy, had had enough. She stood and slinked down the hall into Bob and Mariska's bedroom. The visiting mutt on the sofa remained as if some of its best friends were Captain Hook Spider Wigs.

"What is *that*?" asked Mariska, finding her voice.

"It's a sloth," said Kelly. Her brow knitted. "Did I forget to tell you he was a sloth?"

"*Yes*, you forgot to tell me. Look at its *hands*. He has giant hooky *claws*."

Kelly stammered.

"I'm so sorry, but I don't have time to find another babysitter. It's an emergency—my mother is dying, and we need to cross the state to the hospital. I'm desperate. *Please*? I'll pay you double."

That's all Darla needed to hear.

"Double and a half," she said.

Mariska's attention snapped to her.

"*What*? You can't be—"

"*Deal*," said Kelly. She moved to the faux tree, and with some coaxing, the sloth slowly climbed onto it.

Kelly kissed it on the head.

"You don't have to do much. He'll hang there most of the time. I have leaf eater pellets and fiber sticks in a bucket. I'll be back in a week."

Mariska gasped.

"A *week*?"

Darla stepped in.

"Great. We'll take good care of him."

"Thank you *so* much. I'll get his food." The woman flashed a smile and hurried out the front door.

Mariska looked at Darla.

"No *way*," she said through gritted teeth.

"I got you twice your fee," said Darla. She motioned to the sloth. "And look at him. He just hangs around. It'll be the easiest money we ever made."

"*We*? I'm the one living with this nightmare in my house. I'll probably wake up with those claws around my throat."

Darla moved closer to peer into the sleepy animal's face. "Aw, I think he's cute." Her lip curled. "Kinda stinky, but cute."

Mariska stomped a foot. "*No*. When she comes back, I'm telling her *no*."

Darla rolled her eyes.

"Think about the possibilities. We could charge people to see it."

"I'm not running a *zoo*."

"We could let people see him for free but charge them for drinks."

"A bunch of drunk people and a monster baby. Sounds *terrific*."

Mariska stormed to her front door, muttering. No sooner did she disappear around the corner than Darla heard her gasp.

"Oh *no*!"

"What is it?" Darla hustled to the door hoping the woman had a tiger cub, too. They could make a *mint* with a tiger cub.

"She's *gone*," said Mariska.

Darla followed her outside. Two large buckets sat against the house.

"That must be the food," said Darla.

Mariska stared down the street as if her seafaring love had disappeared in that direction right before the storm of the century.

"Tell me that woman didn't leave that thing in my house and drive off."

Darla shrugged. "Come on. Her mother's dying."

"*I'm* dying," said Mariska, pounding her open palm against her chest.

Darla patted her arm.

"You'll be fine. I'll help."

Mariska looked up at the roof of her carport and sighed. "That's what I'm afraid of."

CHAPTER FOUR

"Hey," said Charlotte, walking into Mariska's house. She paused to stare at Miss Izzy, who'd planted her chubby white butt in the office directly across from the front door. The dog stared at her without moving, like she was haunted.

"What's wrong with you? I don't get any love today?" she asked.

Izzy's eyes bounced to the left, the direction Charlotte needed to continue, but other than that, she didn't move.

Charlotte shrugged and headed around the corner toward the kitchen.

"Okay, if that's how you want to—*Gaah*!"

She pulled up short as a long-armed bear hanging on a fake tree in the middle of Mariska's living room turned its head to blink at her.

She pointed at it.

"Is that a *sloth*?" she asked aloud to no one. The room was empty but for her and the monster with the crazy claws staring at her.

"Charlotte?" called Mariska from the back of the house. A moment later, she appeared, trotting down the hall.

"Did you know there's a sloth in your living room?" asked Charlotte.

Mariska's shoulders slumped.

"Yes. I'm sloth-sitting."

"That's a thing?"

"It is today. I was tricked into it. I thought the lady had a dog and then—" She waved a hand at the creature. "She didn't have a dog."

"I guess not, or that's the weirdest beagle I've ever seen."

"What are you doing here?" asked Mariska.

"Declan and I are going to Orlando for a job, and I wanted to see if you could watch Abby for a night or two, but, um—I'm not sure how she'll get along with a sloth."

"Maybe you should leave her with Darla this time," suggested Mariska.

"I think you're right."

"What's in Orlando? You have a case there?"

"Less of a *case* and more of a *job*. Long story short, we're going to a trivia competition hosted by Xander Flummox."

Mariska perked. "*The* Xander Flummox? From *Tiki Trivia*?"

"The very same."

"He must be a hundred years old."

"Ninty-four. I looked it up."

"Wow. That's *exciting*. When are you going?"

"In about an hour." She crept toward the sloth. "Can I pet it before I go?"

Mariska shrugged. "I suppose so. I haven't dared."

Charlotte scratched the critter's head. It leaned into her without opening its eyes.

"It's kind of cute," she said.

Mariska grunted.

"I'll drop Abby off at Darla's. Good luck with your sloth."

Mariska sighed. "Thank you."

Charlotte had one more stop to make before she and Declan got on the road to Xander Flummox's home near Orlando, Florida. She had no idea why the game show host decided to make the dress for his trivia competition *formal*, but she did know she didn't own anything that would work.

Strange, but formal gowns didn't come up very often in fifty-five-plus mobile home parks.

Declan already owned his fancy outfit. No one owned a pawnshop for long before someone walked through the door hoping to sell a tuxedo. When the day came, and the tux fit, he'd snapped it up.

She didn't have time to find something online. Even if she had a few extra days to allow for shipping, she couldn't risk the gown not fitting. That meant she had to go to the only bridal shop in town, owned by Theresa "Taffy" Craddock.

Taffy grew up in the local pageant circuit and once finished fifth in the Miss Florida competition. Since that moment, the apex of her pageant career, she'd founded, run, or judged several pageants in the area. When her third daughter in a row won one of them, the scandal rocked the Charity pageant world.

So much drama.

Forced to retire, Taffy opened her bridal shop Taffy's Taffeta, which became the go-to spot for brides, gala goers, and prom attendees. The next nearest shop was miles away in Tampa, so she'd filled a hole in the market. Charlotte preferred her uniform of shorts and polos and looked forward to trying on gowns about as much as having her teeth drilled.

She entered Taffy's Taffeta to the sound of a bell much more jaunty than the sad one they had hanging at the detective agency. She scanned the room as if wolves lurked behind every tulle-covered gown.

Taffy looked up from her spot behind the check-out counter, all smiles and energy.

"*Hello*," she said, sweeping from behind the register. She wore a tight rose-colored bridesmaid gown with a plunging neckline.

"Hi," said Charlotte, tensing. Running didn't seem like a terrible option. She still had time.

Taffy flounced forward, a flurry of purple, lace, and breasts.

"Welcome to Taffy's. How can I help you?" she asked, eyes sparkling. She clasped her hands together and leaned in to place her face very close to Charlotte's. She smelled like mint and gardenias.

"How can I make you feel like a princess today?" she whispered.

Charlotte recognized the slogan. *How can I make you feel like a princess today?* was written beneath the shop's logo on the sign outside. It seemed innocuous enough when she read it on the way in but, delivered in this intense whisper, it was *terrifying*.

Charlotte took a tiny step back.

"Hi, um, I need a gown for a fancy dress event."

"Like a *ball*?"

"Um, I suppose so, but no dancing."

"A charity gala?"

"No—"

"A wedding?"

"No, it's a trivia contest, actually."

Taffy seemed to freeze, staring at her with wide blue eyes. Charlotte imagined the woman's long, thick, black eyelashes were fake. Either that, or she'd captured a pair of tarantulas with her eyelids, which seemed less likely.

"I don't understand. Did you say *trivia*?" she asked.

"Yes. It's a—" Charlotte decided Taffy didn't need to know all the gritty details. "It's a party. Just a fancy dress party."

"Oh, wonderful," said Taffy, her shoulders relaxing a notch. "Is it, uh, local?"

She chewed her lip, laying in wait for the answer like a cat.

"No. Orlando," she said.

Taffy relaxed again. "Oh. Good. Wonderful. Come with me."

She shimmied beside Charlotte and looped her arm to walk her to the back of the shop as if they were heading down the yellow brick road together.

"What about something like this?" she asked, motioning to a black dress with a bedazzled bodice. Charlotte wasn't sure, but it seemed paired with a cape with a maroon lining.

"That might be a tad *vampire*," she said.

Taffy sniffed.

"Fine. It is an evening event, though, right?"

"Yes. I think so..." Charlotte realized she wasn't sure if the tournament started that evening or the next day.

"Maybe we could try to find something that works either way? It might be tonight or tomorrow or both."

Taffy winced. "Both? It could be tonight and tomorrow?"

"Maybe. I'm not sure."

"And you'd wear the *same* outfit *both* days?"

Charlotte nodded.

Taffy looked at her as if she was a new species she didn't recognize. "Okay..."

She moved to another rack and pulled out an emerald dress with a split in the skirt riding high to reveal a pair of silken shorts.

"Maybe something like this?"

Charlotte shook her head. She imagined how she felt was a little like someone waiting for waterboarding torture to end.

She was drowning in lace and glitter.

"Something more understated, I think?"

Taffy blinked.

"*Understated?*"

Charlotte tried again.

"Plain?"

Taffy's lip curled.

"*Plain*," she echoed.

Charlotte thought she saw her shiver.

She walked through the racks again, this time with less enthusiasm.

"I suppose rhinestones are out," she murmured.

A simple turquoise gown hanging on a sale rack caught Charlotte's eye as they passed on their way toward more glittery pastures.

"What about this?" she said, removing it from the rack.

Taffy eyed the gown.

"It's simple," she said.

"I think it's perfect. Can I try it on?"

Taffy motioned to the changing rooms, and Charlotte rushed to them. Clothes came off, dress slipped on.

She admired the simple slip dress with a cowl neck in the mirror. It fit, had no glitter, no lace, and no cape. On top of all that, it wasn't even a hundred and fifty dollars.

Perfect.

She redressed and exited the changing room. Taffy had returned to her spot behind the register. She looked disappointed.

Charlotte felt a little like she'd broken the woman's spirit.

She bought the dress with little fanfare.

"I'll be planning my wedding soon, so I imagine I'll be back soon," she said, hoping to cheer the dour beauty queen.

Taffy handed her the box.

"Can't wait," she said.

CHAPTER FIVE

Mariska looked up from her plant watering to find Darla walking down the street toward her house with a bouncy, self-confident gait that worried her.

"How'd it go?" asked her friend as she arrived and planted her hands on her hips like a landing Peter Pan.

Mariska frowned and tried to find what happiness she could at the moment. Darla was up to something, but at least she had someone to complain to about her evening.

"I barely slept a *second*," she said.

"Why? Sir Sleepsalot is noisy? He seemed pretty quiet to me."

"No, he didn't make a sound, but that's the problem. I kept waiting for him to come into the room and kill me."

"Did you close your door?"

"Yes. But those *claws*. He could tear right through the door if he wanted to. How am I supposed to sleep knowing there's a monster on the other side of the door?"

Darla dismissed her with a wave. "Oh, you never sleep anyway, silly. That thing is harmless, and you know it. What did Bob think of it?"

Mariska scowled. "He came in, looked at it, and said, *Mariska, did you do something different with your hair?*"

Darla cackled.

Mariska couldn't help but laugh, too.

"He's such a pill." She shot a stream of water at her hibiscus bush. "Why do these things always happen to me?"

Darla shrugged. "Just lucky, I guess. Come on. We have to plan the party."

"What party?"

Darla held the paper in her hand aloft, and Mariska squinted to read its large, joyous font aloud.

"Come see the sloth. Cheap drinks!"

She scowled.

"You're really selling *tickets*?"
Darla nodded. "I told you I would."
"And I told you, this isn't a *zoo*."
"We'll make a fortune."
Mariska shot another blast of water at her bushes.
"There you go with that *we* again."
Darla slapped her on the arm.
"Come on—we have a lot to do. Show starts at four."
Mariska whirled so quickly that she doused Darla's shins with water before remembering to release the sprayer.
"It's *today*? Tell me you didn't already pass these out?"
Darla stared at her soggy sandals with dismay. "Now I'm all wet. I hate that. These things squeak when they get wet."
Mariska growled. "You're avoiding the question."
"No, I'm not," said Darla, removing and shaking a flip-flop. "I'm trying to get water out of my sandals, but *yes*, it's today, and I've put the flyers everywhere. One on every door, a pile at the rec center—"
As she spoke, she headed for Mariska's front door, shaking her feet with every other step like a wet-pawed cat.
Mariska dropped the hose to follow her inside. She couldn't wring her hands with worry while holding a hose.
"Where are we going to get this booze you promised everyone? We'll need to borrow a folding table and—"
"Where'd you put him?" asked Darla, stopping as she entered the kitchen.
"What?"
Mariska pushed Darla aside to get a better look at Sir Sleepsalot's fake tree.
His *empty* tree.
The sloth was *gone*.
Mariska sucked in a breath.
"Freeze," she whispered.
Darla squinted at her. "What?"
"Don't move."
"Why? Where is it?"
"I don't *know*, that's why I said don't move. It might be ready to pounce."
Darla rolled her eyes. "It just wandered off. We have to find it."
"It could be *anywhere*. It could be in the attic, preparing to drop like *death from above*."
"I doubt that."

Mariska shook her head. "You don't get it. If it isn't here, that can only mean one thing."

"What?"

"That it's *somewhere else*."

"Oh, for crying out loud."

Darla huffed and strode past the tree to check the lanai.

"Not out here," she reported.

"Did you check under the sofa?" asked Mariska, taking shallow breaths so the movement of her chest wouldn't attract the beast's attention.

Darla glanced back into the lanai and scowled.

"A rat couldn't fit under that sofa."

"They can probably flatten themselves. Get in anywhere."

Darla threw her a withering glance.

"It's a *sloth*, not a palmetto bug."

She squeezed past Mariska into the hall to search the guest room.

"Not here."

"Did you check the closets?"

Mariska heard the closet door roll aside.

"You couldn't fit a can of tuna in these closets. Look at this stuff. You're like a doomsday prepper planning to live on stuffing, spaghetti sauce, and fabric softener sheets."

"It's the damn BOGOs," muttered Mariska. "What about the drawers?"

She heard a drawer open.

"Full of dog treats. Mariska, your dog won't live long enough to eat these—"

Mariska stomped her foot.

"Shut up and *find the sloth*."

Darla reappeared in the hall and glanced into the guest bathroom.

She stopped.

"*Whoa*."

"What?" Mariska gripped the collar of her shirt. "Do you see it?"

"I do."

"In the bathroom?"

"Yep. Come here."

"No. Just get it."

Darla shook her head. "No. You have to see this."

Mariska swallowed and pushed herself down the hall one tiny step at a time until she could peek around the corner into the bathroom.

Her jaw fell slack.

"What—?"

That was as far as she could get. She couldn't find the words.
Darla crossed her arms against her chest.
"Whelp, I guess I can die now. I've seen everything."
Sir Sleepsalot turned his head in slow motion to blink at them.
He sat hovered over the toilet, his long gangly arms supporting his body on the seat.
"What is it *doing*?" whispered Mariska.
"What do *you* think it's doing? It's pooping, silly," said Darla.
Mariska scowled. "Are you sure?"
Before Darla could answer, they heard a gentle splash, followed by several more.
"Yes," said Darla.
Having finished his business, Sir Sleepsalot eased himself to the ground in slow motion. The ladies scrambled out of his way as he flatted his belly to the ground and crawled toward the living room, stretching one long arm at a time and pulling itself forward like an alien bug.
"That is *so* creepy," whispered Mariska.
Darla nodded. "And *slow*. We'll die of hunger before we get out of this hallway."
"Do you think he'll go to his tree?"
Darla looked at her.
"Where else would he go? Clubbing?"
"He might hover around the kitchen, and then I won't be able to get an afternoon snack."
Darla eyed her. "I can see that. You're wasting away already."
"Shut up."
Darla motioned to the front door as the sloth passed the tiny foyer and entered the living room at a scorching negative three miles per hour.
"We can get out the front now. Let's see what you have in your shed for the event while he finishes his forty-year trek across the desert."
Mariska followed her to the door, grumbling.
"This is the worst idea you've had in a while, and that's saying something."
Outside, the two headed into Mariska's attached shed, chock full of gardening supplies, Bob's tools, and forgotten lawn ornaments.
"There's a folding table in here," said Darla, tripping past a push mower.
Mariska bit her lip as she eyed the folding table. "That's not mine."
"It's in your shed."
"I think I was supposed to give that back to Patty months ago."
Darla tugged at it. "Well, good you didn't. We'll set this up in the

driveway, throw a couple of boxes of wine on ice and start collecting cash."

"Then what? People go traipsing through my house to look at Sir Poopsalot?"

Mariska stepped back as Darla wrestled the table free and toted it past her to the driveway.

Darla set the table down with a huff.

"You know, you shouldn't look a gift horse in the mouth. For one, *he used the toilet*. He could have dropped those rabbit pellets all over your floor, but he didn't. He used the toilet like a furry little gentleman."

Mariska grunted. "I guess that's one way to look at it. On the other hand, I don't think I'll ever be able to use that toilet again."

Darla wasn't listening. Instead, her expression blossomed with inspiration—the only thing Mariska found scarier than a crawling sloth.

"Do you think we could get him to poop for *everyone*? That would be worth twice as much."

Mariska shook her head. "He just went."

"He'll have to go again. We could feed him a lot."

Mariska clucked her tongue.

"He's not a pate goose."

"Hold on." Darla pulled her phone from her pocket and typed something into it. Her shoulders slumped.

"Oh no. They only go to the bathroom maybe once a *week*."

"Does it say in there if they eat human flesh?"

Darla rolled her eyes at her. "We blew it. We should have filmed him pooping."

"That's just wrong. You have issues."

"Maybe we could feed him prunes or something—"

Mariska had had enough.

"*No*. I don't know how I got roped into this, but I won't *kill* the thing so you can sell tickets."

Darla grinned and pointed at her.

"See? I *knew* you liked him."

"I *don't* like him. Poor Izzy has been hiding in the bedroom since he got here. I had to move her water bowl so she didn't die of dehydration."

"What about the other dog?"

"He just stares at it. I don't know if he's scared or figuring out how to eat it."

Darla wandered back into the shed to inspect a large tarp folded on a rusting metal shelving unit.

"Do you have any string?" she asked in a strange, dreamy voice.

"Why?"

"I have an idea."
Mariska groaned.
"I hate it when you say that."

CHAPTER SIX

In Declan's car, Declan and Charlotte drove toward Xander Flummox's Orlando mansion wearing their fancy dress.

"You look fantastic," said Declan.

She smiled. "Thank you, so do you."

He pulled at his bowtie. "I feel like someone's slowly choking me."

"But you'll die gorgeous."

He chuckled. "That makes me feel better."

"At least you had the outfit. I had to run the glitter gamut with Taffy." She bounced in her seat. "*Ooh*, I almost forgot to tell you—I stopped by Mariska's, and she's babysitting a sloth."

He looked at her.

"An *actual* sloth?"

"Yep. Long arms, hanging from a tree—the whole thing."

"That's *insane*."

"That's not even the craziest part. Because of the sloth, I had to drop Abby off at Darla's, who told me about their plan to sell tickets."

"Tickets *to the sloth*?"

"Uh-huh. They're going to display it in Mariska's driveway to paying customers, like their own little zoo. Complimentary wine with every ticket."

"Wine? How much are these tickets?"

"Boxed wine, I'm sure. It'll be a shot glass full—just enough that Darla can charge more."

Declan shook his head.

"They'll be running an unlicensed zoo *and* an illegal bar. Nice. They could run the trifecta if they played pirated music during the big reveal."

Charlotte giggled. "In the grand scheme of things, this seems relatively tame for them."

"You say that now, but it won't end well when Frank finds out."

Charlotte agreed. "He will lose his *mind* if he finds out, but as good as Darla is at goofy money-making schemes, she's ten times as good at hiding them from Frank. Whenever he finds out, usually Mariska is the weak link."

Declan sighed.

"I'm a little sorry we're going to miss that. I've never seen a sloth."

"I saw it. It was pretty cute."

They drove for a while, Charlotte staring out the window at the passing landscape of cow pastures and rinky-dink towns.

"You're unusually quiet," said Declan as they passed a penned collection of goats.

She sighed. "Sorry. I was thinking it doesn't feel *right* pretending to be Hollie. I'll almost feel bad if we win."

Declan shrugged. "She said she cleared it with her lawyers, and this job sounds *fun* compared to some of the things we've been dragged into. At least no one's been murdered."

"That was one of the downsides for me," she teased.

She looked at him.

"I guess I'm nervous about the competition, too," she admitted.

"Why? You're going to crush it."

"I don't know about that..."

He placed a hand on her leg. "You'll be great. You're the smartest person I know."

"That's not saying much. You hang out with Seamus," she said, invoking the name of his troublesome uncle.

He laughed.

"Well, even if you don't win, we're getting paid ten thousand dollars for a day's work. That's better than being chased by killers for free."

"Or having your store burned down."

He side-eyed her.

"Too soon?" she asked.

"Little bit." He chuckled. "Don't worry about the contest. If you lose, we still win, and if you win, *bonus*."

"That bonus money would cover us for the *year* while we get the business rolling."

Charlotte glanced at the map on her phone.

"It's a left turn in a few miles up here."

Declan pointed. "I thought so. Look."

A large stone structure dwarfed all other nearby structures. Red and blue banners bearing the Flummox logo waved in the wind above the two turrets.

"It's a castle," said Charlotte.

She had to. There was no way to describe Xander Flummox's home without using the word *castle*.

"Did she mention her great-uncle was King Arthur?" asked Declan.

"She did not. Maybe she didn't know."

Declan slowed, and they pulled onto the long, palm tree-flanked stone driveway leading to the castle.

He leaned forward to squint through the windshield.

"Is that a drawbridge? And a *moat*?"

"I think so."

She pointed to a pair of tall tikis on either side of the drawbridge. A metal parrot sat on each, wings outstretched as if they were about to leap into the air.

"I'm having more trouble with the other decorations. Is he going for a castle or an island vibe?"

"Good point. I don't think there were a lot of parrots in feudal England."

Half a dozen other vehicles sat in the large circular driveway. Declan pulled beside one and threw the car into park.

"The guy is having a trivia contest to dole out millions. He has to be eccentric," he said.

"Sure. I just didn't see the *castle* coming."

Charlotte exited the vehicle and smoothed her teal gown.

"Here goes nothing," she said, taking a deep, cleansing breath.

He slipped his arm around her waist and pulled her to him.

"Do you think it's okay for me to kiss you?"

She grinned. "You *are* playing my fiancé..."

He leaned to kiss her, and she let her fingertips play across his chest as she leaned into him.

She couldn't imagine those kisses ever getting old.

"Tell me again I'm going to be great at this," she said.

"You're going to be *great* at this," he said, giving her a quick second kiss as the sun dipped below the horizon.

Landscape lighting, including the tiki torches lining the castle and parking area, blazed to life.

"Does that always happen when I kiss you?" teased Declan.

She smiled but didn't say what she was thinking.

Yes.

The only way to enter the castle was up the wide stone stairs leading to a drawbridge spanning a moat.

Charlotte peered over the edge of the drawbridge as they crossed. The banks of the moat below flanked the first level of the castle.

In the murky water, something moved.

"Are there *alligators* down there?" she asked.

Declan looked over the edge on the opposite side.

"I see two over here."

Charlotte moved to his side to see two alligators lying like clay statues on the bank. One slipped into the water.

"This guy is a *loon*," she mumbled.

Declan touched the small of her back with his fingertips and led her through a stone archway. Her heels clicked on the stone floor as they entered a great hall, where quiet tension charged the air. Several other people in formal wear stood scattered around the edge of the large room, eyeing one another. Their wary gazes pulled to her as they entered.

It felt strange to have so many *silent* people dressed like party guests. No one talked. No one moved except a waiter wearing a classic black and white uniform. He approached to present a silver tray of crystal glasses filled with either red or white wine.

Charlotte chose white. She preferred red but figured if she spilled white, it wouldn't stain her gown.

"Wow. This isn't cheap stuff," murmured Declan after tasting his red.

"You're saying it's better than Mariska's boxed wine back home?" asked Charlotte.

He pinched the air to show her the difference.

Charlotte scaled the entry gate hanging above the entrance with her eyes. Dark metal fortified the edges of the thick wood. It looked as if it could stop a charging elephant.

"That has to be fifteen feet high," she said.

"*Eighteen*," said a voice to her left.

She turned to find a small-boned man with gray slicked-back hair and a narrow mustache. He wore a black tuxedo and a red paisley scarf draped around his neck that hung past his waist on either side.

"You sound sure of that number," she said.

He nodded. "I am. I visited here as a child. I measured them. I measured everything back then." He made a lazy motion toward the entrance. "That's just the beginning. In addition to the drawbridge, there's a portcullis he can lower in case of attack."

Charlotte chuckled.

"You're not expecting we'll be *attacked*, are you?"

He sniffed. "No, but the portcullis would protect us from battering *and* fire."

She swallowed and took a moment to rein in her nerves. If this guy was any indication, she was standing in a room full of trivia nerds.

She decided to concentrate on playing her part.

"I'm Hollie. This is my fiancé, um...*Elmo*," she said.

Declan coughed into his wine.

"Excuse me," he said, using a napkin to dab his mouth before he shook hands with the man.

"Tristan. Nice to meet you. You're Xander's...?"

"He's my great-uncle on my father's side," said Charlotte. She'd been chanting Hollie's family tree in her head since they left Charity but prayed Tristan wouldn't ask her too many questions.

Their new friend with the fancy scarf seemed at home in the castle. He had the air of a man familiar with the snug fit of a bespoke tuxedo. She wasn't sure what made her feel that way—it might have been the mustache or the well-groomed triangular beard beneath it. He was either very fancy or an aging Robin Hood in disguise, here to rob Xander's riches for the poor.

"And *your* relation?" asked Declan.

"He's my uncle. My mother's brother," said Tristan, though his attention floated past them as he spoke.

"Tristan? Is that you?" called a woman from the opposite side of the room.

Tristan raised a hand to show he'd heard her call, nodded to Charlotte and Declan, and wandered away.

"He seemed totally normal," said Declan, sipping his wine.

Charlotte nodded. "I hope the trivia questions aren't all about medieval doors, or we're screwed."

Declan cocked an eyebrow at her.

"*Elmo*?"

She burst into giggles, twirling Hollie's H necklace between her fingers.

The initial jewelry had worked. Tristan hadn't questioned her identity.

So far, so good.

"I guess we should mingle and see what we're up against," she said, heading toward a striking young woman in a peach gown. She stood beside a gangly man and an enormous unused fireplace.

The blonde looked less than thrilled to be there, but the man's gaze crisscrossed the room with wide-eyed wonder.

"Hello, I'm Hollie," said Charlotte. "Xander's great niece. This is my fiancé El—"

"*Mo*. Call me Mo," said Declan, thrusting out a hand to shake.

"Della," said the blonde.

She seemed bored.

Charlotte studied the man at Della's side. It seemed she wouldn't be introducing him.

"Timmy," said Della's bespeckled date, shaking hands with both of them.

His palms were clammy, and his ill-fitting tux made him look like an absent-minded professor. The fabric was cheap—Charlotte guessed *rental*.

The two of them made a strange couple. Della looked like a sorority princess from a nearby college campus. Timmy looked like he'd never kissed a girl.

Della leaned forward, giving Declan a prime view of the cleavage spilling from her tight gown.

Charlotte decided she didn't like her.

"Oh, they're passing the canapes. I'm *starving*," Della said, striding off without another word.

Timmy offered Charlotte and Delcan an apologetic glance and then hurried after her.

"I think we found a ringer," said Declan.

Charlotte watched the couple as they left. "She didn't say how she's in the mix. What do you think? Grandaughter?"

"She's young. Grandaughter is as good a guess as any."

Charlotte noticed the older woman who'd called for Tristan staring at them. She smiled, and the woman, alone again now that Tristan had wandered off, moved to them as if Charlotte's attention was a tractor beam.

"I'm Mildred," she said as she neared. Her unnaturally strawberry blonde hair was wrapped into what looked like a lowrise beehive.

"Hollie and, uh, Mo," said Charlotte. She squinted at the woman. She couldn't shake the feeling she knew her.

Something about the beehive...

Mildred pointed to them, each in turn. "Is it you or him who got the invite?"

"Me. Grandneice."

"Ah, Hollie, right. I don't think we've met. I was Xander's *Vanna White*."

Charlotte gasped. "*Mildred*. I remember you now. I knew you looked familiar. You were on *Tiki Trivia*."

The woman nodded. "Forty years."

"You're competing?" asked Declan.

She nodded. "I *am*. Fun of him to invite me, wasn't it? I guess he wants to know if I was paying attention all those years."

"We'll have to keep an eye on you. You have the inside track," said Declan.

The woman tittered.

"Do you know the others?" asked Charlotte.

"I think I've met everyone," she said, turning to survey the group. "There's Tristan, you met. You were talking to Timmy and Della. There's me, you, and then the twins over there. Jarett and the one in black, Barett. His sons."

"Jarrett and Barrett?" echoed Declan. It was clear from his tone he found the rhyming names amusing.

Charlotte scowled. "Xander's *sons*? I assumed he didn't have children—" She pulled the reins on her comment and bit her lip.

Wouldn't *Hollie* know her great-uncle had kids?

Shoot.

Mildred didn't flinch.

"He *thought* he was childless until twenty-five years ago," said Mildred, lowering her voice. "The twins were the product of a brief affair. He didn't meet them until they were in their teens." She touched Charlotte's arm and leaned in to add, "Xander was a bit of a *scoundrel* in his day."

"Oh," said Charlotte, eyeing the middle-aged twins. Their matching auburn hair, piercing blue eyes, and heart-shaped faces made it clear they were siblings. She thought they resembled Xander from his earlier days on *Tiki Trivia*. It would have been hard for him to deny being their father even without a paternity test.

"Look at them wearing black and white. They look like chess pieces," said Mildred with a chuckle.

"I guess it's to help us tell them apart," suggested Charlotte.

A voice boomed overhead that made everyone jump. Mildred's wine sloshed to the stones and splashed on Charlotte's bare ankles. Luckily, she, too, had chosen white.

"*Welcome, all! Please gather in the center of the room,*" said a booming voice.

The voice came from *everywhere*. It took Charlotte a moment to spot the source—a man on the second-floor balcony wearing a loud, baggy Hawaiian shirt and khaki pants, in sharp contrast to the fancy dress of his guests. He wore a ball cap pulled low with long gray hair sticking from either side.

"Pretty perky for ninety-four," mumbled Charlotte as they shuffled toward the center of the grand foyer.

The room's energy shifted to excitement. The penguin-dressed server disappeared, and only the competitors remained—the twins, Mildred, Tristan, Della and her ringer, Timmy, and Team Charlock Holmes.

A rumbling shook the room as the drawbridge began to rise. When it crashed shut, a second clanking began.

"He's lowering the portcullis," noted a giddy Tristan.

He sure loved doors.

Charlotte realized she'd lost her chance to run to the car and drive away. She sighed and took a sip of her wine.

I'm in it to win it now.

The announcement continued over the loudspeaker.

"Those doors won't open until someone solves the puzzle or the sun rises, whichever comes first," said Xander.

"All night?" peeped Charlotte. She couldn't help it. She was more of a morning person, and she'd hoped to at least change out of the stupid gown before things started.

"There are multiple clues in every room on the first and second floors. The third floor is off-limits. Anyone who takes, hides, or tampers with another player's clue will be disqualified."

"And again, the contest with no rules has rules," mumbled Declan.

The old man poked his hand at the sky.

"Let the games begin!"

Charlotte turned her head to say something to Declan but never got the chance.

The floor beneath them dropped away.

She was falling.

CHAPTER SEVEN

A crowd of Pineapple Portians gathered on Mariska's driveway to mill about sipping lukewarm boxed pinot grigio at ten dollars per person. Behind a folding table at the back, a tarp hung from an intricate string lacing, blocking the crowd's view of the sloth hanging on his treestand behind it.

Darla stood vigilant beside the folding table, pouring wine and turning away looky-loos attempting to steal a free peek. She'd been delighted at how easy it'd been to get Sir Sleepsalot outside and into an optimal viewing position. She'd walked to his tree and held out her arms.

That's all it took. The creature reached out and hung from her like a furry Baby Bjorn.

Mariska lugged the empty tree outside while Darla walked like a mummy, hands in front of her, sloth on her chest, through the front door. By the time she reached outside, her arms had naturally folded around the sloth.

"He's actually kind of cuddly," she said.

"Better you than me," said Mariska. "Put him on the tree."

Sir Sleepsalot seemed happy to be outside, though he always smiled, so it was hard to tell.

"Do you think this is illegal?" asked Mariska.

"Sloths?"

Mariska moved closer and lowered her voice.

"Selling *booze*."

"No. We're *not*. We're selling a look at the toilet-pooping long-armed bear. The wine is shared with friends."

"Half these people wouldn't be here if it wasn't for the *free* wine."

She made air quotes around the word *free* as she said it.

"That's *your* opinion."

Mariska frowned. "I'm pretty sure it would be your husband's opinion, too. You remember him, right? Frank? *The sheriff?*"

Darla scoffed. "What Frank doesn't know doesn't hurt him."

"If what Frank didn't know did hurt him, he'd be dead," muttered Mariska. "Why do we need the wine at all?"

Darla leaned in and hissed.

"*So we can boost the cost of the tickets.*"

She turned as an elderly woman with a walker started clomping up the strip of grass between Mariska and her neighbor.

"Where are you going?" asked Darla.

The woman squinted at her.

"Nowhere."

"You're trying to sneak a peek. Get back on the driveway."

"I'm just going for a walk. I get blood clots if I don't keep moving."

Darla pointed. "Then keep moving in *that* direction."

The woman huffed and clomped back toward the sidewalk.

Darla shook her head.

"These people. I swear."

Mariska spotted Bettie Giraffe in the crowd. Bettie didn't live in Pineapple Port but was good friends with many residents and often stopped by for lengthy visits. That's how she spent her year—traveling from one friend to another—though she lived in a nice rent-controlled apartment in New York City.

"Bettie, I didn't know you were in town," said Mariska, waving to catch her attention.

Bettie turned her head and sent her giraffe earrings swinging. That's how she got the name Bettie Giraffe—they were her favorite animals, and she always wore one or two things giraffe-themed.

"Hello, Mariska, how are you?" she said, weaving her way to the table.

"Wonderful. And you?"

"Oh, I'm wonderful. I came to see the sloth."

She held out a ten-dollar bill.

"I thought you only liked giraffes," teased Mariska, handing her a ticket.

"Oh, I like all animals."

Mariska poured her a glass of wine.

"You just like wearing giraffes?"

Bettie shook her head.

"No—when my kids were little, I told them I like giraffes. They got me a giraffe sweater for Christmas. Then my birthday—*more giraffes*. Mother's Day, *giraffes*." She shrugged. "That was forty years ago. The kids, my friends—you don't know how many things there are in the world with giraffes on them until you make the mistake of telling your children you like giraffes."

"I think I've gotten you giraffe gifts," said Mariska.

"Oh, that's wonderful. I love them now. It's me, *Bettie Giraffe*."

Mariska leaned toward her to whisper. "I won't tell anyone you're looking at sloths today."

Bettie turned to look at the crowd behind her. "Oh, I think they can see me."

Mariska nodded and let it go.

Bettie wasn't always the sharpest cheese on the charcuterie tray.

Darla stood staring at them until Mariska caught her eye.

"What's wrong?"

"Nothing," she said, snapping out of her trance. "I just realized we should have sold tee shirts."

Mariska surveyed the crowd. The glances at the tarp were increasing. She caught a couple of people checking their watches.

She glanced at her own and pulled Darla aside.

"I think we should start now."

Darla frowned. "I don't know. I've had a couple of people buy extra tickets to get another glass of wine. We might be on to something."

"It's called opening a bar."

Darla nodded. "Maybe we should open a bar. That's not a terrible idea. It seems like a license to print money."

Mariska sighed.

"For today, we're running out of wine. Let's unveil the sloth?"

"We'll get more. You can run to the store while I man the fort."

"Your husband will be home from work in fifteen minutes."

Darla glanced at her watch and huffed.

"*Fine.*"

She put her hands over her head and yelled at the crowd.

"Ladies and gentlemen!"

All eyes turned to her.

"Prepare to be amazed!"

"It's a sloth, not Houdini," muttered Mariska.

Darla ignored her and climbed the ladder beside the tarp. She gathered the scissors she'd left at the top of the ladder and nodded to Mariska to hit play on her phone.

The tinny sound of the *2001: A Space Odyssey* theme played.

"I present to you... *Sir Sleepsalot!*"

Darla cut the strings holding the tarp. It swung to one side and dangled there.

"It's a stick," said someone.

"Hm?"
Darla and Mariska turned.
Both of their jaws dropped.
The tree was empty.
"Oh *no*," said Mariska.
"I paid to see a sloth," said someone.
"Are you saying that thing is loose in the neighborhood?" asked another.
"I want my money back," said a man, guzzling the last of his wine. Several others echoed the sentiment.
"You got *wine*," said Darla, hustling back down the ladder.
She grabbed Mariska's arm.
"I'll look out here. You check the toilet."
Mariska hurried inside as Darla scrambled around the area, circling Mariska's house.
"He's not inside," Mariska reported, returning to the driveway.
Darla had returned, shiny with sweat.
"He can't have gotten far," she said.
She tried to sound upbeat.
Mariska didn't feel optimistic.
Sir Sleepsalot was gone.

CHAPTER EIGHT

Charlotte felt Declan grabbing for her as they dropped through the open air. They bounce-landed on cushy plastic before the horror of what was happening had time to gel.

Around Charlotte, a symphony of *oof!s* played as the others landed around her.

"Are you okay?" asked Declan.

"I'm fine," said Charlotte bobbing on the giant air mattress.

The room into which they'd dropped had little light, but she could make out the shapes of the people around her as they sat up.

She heard a hiss and felt the cushion beneath her deflating, lowering them to more stable ground.

Declan stood and helped her to her high-heeled feet. He didn't look happy.

"This whole thing has gone from weird to dangerous. Someone could have been hurt," he grumbled.

"Like *me*," said Mildred from the ground beside them. "I'm much too old for this nonsense."

Declan helped her up. He motioned to help Tristan, who waved him away and clambered to his feet, muttering.

Charlotte straightened her gown and scanned the room. The giant air mattress lay flat on the ground like a plastic rug. The ceiling had closed as quickly as it opened. A few small light sources dotted the walls—all looked more like portholes than windows. The room's only illumination shone through them—compliments of the castle's outdoor lighting.

"It's cruel to make us dress up and then throw us around," said Charlotte to Mildred. "I was hoping to change into sensible shoes."

"After forty years of heels, I'm *always* in sensible shoes," said Mildred, motioning to the black flats that matched her black pants and bedazzled tunic.

Charlotte wondered if Mildred's long history with Xander and *Tiki Trivia* might make her a good ally for the competition.

"Are you familiar with the castle? Do you know where we are?" she asked.

Mildred looked around. "We're in the library."

"Get away from me," snapped Della, somewhere to Charlotte's right. She turned to see Timmy attempting to pull her to her feet. The blonde slapped away his helping hand.

The beefy twins, Jarrett and Barrett, stood beside each other like a pair of confused middle-aged bouncers. They seemed unsure of what to do but had clearly planned to stick together.

"Look for a light switch," said Declan, loud enough for everyone to hear.

The group gravitated toward the room's outer edges. The library wasn't round or square—Charlotte noted the angles in the walls and declared it an octagon.

She snorted a laugh.

The Octagon. Just like UFC fights. That seems appropriate.

"I found it," said a male voice Charlotte didn't recognize. She guessed it to be one of the twins.

She heard a click, and bookshelf lighting burst to life, revealing rows of books covering every wall, with shelves rising to the approximately twenty-foot ceilings. She fought the urge to ask Tristan their exact height, fearing he'd tell her.

Everyone spun in slow motion, admiring the collection of leather-bound books and fancy lighting.

"This would be impressive if I wasn't so angry," said Tristan, brushing at his jacket.

Charlotte spotted the only door and tried the knob.

"We're locked in," she reported.

The knob felt strangely modern for such an old-timey ornate library, and she bent to take a better look.

"It's a combination lock."

"The combination must be in here somewhere. It's part of the puzzle," said Timmy.

Della rolled her eyes. "Ya *think?*"

"There's a note," said Mildred. She stood near a large table so seamless and ornate it appeared carved from a single giant redwood.

The group moved in as she read the note aloud.

"*For your first test, you'll need to work together to escape. You've got sixty minutes, or you all lose. The game is afoot.*"

"It's an escape room," said Timmy.

"That's it?" asked the twin in black. "That's all it says? There's no clue?"

Mildred flipped over the sheet. "That's it."

"Sherlock Holmes," said Charlotte and Della in stereo.

The others looked at them, and they looked at each other.

"The note ended with *the game is afoot*. That's Sherlock Holmes' line. The code must be in a Sherlock Holmes book," explained Charlotte.

Della didn't feel the need to explain. She was already moving, her finger dragging along the spines of the books as she searched for Sherlock Holmes.

"Spread out. They have a pattern," she announced. "This section is all science and medical books."

The others moved to different walls.

"I've got historical stuff," said the twin in white.

"I've got fiction, but *old*—Shakespeare, Chaucer..." said Charlotte.

"I've got all mysteries," said Declan.

Everyone gravitated to his wall to search. One of the twins elbowed Tristan out of the way, and he scowled at the younger man.

"No need to be rude, *oaf*," he muttered.

"Nothing but Agatha Christie, Dorothy L. Sayers, and Raymond Chandler," said Mildred, looking at the shelves above their heads. "What about up there?"

As the tallest in the group, Declan checked the highest shelves he could reach, but three more sat above those. He dragged over a chair to stand on it, gaining access to one more shelf. Finding nothing, he glanced back at the table.

"Even if we could move that table, I can't reach the top shelf."

He hopped off the chair.

"How can there not be a ladder in here?" asked Della.

"I suspect he removed it on purpose," said Tristan, pointing to the track where the library ladder should hang. "That makes it all the more likely the book we want is on the top shelf."

"I can maybe *climb* the shelves?" suggested Timmy.

He put his foot on one of the lower shelves and pushed up to grab one above his head. As he pulled himself up, the shelf from which he hung snapped, sending a dozen or more heavy hardbacks down on his head as he hit the ground butt-first.

"Or not," he said sheepishly.

"The note said we had to work together," said Declan. "Char—er, *Hollie*—stand on my shoulders."

Charlotte kicked off her heels as Declan squatted down. She stepped on his shoulders, with one of the twins standing nearby to steady her. She used the shelving to balance herself as she straightened her knees—careful not to put too much weight on them and end up on the ground like Timmy.

Wobbling, she scanned the second to the top shelf. Finding no Sir Arthur Conan Doyle, she strained to grab the top shelf books. She was tall enough to pinch and pull them but not tall enough to read the faded spines.

"Heads up!" she called down before whipping them one after the next from the shelf. As soon as she finished bombing, the group moved in to investigate.

The twin in white looked at his brother.

"You got something, Barrett?" he asked, ending the mystery of which was which for Charlotte.

Barrett's in black. Got it.

Barrett nodded and held the book in his hand aloft.

"Sherlock."

He shook the book to see if something fell out. When nothing did, he flipped through the pages.

"Give it to me," said Della, snatching it from his hands.

He frowned but let her have it. She ruffled through it more slowly and then plopped it on the table.

"Nothing. I'll have to go through it page by page."

"Maybe we have the wrong book. Are there any others?" asked Mildred.

The twins shook their heads in unison. It seemed they'd found the only Sherlock Holmes book—a large one—the collected works. It would take Della days to flip through a page at a time, looking for clues.

Time would run out long before then.

Charlotte shook her head.

That can't be right.

She picked up the original note Mildred read aloud and scanned it, wondering if they'd missed a clue.

"*A foot*," she said, holding up the note. "This doesn't say *the game is afoot*—it says the game is a *foot*. Two different words."

She left a lengthy pause between *a* and *foot* to drive home her meaning.

Mildred plucked the sheet from her hand and reread it.

"Oh my stars, you're right. My mind filled in where I thought it was going." She pointed to the wall where she'd started her search. "The medical books—maybe there was one about feet?"

Everyone moved there to search the shelves again.

"We're going to run out of time," moaned Timmy.

Tristan whooped and jerked a book from the shelf. "Here! *Diseases of the Foot*, by Dr. Emil D. W. Hauser," he said, ruffling the yellowed pages.

A paper too white to belong to the aging book fluttered out, and the group pounced. One of the twins knocked Mildred into the shelves.

Furious, she regained her balance and slapped him on his arm.

"Calm yourselves, you *animals*."

Jarrett grabbed the paper first and spun away, reading silently.

"We're working together on this one, remember?" asked Della, words soaked with disdain.

He nodded and read aloud.

"You'll think I'm a stinker, but this one's a thinker."

"What the heck is that supposed to mean?" asked Mildred.

"Philosophy section?" suggested Declan.

Several heads nodded, but Charlotte's attention pulled toward the shelf across from her. She pointed.

"*There*."

She strode to a shelf where a bookend shaped like Rodin's statue, *The Thinker,* sat on his rock, pondering life as the knockoff of a famous statue.

Lifting the ivory-colored bookend, she felt the notches of its surface until her fingertips discovered small hinges on the back. She opened it to reveal a small bronze key inside the hollow body.

"There's a key," she said, holding it up for all to see.

"That's it," said Barrett, moving toward the door.

She shook her head. "The door has a combination."

"Then what's the key for?" asked Mildred.

Della eyed the woman.

"Do you have an *endless* supply of unhelpful questions?" she asked.

Mildred pointed at the girl like a mother scolding her child.

"You mind your manners."

"Check the desk," said Tristan, oblivious to the drama between the women. He pointed to a desk against the wall. The twins reached it first.

"This drawer is locked," said Jarrett, jerking on the gold-plated handle.

Charlotte hustled the key over to him. After some fumbling, he used it to open the drawer. A rolled parchment inside rocked forward as if begging to be grabbed.

Jarrett carried it to the table and unfurled it, smoothing it with his freckled hand.

"It's a map."

The others gathered around him.

"That's a map of somewhere outside, not the house," said his brother. Charlotte agreed. The map clearly marked woods and mountains. She made a quick three-sixty to see if there was a tapestry or painting in the room containing an outdoor scene but found nothing.

"The legend isn't right," said Della, pointing to where the map's legend should be. Instead of explaining how to use the map's symbols, the cornered-off section contained one sentence.

This map will illuminate the clue.

Charlotte and Della exchanged a look.

"What is it?" asked Declan, noticing.

"No one uses the word *illuminate* in puzzles like this unless they mean a light source," said Charlotte, pulling out her phone.

"The phones don't work here. I tried," said Jarrett.

"The flashlight does," said Charlotte, pointing the beam on the map. Nothing jumped out at her.

Della held the parchment up. "Try again."

Charlotte ran the light over it again and thought she saw something shadowy in the background of the landscape.

"There's something there, but it isn't easy to see," mumbled Charlotte.

"I don't see anything," said Mildred, peering over her shoulder.

"It's on this side," said Tristan, who'd hung behind the group when they rushed to the table to see the map.

The rest shifted to peer at the back of the map, where letters were visible with the glow of Charlotte's flashlight behind them.

"*I'm an amateur, not a better yeoman,*" read Tristan.

"What the heck is that supposed to mean?" Mildred dropped her head into her hand. "Why is this so hard?"

The group stared at the words, silent. Charlotte found a pencil on the desk and wrote the phrase on the back of an empty envelope so she wouldn't have to refer to the map.

"Ringing any bells?" she asked Della.

Della shook her head. "Nope. I feel like it has to do with the word *yeoman*. It's such an odd word."

Charlotte realized the others were staring at them. Apparently, they'd pulled ahead as the group's go-to puzzle solvers.

Tristan wasn't looking at them. His focus floated toward the ceiling before dropping back to the group.

"It's an anagram," he said with confidence.

"*Yes,*" said Della, poking a finger in his direction. "Good call. Let's try."

Jarrett and Barrett glanced at each other. They seemed confused.

Della found typing paper in one of the desk drawers, and she and Charlotte wrote the phrase on several sheets before handing it out.

"That's the scrambled letter thing, right?" asked Mildred as Charlotte handed her a sheet.

"Yes. The letters in that phrase unscramble into another phrase or clue."

"Oh..." said Barrett and Jarrett in stereo.

"I'm terrible at those." Mildred frowned. "What if it *isn't* an anagram?"

Charlotte sighed. She suspected Mildred wouldn't be much help with the puzzle, but the woman wasn't wrong either—the phrase might be a *clue* and *not* an anagram.

She decided to keep a few eggs out of their proverbial basket.

"Tell you what, Mildred, you look through the history section over there," she said, pointing. "See if you can find any books with *yeoman* in the title. Something medieval."

Mildred nodded and toddled toward the history section.

"We'll help," said Barrett.

The brothers followed Mildred.

The others sat at the table and worked on the puzzle.

"We're not going to finish in time," said Timmy. "This is too long. There are too many options."

Charlotte worried he was right. She'd started making a string of small words like *was, and, are* and worked with what she had left using letters that went well together, like double Ts and consonate blends like *tr* and *br*.

She stared at how she'd rearranged the letters, fighting the urge to get frustrated or look at her watch.

Finally, something caught her eye.

She'd written *letter man*. She saw there was a *b* and changed it to *better man*.

That sounded familiar.

She wrote out her hunch and found it worked with the remaining letters.

"I've got it!" she yipped, holding up her unscrambled words.

You're a better man than I am.

"*Gunga Din*," said Tristan, noting the work in which Rudyard Kipling wrote those famous words.

Timmy looked at his watch. "We only have three minutes left."

They rushed to the shelves of classic literature, where Tristan pulled a Kipling collection. He flipped through the pages until he found the poem they needed.

"This is it," he announced.

Charlotte leaned in to see. Next to the poem, someone had penciled in a string of numbers.

"There are numbers," she said to alert the room.

Jarrett set himself up next to the door, his finger hovering over the keypad.

"Read them," he barked.

Tristan called them out.

"Four, six, eight, one, one, three."

Jarrett punched in the numbers, and Charlotte heard the latch mechanism whir.

CHAPTER NINE

Once the library door opened, the contestants filed into the hallway to find *nothing* waiting.

The group milled around. A hallway cut a square path around the center stairs. Rooms flanked the hallway—some with doors opened and some closed, but none with anything that offered a clue as to what they were supposed to do next.

Charlotte moved to the window across from the stairs and pushed aside the heavy drapes for a view of the moat outside.

Not promising.

As she returned to the group, Tristan passed in the opposite direction, heading for the stairs. The others remained staring at each other.

"What now?" asked Mildred.

Della shot her a look but didn't say anything. Even cranky Della couldn't be angry at the woman for saying what everyone was thinking.

"Thanks for your help in there," Charlotte said to Della, lowering her voice. "You're good at this. It doesn't seem like you needed to hire Timmy."

She thought the comment might draw Della to her. While Mildred felt less of an asset than she'd hoped, Della had proven herself a talented puzzle solver. It might behoove them to team up.

Della laughed at her comment hard enough to start her blonde curls rocking.

"Hire *Timmy*? I didn't hire Timmy. He's Xander's grandson. He hired *me*. His grandmother is friends with mine, and he found out I'm a trivia buff. He couldn't win a trivia contest if the answer was his own name."

"*I'm right here*," grumbled Timmy.

Della side-eyed him.

"Am I wrong?" she asked.

He paused and then shook his head.

"Maybe we should work together?" suggested Declan. "For a little bit?"

Della scoffed.

"No, thanks. Come on, Tim," she said, following Tristan's path.

"*Timmy*," he corrected, falling in line behind her.

Della shook her head without turning.

"Grown men aren't named *Timmy*, Timmy."

The twins watched them go and then, with a final glance at the others, followed.

Mildred blinked at Charlotte and Declan.

"Do you mind if I come with you? Just for a little while?" she asked. "You offered to work with Della," she added with a pronounced pout.

Charlotte exchanged a look with Declan.

He shrugged.

"Sure. For a bit. Let's make some progress," he said.

They walked down the hall to the stairs leading to the second floor and paused to decide their next move. Charlotte found it hard to think. Through a door to their right, she saw and heard the twins yanking drawers out of kitchenette cabinets, searching for *something*.

"Are they on to something?" asked Declan.

Charlotte shook her head. "Somehow, I don't think so."

"Like bulls in a china shop," murmured Mildred.

"Up the stairs?" suggested Declan.

Charlotte grimaced through the loud clatter of silverware raining onto the castle's stone floor.

She wasn't sure *what* to do. She glanced at the twins again.

She knew what *not* to do.

"Randomly searching seems like a bad idea. Maybe we missed a clue somewhere?" She looked up the stairs. "Yes, let's try going back to the beginning."

The stairs led them back to the grand hall, where they'd enjoyed wine before being dumped into the library. Charlotte looked to the balcony to see if Xander still watched over them.

He'd gone.

A large round table holding a collection of white envelopes stood in the center of the room—exactly where they'd been standing when the floor gave way. While they were trying to find a way out of the library, someone had pushed the table into place.

Declan eyed the table and its suspicious location.

"This feels a little like a trap, doesn't it?" he asked.

Charlotte agreed. "Fool me once..."

Mildred didn't notice them conferring.

She walked directly to the table.

They watched to see if the center of the room would drop away.

It stuck.

"Not a great puzzle solver, but she does come in handy," whispered Charlotte.

"We'll just throw her at anything that looks like a trap," said Declan.

Charlotte giggled as they followed her to the table.

"They have our names on them," announced Mildred, choosing her envelope.

Charlotte took the one marked *Hollie*.

Tristan and Timmy's envelopes were missing.

"Looks like Tristan and Della thought to return to the scene of the crime. They beat us here," said Charlotte.

She opened her message. Inside was a slip of paper with a typed question she read aloud to Declan.

"What rare and expensive wood is often used to construct grand pianos?"

PS: Don't forget—if you disturb the other players' envelopes, you'll be disqualified.

"That last bit explains why Della didn't steal all the envelopes," said Declan.

Charlotte chuckled. She hadn't known Della for long, but that did feel like something the woman would have done if given the chance.

"For a contest with no rules, *more rules*," she said.

"Do you know the answer?"

She nodded. "I think it's *ebony*."

Declan nodded. "Okay. Great. Now what does that *mean* exactly?"

A second sheet of paper hung stapled to the first. It bore a simple house map with large labels naming each room.

"There's a music room," she said, pointing to it.

"Seems like a good place to start looking for...?"

He let the sentence hang.

She shrugged. "Something black?"

"I have a different clue," said Mildred. "*What former governor of California has been on the cover of Cigar Aficionado magazine?*" She grinned. "I know that. Arnold Schwarzenegger."

Charlotte glanced at her map. "There's a smoking room. I think you're supposed to start there."

Mildred frowned.

"We don't all start in the same room?"

"I guess he doesn't want us working as a group anymore. We'll stagger based on how fast we solve things. Maybe we'll come together again in the end."

"He never was one for making things easy," Mildred huffed. "I guess this is where I leave you. See you soon."

She wandered off, yipping as she clipped her shoulder on a doorway. She'd been staring at the map instead of where she was going.

Charlotte patted Declan's arm. "Let's hurry—Della's already ahead of us."

They followed the map down a wide hallway covered in grasscloth wallpaper—another nod to Xander's tropical leanings—until they reached the music room.

The heavy wood double doors opened with a subtle creak, and Charlotte paused to admire them.

"Not as antique as you might think," she said, pointing to the carved image of a shark leaping out of the water to catch a fiddle-playing monkey.

"Classy," said Declan, stepping inside.

As promised, a vintage Steinway grand piano served as the centerpiece of the room. The instrument's jet-black polished surface gleamed like a mirror, reflecting the dim, golden light from the classic chandelier above.

"That looks a little more expensive than the doors," said Declan, nodding to the piano.

"Maybe," said Charlotte studying the bookshelves and two tall, narrow stained-glass windows. Each featured a lizard in the center that glowed green against the landscape lighting outside.

She tittered.

"This place is like a *Connecticut Yankee in King Arthur's Court*—if the Yankee was Jimmy Buffett."

Declan lifted the cover over the piano keys, discovering a white notecard, which he held up for Charlotte to see.

"That was easy," he said before reading. "*What song was on the first twelve-inch vinyl record?*"

Charlotte blinked.

"I don't like that look," said Declan.

"You shouldn't. It's my *I have no idea* look."

He frowned. "Me neither. I shouldn't have said *that was easy* out loud. I cursed us."

Charlotte took a deep breath and huffed it out.

"Let's see. There has to be a way to figure this out." She pulled out her phone and attempted to search for the answer. She had no signal.

"Surprise, surprise—the phones don't work, so that's not an option..."

Declan pointed to a slick modern record player sitting on a cabinet behind her. The bottom half of the cabinet held hundreds of vinyl records.

"The clue must be on a record, right?"

"Good thought...and Xander is old enough he might *have* the first vinyl record here."

They moved to the cabinet and flipped through the record collection.

"This could take forever," said Declan.

Charlotte agreed. "The problem is they're mostly from the last fifty years. The first recording has to be older than that."

She scanned the room, hoping for inspiration. The dark paneled walls offered little help. Standing to stretch her legs, she noticed several white busts decorating a shelf and wandered to them.

"The first record would probably be something classical, right?" she asked.

Declan held a black album aloft. On it, a man in a white suit pointed to the sky. "Safe bet it wasn't the soundtrack to *Saturday Night Fever.*"

"How about Mozart?"

A gold plaque on the first ivory bust bore that composer's name. She lifted the statue, pulling and pushing to see if it would open like the one in the library.

Nothing moved.

She grabbed the next one. *Beethoven*. Turning it over, she noticed a hole in the bottom leading to its hollow center. She poked her fingers inside to pull out another card.

A shot of excitement ran through her body.

"Found a card in Beethoven's head," she reported. "It's orange."

Declan leaped to his feet. "Orange? I wonder if that means something. What's it say?"

"*The first twelve-inch LP was Beethoven's Symphony No. 5 In C Minor by the Philadelphia Orchestra conducted by Leopold Stokowski.*"

Declan scoffed. "And you didn't know that?"

She stuck her tongue out at him. "It goes on with the next clue. *This can spur you on, line you up, or get the ball rolling.*"

"More of a riddle than trivia, isn't it?"

"Yes. Seems ol' Xander has been playing fast and loose with everything—rules in a game without rules, riddles in a trivia contest, floors that disappear..." She studied the card. "He mixed spelling on this one, too."

"He typoed?"

"No, the answer is a *cue*—you can take your cue, use a cue to get a pool ball rolling, and a line of people is a queue, but that's spelled q-u-e-u-e."

"I think I know what that means," said Declan as he pulled the map from his pocket. "There was a billiards room. I bet the orange cards signify a move to the next room."

She nodded. "That makes sense."

As they exited the music room, she thought she saw a flash of Hawaiian print running by at the end of the hall.

"I think I just saw Xander run by," she said, pointing.

"*Run* by? Didn't you say he's ninety-four?"

"Yes—I'm starting to think the real prize is finding out what that guy eats. Should we try to catch him?"

"Why?"

She sighed. "For one, I'd like to ask him what made him think it was okay to drop us twenty feet to the ground. But you're right. I guess it doesn't make any sense. We need to stick to winning this thing. I doubt he'd give us clues even if we caught him."

Declan chuckled. "He's not a leprechaun."

"Who knows? Maybe he is. Maybe that's his secret."

They walked ten feet down the hall to make a right into the long, narrow billiard room. Like the music room, it featured dark cherry wood panels reaching from floor to ceiling. Persian rugs worn thin with use lay scattered on the stone floor, patterned in faded colors. A chandelier created from a pod of leaping iron dolphins lit the space.

In the center sat an enormous pool table with green felt, crafted from the same dark wood as the walls. The carved legs featured monkies, parrots, and flamingoes instead of the eagles or lions one might expect to find on castle furniture.

Heavy drapes hung from brass rods above large sealed windows. Rows of cues occupied a section of one wall, and deep cushioned chairs lined the room.

"I'll check the table. You check the cues," said Declan, peering into a corner pocket.

Charlotte twisted and pulled each cue in turn, searching for anything interesting.

"Nothing here," she reported before wandering to the table to check the ball return. She grabbed a few balls and rolled them one at a time at the pockets, waiting for each ball to return to her before throwing the next.

The ball thrown into the left side pocket remained missing in action.

"Something's in the return for that pocket," she noted.

She lay on her back and slid under the pool table where the winding ball return tracks led to the far end. She spotted the missing ball, blocked from its destination by a white card wedged in the track.

"Found it," she said.

She was about to slide out when she noticed something red sticking from a wall panel. She would have never seen it had she not been on the ground.

"What's that?" she said, crawling toward it. "Something's sticking out of the wall paneling down here."

"Maybe he didn't hide a clue as well as he thought," said Declan, walking around the table to her. "Maybe we can jump the line."

She pushed aside one of the padded chairs and pointed at the red tag poking from the baseboard. She squatted to get a better look and tugged at it. The fabric extended another four inches before catching.

Charlotte gasped as the fabric's pattern revealed itself.

I know this pattern.

The silky fabric had navy blue paisleys dotting the surface. She rubbed it between her fingers.

"This looks like Tristan's scarf," she said. "Why is it *here*?"

Declan ran his hand along the edge of the panel. "This wall must open."

"Tristan? Are you hiding?" called Charlotte, knocking on the wall.

No one answered.

Charlotte stood to help Declan look for a lever to release the hidden door. The two felt along the panels until a section of the trim work depressed beneath Declan's fingers.

Something clicked.

The wall popped open a crack. Using fingertips to pry the panel, they swung it open to reveal a narrow hidden passageway.

Tristan lay sprawled on the ground, still attached to his scarf. His wide eyes stared up at them, his pale flesh nearly glowing against his dark mustache and triangle beard.

"Tristan?"

Charlotte squatted to feel his neck for a pulse. She found no heartbeat. She suspected there hadn't been one for some time. His flesh had cooled to an unnatural temperature.

She looked up at Declan.

"He's dead."

CHAPTER TEN

"We need to get ahold of Charlotte and Declan so they can help us find Sir Sleepsalot," said Mariska, dialing Charlotte.

"I don't know if this is their thing," said Darla. She was still shiny with sweat. It had taken them an hour to get everyone to leave by selling the crowd empty promises for future sloth-viewing and free glasses of wine. After the people cleared, they scoured the area one more time, to no avail.

They were both sweaty and tired.

"Remember when Charlotte first started being a detective? She used to find dogs for people." Mariska hung up with a pout. "But she's not answering. Neither is Declan. It's not like them."

"Weren't they going to be in some sort of contest with Xander Flummox? They probably can't be on the phone during whatever that is."

Mariska lowered the phone and let her shoulders sag.

"This is terrible. What are we going to do?" She sat up. "Do you think that thing was worth a lot of money?"

Darla scoffed. "The sloth? Probably, but I wouldn't get your panties in a bunch about her suing you. She threw his food at the wall and pulled a runner."

"I suppose I could argue that I never even agreed to watch it."

"You *didn't*. I'll be your witness."

Mariska frowned. "I think *you* did, though."

"Maybe, but it's your house. I had no right."

"Can I record that?"

Darla shook her head. "Never mind all that. We're getting ahead of ourselves." She stomped her foot and offered Mariska a motivational fist pump. "We have to charge ahead and stop thinking about consequences."

Mariska blinked at her.

"I just figured out why you always end up in trouble."

Darla ignored her and paced Mariska's kitchen.

"Let's walk through it. We put the thing on the tree and hung the tarp, and we were right there...he was behind the tarp...and then...he just *wasn't* there."

"He disappeared, *poof*, and the thing moved like molasses. It doesn't make any sense. Where could he have gone in that little bit of time? It couldn't have crawled away, looking like something out of a horror movie, without *someone* noticing."

Darla pressed her lips together. "Which means someone must have taken it."

Mariska's eyes widened.

"You think he was *slothnapped*?"

Darla nodded. "Had to be. It wouldn't have been hard. He *is* a cuddly thing. When I went to take it outside, he jumped into my arms like he'd been waiting to do it all day."

Mariska tapped her chin with her fingers, thinking.

"While we were selling wine, someone sneaked back there—maybe came from the back of the house where we wouldn't have noticed them—and Sir Sleepsalot jumped into their arms." She cocked her head. "Do you think someone *meant* to take him? Maybe he jumped into their arms, and they didn't know what to do?"

"And they ran off with a sloth stuck to them, silent screaming?" Darla shook her head. "I don't think so. I mean, maybe once they had it, *slothnapping* seemed like a good idea, but it's more likely they planned to steal it all along."

"But *why*?" moaned Mariska. "How did they even know it was there?"

"The same way everyone else knew it was there. The flyers."

Mariska growled. "You and your stupid flyers. I knew this wasn't a good idea."

Darla lifted her hands into the air and let them drop to her sides.

"How were we supposed to know someone would steal it? Why would someone steal a sloth?"

"Like I said, it's probably worth a few bucks to the right weirdo." Mariska hung her head in her hands. "If they planned all along to sell it, then we won't get a ransom note."

"Ransom?"

Darla perked, looking hopeful.

"Why do you look like you thought of something?" asked Mariska.

Darla pointed to the front door.

"What about your doorbell camera? Did that have a clear view behind the tarp?"

Mariska gasped.

"*Yes*, you're right. I'll look."

She picked up her phone and scrolled to her camera app.

"Hold on, here it is..."

"Let me see," said Darla, slamming her hip against Mariska's as she jostled to get a peek at the screen.

Mariska scrolled through the clips until she reached one where the preview image showed a figure approaching Sir Sleepsalot as he hung on his tree behind the tarp.

Mariska poked the phone so hard it almost slipped from her hand.

"*Look*. This is *it*."

She tapped on the video to start it playing. Darla leaned against her harder.

"You're going to knock me over," grumbled Mariska.

She squinted at the screen as Sir Sleepsalot appeared on the screen, hanging on the tree behind the tarp, alone. They saw themselves selling tickets and pouring wine on the opposite side of the tarp.

"Have I gained weight?" asked Darla.

"*Shhh*."

A figure rounded the corner of the house.

Mariska gasped.

"There he is!"

"That's a *man*," said Darla.

A thin man wearing a hooded sweatshirt slipped behind the tarp and raised his arms to the sloth. The poor sleepy thing wrapped its crazy arms around him, and the man returned the way he came, gripping the sloth against his chest.

"Someone *did* steal it," said Darla, breathless.

Mariska raised a hand to her mouth and nodded, still finding it hard to believe her eyes.

"We were right in front of the tarp while this jackass was walking away with Sir Sleepsalot."

Mariska threw back her head and moaned.

"What are you doing?" asked Darla.

"What am I doing? We let this woman's sloth be *stolen*. What are we going to do?"

"We'll find him. Rewind it. Play it back."

They watched again.

"I can't see his face," said Mariska.

"No. He kept it covered. He moves like a *him*, though."

"Definitely a man."

"Yes. Of course, it is. Jackass. Younger, too, don't you think?"

Mariska nodded. "Yes. For a second, I was hoping maybe it was Bob playing a trick on us."

"No such luck."

Darla eyed her warily, and Mariska realized she was scowling.

"*What*? Why do you have that look on your face?" asked Darla.

Mariska touched her hand.

"We have to tell Frank."

Darla closed her eyes and shook her head like a wet dog.

"*No*. Not yet."

"We *have* to. We need to police."

Darla writhed as if she were in pain.

"You don't understand. If we tell him, I'm going to have to hear about this for months..."

Mariska's phone dinged, and she lifted it, knowing it would be a while before Darla overcame her tantrum, gave in, and called Frank.

She hoped it was Charlotte.

It wasn't.

Someone from an unfamiliar number had sent her a text.

1000 or yu never see it agin.

Mariska gasped, and Darla stopped her theatrics.

"What is it?"

"I think it's a ransom note."

"*What?*"

Darla snatched the phone from her to read the text.

"Who's it from?" she asked.

"How would I know? You think it's one of my good friends?"

"No—but how did they know your number?"

"I don't *know*. Did you put it on the flyers?"

"Did I—?" She frowned. "Yes. Maybe."

Mariska huffed.

Darla started typing.

"What are you doing?" asked Mariska, horrified.

"I'm asking who they are."

"They're not going to tell you that."

"I have to *ask*."

Darla stopped typing. Her eyes widened.

"What *now*?" asked Mariska.

Darla turned the screen to her. The kidnapper had sent them a picture of Sir Sleepsalot on an ugly green sofa, lying across the back of it, eyes closed.

"He could be dead for all we know," said Darla.

Mariska nodded. "Kind of hard to tell with that one."

The phone dinged with a new message.

Send Bitcoin.

Mariska scowled. "*Bitcoin*? I don't even know what that is."

Darla grabbed the phone again. "Just as well, we don't have a thousand dollars in Bitcoin, or wampum, or rare bottlecaps, either."

She tapped another message.

"Now what are you saying?"

Darla huffed. "I'm telling them we couldn't get our own mothers back if it required Bitcoin."

"Don't piss him off."

"I'm *not*. It's just a fact."

After a minute, a response came.

I send diff way.

"What's a *diff way*?" asked Mariska.

"He means he'll send us a different way to pay."

Mariska grunted. "I hope he plans to use the money for schooling. His grammar is terrible."

"We're not giving him money. There must be a way to track down this number." She tapped her front tooth with her fingernail. "Oh! Who's that computer guy Charlotte uses?"

Mariska thought for a moment. "It's that guy over on Penny's street. The one who walks his cat on a leash."

"Right. I think his name is Gryph? We should ask him. He can probably hack your phone or whatever."

Mariska set her jaw. "Let's go."

They walked the few blocks to Gryph's house, Mariska grumbling.

"It wasn't a bad idea," Darla argued.

"It was a *terrible* idea."

"We made, like, a hundred and fifty dollars."

Mariska grunted. "*Great*—except now we owe some thief—who has my phone number and address—a thousand Bitcoins."

She pounded on Gryph's door, still seething. A heavy-set man with a wavy-haired gray cat perched on his shoulder opened the door to stare at them without speaking. He wore a light blue tank top and striped pajama bottoms. The cat sported a pink harness and a miserable expression on its oval face.

"Must be related to Miss Izzy," muttered Darla, motioning to the cat's cavernous ears.

Mariska elbowed her arm.

"Ow. *Hello*," said Darla.

Gryphon and the cat continued to stare in stony silence.

Darla plowed on. "You're Gryph?"

Gryph pursed his lips. "Depends. Who's asking?"

"Um, you don't know us, but we're friends of Charlotte's—"

"Like her *mother*, really," interjected Mariska.

Darla nodded. "That's true. We're like her mother. Collectively. *Anyway*, we need you to hack our phone."

Gryph's right eyebrow arched.

"You want me to hack *your* phone?"

Mariska nodded and held up her phone. "Someone stole our sloth—" He tucked his chin and scowled at her.

"You're the ones who stuck the sloth flyer on my door?"

"That was me," admitted Darla.

"There was *really* a sloth?"

Darla blinked at him.

"*Yes*. Why would we stage a whole sloth party without a sloth?"

He shrugged. "I don't know. I guess I thought it was a joke."

"It kind of is, *now*," grumbled Mariska. "*We're* the joke—"

Darla cut her short.

"It wasn't a joke. We had a sloth until someone stole it. The kidnappers texted us a photo of it with a ransom note."

"And you want me to see who sent the message?"

"*Yes*. We have to get the sloth back."

Gryph grunted. "Five hundred."

Darla's eyes popped wide. "*Dollars*?"

"We don't have five hundred dollars," said Mariska.

Gryph frowned. "A hundred?"

Mariska glowered at Darla.

"That's everything I'll make for babysitting."

"Considering what a bang-up job you're doing..." said Gryph. He chuckled, and the cat imitated him with its own wheezy laugh.

The ladies stared at the cat until it stopped.

Mariska turned her focus on Gryph.

"What do you know?" she said under her breath.

He smiled.

"I know you're short one sloth."

She thrust her phone at him. "*Fine*. One hundred."

He took it.

"Come to my workshop."

He leaned through his door to look left and right as if he were worried snipers lurked nearby, waiting for their chance. Satisfied he'd make it from the front door to the workshop alive, he led them to the adjacent garage, the cat balancing on his shoulder like a furry, wide-eyed parrot.

He punched a code into a panel.

"Aren't you the guy who walks his cat?" asked Darla as they waited for the door to rise.

"I hate the smell of litter boxes," he said.

The door locked into place above their heads, revealing Gryph's messy workshop. A built-in table ran along the room's outer edge, covered in computer parts and bits of technology. Along one wall, a squadron of drones sat on shelves, waiting for action.

"I can probably pull the geolocation data from the photo," he said, sitting on a torn rolling chair.

"Good. Do that," said Darla.

He plugged the phone into one of the few computers that looked like it might work and typed away.

"Reverse lookup says it's a cell, but that's all I've got."

Ten minutes later, he shrugged.

"Nothing."

"*Nothing?*" Mariska echoed.

"We're not paying for *nothing*," said Darla.

Gryphon nodded and began typing again. "Hold on..."

"You see something?" asked Darla.

"Yep. I've got him now."

Mariska yipped with joy. "Who is it? Where are they?"

Gryph sniffed. "I'm not telling you until you pay me."

Darla shook a finger at him. "We're not paying until you tell us."

He shrugged. "I can wait. When's the owner of the sloth coming back?"

Grumbling, Mariska reached into her purse and pulled out five folded twenty-dollar bills.

"Here. This is all my emergency money."

Gryph took it and wandered out of the garage.

"*Where is he?*" asked Darla, chasing after him.

Gryph motioned for them to follow him. Once they'd left the garage, he shut the door and headed back to his house.

"Hey!" barked Mariska. "Where's the thief?"

He shrugged. "I don't know. There was nothing there."

"But we *paid* you," said Darla.

"To look, not to find."

The cat turned to wheeze at them again as Gryph entered his home.

"I don't think I like that cat," said Darla.

Mariska rubbed her eye with her hand. "I need a snack to think. My blood sugar is low."

Darla clapped her on the back.

"Me, too. Half a sleeve of Girl Scout Cookies, and I bet we'll figure everything out."

Mariska started walking.

"I think this is a *full-sleeve* think."

CHAPTER ELEVEN

"We didn't sign up for *this*," said Declan as he and Charlotte stared at Tristan's cooling body.

"No. This is *not* good. Ten thousand suddenly doesn't seem like enough."

Declan pulled out his phone and flipped on the flashlight. "Was it a heart attack? Did he maybe find this passageway as one of his clues and then happen to *die*?"

As soon as the light hit the body, they had their answer. Blood stained Tristan's chest.

"Stabbed, by the look of it," muttered Declan inspecting the wound. "Looks like someone wants to win a little more than the rest of us."

Charlotte rubbed her temple. "This is *insane*. They can't kill *all* of us. We need to get out of here. This isn't fun anymore."

"The problem is the old man made a big show of sealing us in. The place is *literally* a fortress."

"We'll break a window."

"And swim through the unscalable alligator-infested moat?"

Charlotte frowned.

"Forgot about that."

"What we need to do is find Xander. He must have a way to communicate with the outside world, and he knows how to open the drawbridge."

Charlotte frowned.

"Can we trust him? What if *he* killed Tristan? Remember? I thought I saw him in the hall—"

"He's *ninety-four*. If a ninety-four-year-old guy can kill us all, frankly, maybe we deserve to die."

Charlotte snorted a laugh. "I can't think of any motive he'd have for killing his heirs, either. Unless he just *hates* his family tree. In which case, he didn't have to stage an elaborate contest—he could have just poisoned the reception wine.

"Right. I think all that makes him the one person we *can* trust."

Charlotte agreed.

"Here's the other question. Do we warn the others?"

Declan frowned. "Maybe not yet. One of them probably killed Tristan, and if we let everyone know *we* know what's going on—"

Charlotte ran her finger across her throat.

He nodded.

"Right. *That*."

She glanced into the darkness of the passageway behind the wall. "Let's not go that way. And let's close the door so the killer doesn't know we're on to him."

"Him? You think you know who it is?"

"No. But stabbings are usually a *him*."

"Sure, but guns make a lot of noise."

Charlotte huffed. "I'm going to call him *him*."

"Fine. Which way did you see Xander heading?" asked Declan.

"Down the hall and to the left. How fast can he move? If we hurry, maybe we'll catch him."

They jogged into the hall and made a left, nearly smashing into the twins, who were headed in the opposite direction, looking flustered.

"Have you seen Xander?" asked Charlotte.

The men scowled in unison and pushed past them without answering. Charlotte noticed stapled sheets of paper in Jarrett's hand.

"Okay, thanks, good talk," she called after them as they disappeared around the corner.

"Friendly guys. We should get a beer after this," said Declan.

"They were a lot nicer when they needed our help to get out of the library." Charlotte sighed. "They're probably stressed. They're behind. It looks like they just figured out to check the foyer for a starting point."

"After tearing apart half of downstairs."

They continued down the hall, taking another left that led them back to the great hall. They moved to the bottom of the curving staircase and stared up at the third-floor landing, hoping to see Xander.

No one was there.

"He probably went back to his room to stay out of sight," said Charlotte.

"We were forbidden to go to the third floor. Going up might disqualify us."

"Does it matter at this point?"

Declan snorted a laugh.

"No. I guess not."

They mounted the stairs.

Though the layout of the third floor wasn't on the provided house map, a quick look made it clear it held nothing except bedrooms and adjoining baths. After poking their heads into a few guest rooms, they reached the end of a hall to find a door marked 'DO NOT ENTER' with a large plastic red, white, and black sign.

"This has to be his room," said Charlotte, knocking.

There was no answer. Declan tried the knob.

"Locked."

Charlotte eyed him.

"How's your shoulder? Feeling strong?"

Declan winced.

"You think we should kick in his door?"

Charlotte shrugged.

"If there was a dead guy in your billiards room, would you want someone to let you know? Or should we wait until someone takes out Mrs. Peacock in the conservatory with a candlestick?"

Declan smiled and shook his head.

"Fine. Good point, but I think this is more of a *foot* situation."

He stepped back and kicked to the right of the knob.

The lock exploded, and the door flung open.

Charlotte expected Xander to come running, but nothing happened. Though the crack seemed loud in the big quiet house, no one appeared at the foot of the stairs, and nothing moved in the bedroom.

"That was anticlimactic," said Declan.

They walked into a large bedroom featuring an odd mix of garish tropical décor and sterile medical equipment. Oversized palm trees and hibiscus flowers dotted the wallpaper. Someone had stapled palm fonds to the ceiling, and heavy, gothic furniture loomed beside flimsy wicker pieces.

"It's like a cheap Hawaiian hotel barfed in here," muttered Declan.

In stark contrast, a medical bed with guardrails and a cold, off-white metal frame sat in the center of the room. An array of medical machinery hovered around the bed like worried relatives. An IV pole stood nearby, its clear tubing snaking to nowhere. The bed was empty.

"Xander?" called Charlotte.

She entered the attached bath, where the tropical nightmare continued. A shower curtain covered by a dizzying array of toucans and parrots hung half open, saving her the nervewracking exercise of throwing it open. Shell-shaped sconces flanked the gilded bamboo bathroom mirror. A brass monkey held a toilet paper roll at the ready. The walls throbbed with vibrant turquoise.

Xander hadn't missed adding his tiki flair to a single accessory. A soap dispenser shaped like a pineapple sat beside a tiki idol toothbrush holder, and a bronze dolphin poised at the ready to spit water into the sink.

Declan stepped in behind her. She looked at him.

"On house renovation shows, they always say the bathroom is the place to take risks, but...*damn*."

He nodded. "This is a risk, alright. A *seizure* risk."

"I think this wins the prize," she said, pointing to the toilet seat. Pointed teeth made the porcelain throne look like a grinning shark, its mouth wide and eager to bite any tush dumb enough to sit on it.

Declan laughed.

"That is something special."

"A lot of *something* in here, but no Xander."

"No. Why build a castle and then retrofit it to look like a dimestore Tahiti? Why didn't he build a giant thatched hut?"

"That's an excellent question. Almost as good as, *Hey, Xander, any idea who's killing your contestants*?"

Declan put his hands on his hips. "I thought we'd find a landline phone in here, but nope. Now what?"

"I guess he's still running around the house. We'll have to find him."

"Is this guy *sure* he's going to die soon? He seems awfully spry."

"Speaking of which—if someone's willing to kill the other contestants, doesn't it follow they'll kill Xander, too? They don't get anything until he's dead. It might be we need to warn him more than anyone. Warn him and *then* call in help sorting out the others."

Declan nodded. "Getting out of here is priority one. Figuring out who we can and can't trust is impossible. We'll call the cops and let them figure it out."

"For what it's worth, I can't see Mildred stabbing Tristan."

"No, but Tristan wasn't a big guy and could have been caught off guard. We can't even cross her off our list."

"Della's mean enough. Timmy's a strange, squirrelly little guy, but that could be an act."

"The twins have the strength and numbers. They were nearby when we came out of the billiards room, too."

"Long story short, we can't trust any of them." Charlotte started for the door and then paused to sniff. "Do you smell that?"

Declan took a whiff and scowled. "Yes. Ugh. What is that?"

Charlotte took a few steps toward the large wardrobe, nose twitching like a rabbit's.

"It's over here..."

She opened the wardrobe's door, her attention dropping as a hand fell out and slapped her naked toes.

She yipped and jumped back. Declan grabbed her shoulders to steady her.

"Not again," he said.

A body lay bunched at the bottom of the wardrobe. With the door open, the stench filled the room.

"That's Xander," said Charlotte, recognizing the man's pale face. He was twenty years older than the last time she'd seen him on television, but it had to be him.

He wore bunched-up light blue pajamas dotted with bananas.

Charlotte pointed to a visible section of his back where his pajamas had bunched. The skin had turned dark blue.

"Lividity. His blood already pooled." She touched the arm now hanging from the cabinet. "He's not stiff. He's probably been dead for a day or more."

"How could he have been dead that long? We saw him on the balcony two hours ago, and you thought you saw him in the hall."

She frowned. "Or we didn't, which means the players aren't the only people in the house. Someone else is here, pretending to be him."

Declan nodded.

"And they've already killed two people."

CHAPTER TWELVE

Charlotte pushed Xander's hand back into the wardrobe. When she thought she had him secured, the hand flopped back out. The faster and harder she tried to close the door, the quicker the hand blocked her.

"I think he's doing this on purpose," she grumbled as his fingers prevented a seal for the third time.

Declan stood at the doorway, waiting.

"Cut it out before we have to explain why every bone in his hand's broken."

Charlotte huffed and gave up.

"Getting Xander's help is no longer an option. What's plan B?"

"I think we're on plan Q at this point."

Declan's gaze pulled toward the front of the house.

"He said the gate would rise in the morning or when someone solved the puzzle, right?"

"Right, but that wasn't him, so who knows?"

"True. But do you think they were reading his script? That it still might be the truth? Maybe the gate is on some kind of timer?"

"The voice did sound like an old guy. He could have pre-recorded it. Of course, he could have planned on being alive to open the door, too."

She glanced down the stairs to the great hall.

"It's probably safe to assume the mystery killer wants everyone dead, so they're the last man standing to win everything. But, if you plan on killing everyone anyway, why run the event?"

Declan blinked at her. "That's a good question. Why are they going through the motions?"

"The only thing I can think is that they must *need* to really win the game. There must be some prize or token at the end that they can turn over to Xander—or, since he's dead, his *lawyers*—to prove they won."

"Someone has to actually win..."

Charlotte sighed. "If that's the case, I guess we better be sure it's us. Plan Q is we go back to winning the contest."

Declan peered back at Xander's lolling hand. "What about him?"

"Even if I could shut the wardrobe, we can't fix the bedroom lock, so it doesn't matter. We'll shut the door and hope the bad guy doesn't check on him."

They pushed the bits of broken lock into the bedroom before shutting the door as best they could.

"One other thing is bothering me," said Charlotte as they trotted back down the stairs to return to the billiard's room. "Say the bad guy wins and gets the proof—how does he explain Xander in the wardrobe?"

"Or Tristan, or the rest of us, for that matter."

"They might be planning on framing one of us for everything."

Declan rolled his eyes. "Great. More to worry about."

They'd nearly reached the billiards room when they spotted Della alone. She had her arms crossed against her chest, scowling at the ground. She seemed more annoyed than scared.

She looked up as they approached.

"Have you seen Timmy?" she asked.

Declan and Charlotte shook their heads. Charlotte found it hard to keep from warning her. As far as she knew, Della *was* the killer, but it still felt wrong not to let her know about the dead bodies piling up.

Come to think of it...

Was it strange she'd lost Timmy? Did she kill him? Was she pretending not to know where he was to create an alibi and put them at ease so she could stab them at her leisure?

Charlotte squinted.

I knew I didn't like this chick.

"Haven't seen him," said Declan.

Della huffed. "He said something about having to go to the bathroom, and then he just disappeared." She eyed them. "How many rooms have you cleared?"

"Just one," said Charlotte.

Della snorted a laugh and continued down the hall.

Charlotte looked at Declan.

"Do you think she killed Timmy?"

"Certainly possible."

"Either way, I get the impression we're falling behind clearing rooms."

"Me, too. Do you still have the card you found under the table?"

"Oh, yes." Charlotte pulled the card from the bodice of her gown as

Declan looked on, clearly bemused.

"They don't make gowns with pockets," she explained, unfolding the card to read the clue.

"*The colors in order and the sum.*"

"So again, not trivia. A riddle," said Declan as they entered the billiards room. "How about you figure it out, and I'll keep watch to be sure no one kills us."

"Seems fair." She motioned to the secret passage where Tristan lay hidden. "Don't forget to watch the walls, too."

He nodded and split his time watching the hidden door and the hall while she wandered around the pool table, thinking.

The colors in order...

What colors?

The games so far had stuck to the room themes, so the clue *had* to reference the pool balls' colors.

Right?

She released the balls from the triangle rack and lined them up numerically. The solid-colored balls from one to eight were yellow, blue, red, purple, orange, green, maroon, and black.

She stared at them.

Great.

Now what?

The rest of the clue was *and the sum*. Obviously, she was supposed to add something up. Again, she assumed the balls. One through fifteen added up to one hundred and twenty.

Fantastic.

A row of balls and the number one twenty—she had everything and nothing.

"Could you speed things up?" asked Declan.

"Very funny. The balls have both colors and numbers. It has to have something to do with them."

"Do they open?"

She'd already worked on them as she laid them in a row but went through them again. Nothing opened or broke away.

"No. They're normal pool balls."

She put her hands on her hips and stared at the faded rugs.

Hm.

The rugs were colorful, even if they were faded. Yellow, blue, red, purple, orange, green, maroon...

She dropped down and rolled up the parts of the rug *not* bearing the weight of the pool table, exposing a metal square embedded in the stone.

"*Ah ha!*" she said, motioning to it for Declan to see.

He nodded approvingly.

"Good job."

She pried at the metal square with her fingernails until it gave way, revealing a safe with a keypad combination lock beneath it.

"There's a floor safe," she reported.

"Awesome. Do you know the combination?"

"I actually think I do."

Charlotte punched in one-two-zero.

Like a hotel safe, it beeped and unlatched. She opened the door.

Inside sat an orange card.

"We have orange," she announced. "We're getting out of this stupid room."

"Good. What's the clue?"

"*What food never goes bad?*"

Declan shrugged. "We're back to trivia, but I don't know."

She smiled. "Luckily, I do. *Honey.*"

"Honey? Why not?"

"Something to do with acidity and a lack of moisture."

"Hm. You learn something new every day. Well, you do, apparently. I don't think I do. Does Xander keep bees?"

"Not indoors, I hope, so since we can't get out of this stupid castle, I think the kitchen is our next stop."

Charlotte shut the safe and rolled the rug back over it.

"Next stop, the kitchen."

They followed the map to the large, if outdated, kitchen. The brown, speckled countertop granite and walnut cabinets made the room feel dark.

A professional-grade, six-burner gas range, wine fridge, and double-door refrigerator redeemed the space on the technology front. The enormous island ensured plenty of space for cooking, but the room felt as if it had gone largely unused for some time.

A breakfast banquet occupied one corner, its cushions faded and flattened from years of sitting. After moving through so many impressive spaces, the kitchen felt like a letdown.

"It looks like he hasn't been here in years," said Declan.

"He probably had kitchen staff, and what he doesn't see, he doesn't upgrade."

Charlotte traced her finger along a dusty countertop corner and added, "It's also getting eerie that we haven't bumped into more people."

Declan nodded. "I was just thinking that. It's a big house, but it isn't *that*—"

As if on cue, voices and the sound of a struggle echoed from the hall. People grunted. Someone yipped in a higher, feminine voice. A moment later, Della and Barrett burst into the kitchen, their expressions angry.

Della held a large kitchen knife in her hand.

"*Get back*," she hissed, waving the weapon at Barrett.

Barrett was bleeding—red stained the upper arm of his white tuxedo.

Charlotte looked at Declan.

"Ah, there's people now."

CHAPTER THIRTEEN

"We have to think this out," said Mariska, slipping a cookie into her mouth as they walked out of the food store.

She remembered she'd eaten all the Girl Scout Cookies, but their mouths were so set they went to the store to buy a box of Thin Mint knockoffs.

Darla held out a hand so Mariska could hand her a cookie from their already dwindling supply.

"We better think of something soon, or you'll be a thousand pounds. You ate a sleeve before we even got out of the store."

"I did not." She eyed the half-empty package and grunted. "Anyway, it doesn't matter. I always think best when I'm eating or food shopping."

"So you should be able to cure cancer doing both." Darla unlocked her car, and they placed their few other groceries on the back seat before entering. "Try Charlotte again."

"I did when you were checking out. She's not answering. What a time for her to be out of town." Mariska looked at Darla with her best puppy dog eyes. "Please let me get Frank involved now?"

Darla shook her head. "I've got a better idea. We should go to the bar."

Mariska scowled. "Some of the dumbest things Bob ever said came out of his mouth when he was drinking. Drinking never solves anything."

"I don't totally agree with that—I mean, I *do* agree Bob has said some stupid things—but I don't mean we should go to the bar to get drunk. We should go to talk to Seamus."

Mariska perked. "He was a policeman in Miami before he came here, wasn't he?"

"Something like that. And he's crafty. He'll know what to do."

Mariska bounced in her seat, clapping her hands. "Yes, good idea. Go to the bar. Go, go, *go*."

Darla motored to Seamus's bar, The Anne Bonny, and the two women hustled inside. The air felt like ice, and they jostled against each other as their eyes adjusted to the dark.

Seamus stood behind the bar chatting to a pair of women with pink cocktails in front of them.

"Seamus, we need your help," said Darla.

Seamus spread his arms wide. "I'm here to serve. How can I help you, ladies?"

He grinned, his teeth especially white against his new closely cropped salt-and-pepper beard. Mariska thought it made him look more like a seafarer, which matched the theme of his bar.

"Someone stole our sloth," she said, clawing through her purse. She pulled out her phone, unlocked it, and handed it to him.

"I'm sorry. Can you repeat that? I thought you said *sloth*," he said, taking the phone.

Darla nodded. "She did. We were babysitting a pet sloth, and someone kidnapped it."

Seamus's gaze drifted from Mariska to Darla and back again.

"Okay. I think I got it. Kidnapped sloth. How do you know it didn't wander off?"

"We got a ransom text with a photo, and we have doorbell camera footage of the weasel who took it," said Mariska.

Seamus frowned.

"Are they asking for a drop?"

"A what?"

"How did they want you to pay them?"

"Oh. With Bitcoin."

Darla snickered. "I told them good luck."

"What did they say to that?"

"They said they'd find a *diff way*."

"So your sloth was stolen by a weasel," muttered Seamus as he scrolled and poked through her phone.

"That sounds like a children's book," said one of the two younger women at the bar. The redhead of the pair giggled.

Darla side-eyed them and continued, "We had the nerdy guy, Gryph, look at the photo, and he tried to get map information off the photo—"

"Geodes," said Mariska.

"*Geolocation*," corrected Seamus. "Geodes are rocks."

"Whatever. He didn't get anything and still took our money," grumbled Mariska.

Seamus looked up. "Yer sayin' this is a paying gig?"

The ladies hemmed, and he laughed.

"I'm kidding. I'm kidding. Let's see. What do we *know*?"

"They have terrible grammar," said Mariska.

"That narrows it down to *everyone* these days," muttered Darla.

"Did you try to reverse lookup on the phone number?"

"Gryph did. He said it's a cell, but that's all he could get."

"Did you call the exotic animal shops, pet stores, and vets? They have to feed it."

Darla nodded. "That's a good idea. I'll make some calls."

She peeled off to sit at the back of the bar.

Seamus looked up from his inspection of Mariska's phone.

"Did you ask your neighbors if they have footage from *their* cameras? Maybe we can get a peek at the getaway car."

Mariska nodded. "That's a good idea too. You're full of good ideas."

"Let me put the kidnapper's phone number in my phone," said one of the young women. "I'm on all the socials. It might connect me to an account."

"I t'ink you just got yerself a free drink, lass."

Seamus winked at her. His accent always grew thicker when talking to attractive ladies.

The women cheered as he poured them a second round. When finished, he wrote the number on a bar napkin and handed it to the girl.

"What's that it says on his sweatshirt there?" said Seamus, squinting at the phone again. "Ocean-something-Surf? Maybe Skate and Surf? Maybe it's something you can get at a surf shop around here? It's a long shot, but—"

"Nothing showed up," reported the redhead, holding up her phone.

Mariska sighed. "Darn it. That sounded like a fine idea."

"What about Frank?" asked Seamus.

Mariska winced. "Darla's hoping to keep him out of it."

Seamus nodded. "And Charlotte and Declan are out of town. You picked a bad time to misplace your sloth."

"You're telling me."

He handed Mariska's phone back to her. "I'd check your neighbors' cameras next. See what that gets you. Maybe I can come around after work and see if I can help."

Mariska collapsed on the bar theatrically. "Oh, I would *so* appreciate that. We are at our wits' end."

She walked to Darla, who hung up as she approached.

"Anything?" they asked each other at the same time.

Both shook their heads.

"I never thought about the kidnapper having to feed the thing," said Darla.

"I know. I still have the sloth food in the house. I guess since they're asking for ransom, it means they're not trying to sell it?"

Darla shrugged. "Not necessarily. Maybe the Bitcoin bit was meant to delay us while they found a buyer."

Mariska groaned and stared at her phone. "This is terrible. Seamus said he'd come around after work to see if he could help. He said, in the meantime, we should see if my neighbors have anything on *their* cameras. Maybe the getaway car?"

"That's a good idea."

"And then maybe we should check surf shops."

"Surf shops?"

Mariska tilted the phone and hit play to run the doorbell video of Sir Sleepsalot's kidnapping.

"His sweatshirt says Ocean Skate and Surf, I think."

Darla peered at the screen.

"No, it doesn't."

"Hm?"

"Not *skate* and surf. It says Ocean *State* Surf."

"Oh. Well, whatever. Maybe he hangs out at surf shops or something—"

Mariska stopped, noticing a strange look on Darla's face.

"What is it?" she asked.

"Rhode Island Rose and Pete are from Rhode Island."

"Yes. So?"

"That's the Ocean State."

"Is it?"

"I'm pretty sure. Give me your phone."

Darla took it and did a quick search. "It is."

"But Rose and Pete wouldn't steal anything, and that person—that's a young person. That doesn't look like either of them."

"No, but maybe they know other people from Rhode Island. We should check with them, too."

"Okay. We'll stop there first."

With a final wave to Seamus, the ladies left The Anne Bonny and returned to Pineapple Port to pull into Rose and Pete's driveway.

They knocked, and a moment later, the woman people in the neighborhood affectionately called Rhode Island Rose answered, sporting her dark, short helmet of hair.

"Mariska, what are you doing here?" she said before noticing Darla

behind her. "Oh, Darla. You two—I heard about your sloth. Is he still sick?"
"Sick?" asked Darla.
"We told everyone it was sick," mumbled Mariska.
Darla nodded. "Oh, *right*." She focused on Rose. "Between us—it isn't sick. It was kidnapped."
Rose gasped. "*Kidnapped?*"
"Slothnapped. Do you mind if we come in for a moment?" asked Mariska.
Rose took a step back to make room. "No, not at all. Come in."
They walked into a foyer adorned with an eclectic collection of mismatched, hand-painted tiles, each telling the story of a place she and Pete had visited. The couple were avid campers, and the tiles reminded Mariska of the large mobile home the pair kept parked at a nearby lot.
Rose let them into the living room, where a cuckoo clock featured a parade of moose that marched out to announce the hour. The shelf beside it supported a family of knitted owls, each wearing miniature reading glasses.
Somewhere in the back of the house, upbeat and strangely modern music played.
"I didn't take Pete for a rocker," said Darla as they entered the kitchen.
Rose didn't appear to hear her.
"Who do you think took it?" she asked, motioning for the ladies to sit on her slip-covered plaid sofa.
"We don't know, but they sent us a ransom note."
Rose shook her head. "That's *horrible*."
Darla nodded. "It is. We don't have a lot of clues, but we were wondering if you could look at this video?"
Rose placed a hand on her chest.
"Me? I don't know how much help *I* can be. Pete would be better at this sort of thing, but he's bowling."
"It's nothing like that. We think the kidnapper is wearing something from Rhode Island."
"Really? I'm from Rhode Island."
Darla nodded with wide eyes. "*Right*. That's why we were hoping you could take a look? Maybe you'll recognize him or know someone else from Rhode Island we could talk to?"
Rose chuckled as Mariska handed her the phone. "It's a small state, but it isn't like we all *know* each other."
"We know. It's a shot in the dark. We're running out of ideas," said Mariska.
Rose slid her glasses from her head to her nose.

"I'll give it a shot."

Mariska played the video for her. Rose watched, and as she did, her animated expression drooped. She grew very *still*.

"Rose?" asked Darla. "Do you recognize him?"

Rose looked up, her eyes wide.

Someone entered the room from the back.

"Nan, I'm going to—"

Rose's gaze shot past the ladies to the young man standing at the end of the hall.

Time stopped as Mariska read the words written down the sleeve of the young man's hooded sweatshirt.

Ocean State Surf.

Then, just as suddenly, the world burst back into motion.

The young man swore and bolted for the front door as Darla and Mariska both jumped to their feet.

"Who was *that*?" asked Darla.

She didn't wait for an answer. She ran after the boy.

Rose looked at Mariska.

"It's my grandson. He's been staying with us. His mother needed an, um, *break*."

"A break?"

Rose sighed. "He's a troubled kid—always getting into trouble. He'd moved out, lost his job, and moved back home." Rose sighed, then added, "Having that brief moment of freedom and then having it yanked away was more than my poor daughter could handle. She sent him down here to live with his aunt, but *she* kicked him out after a couple of weeks. He ended up here."

Mariska frowned. "I'm sorry, Rose, but he stole our sloth."

"Are you *sure*?"

"You saw the video."

Rose nodded sadly.

"He's a good kid at heart," she said.

"Is he?"

Rose looked at her.

"No. He's *horrible*." She sighed. "Have you told Frank or the police?"

"No, but that isn't his worst problem."

Mariska looked out the front door.

"God help him if Darla catches up to him."

CHAPTER FOURTEEN

Sheriff Frank looked up from his desk as Mariska's husband, Bob, entered his office wearing his usual tee shirt and the baggy cargo shorts hanging off his non-existent butt.

His neighbor rarely came by the station.

Frank's dread and curiosity piqued.

"What are you doing here? Something wrong?" he asked.

Bob dropped into the chair across from him.

"Nah. Just getting out of the house. It smells like sloth."

Frank nodded before the sentence fully processed in his brain. When it did, his head cocked.

"It smells like *what*?" he asked.

"*Sloth*. Mariska has a sloth."

Frank blinked at him, wondering if this was that moment some of his older friends often told him about—that moment you realize your friend is one slice short of a loaf.

Frank leaned back in his chair, bracing himself for whatever nonsense Bob had planned.

"I'm going to need you to explain that to me," he said.

Bob focused on a Matchbox police cruiser someone had given Frank years ago. It had been sitting on his desk for almost as long, and most people didn't give it a second glance.

Bob *had* to touch it.

He pushed it around the desk as he spoke.

"Someone tricked Mariska into babysitting a sloth instead of a dog."

Frank sat back up. Bob's explanation had been shockingly straightforward.

Insane but straightforward.

"A real sloth? Like the kind that hangs from trees? With the smiley face and the long arms?" he asked.

Bob opened a stapler on Frank's desk to create a ramp for the tiny car.

"Yup."

He used the stapler ramp to help the toy cruiser perform a slow-motion leapfrog over a tissue box.

"How long does she have to watch that thing?"

Bob wove the mini-cruiser between a cup full of pens and a small plastic cup of paperclips.

"Hm? I don't know."

Frank leaned forward to snatch the car out of Bob's hand.

He placed it near him, out of Bob's reach.

"I've had field trip school children in here less annoying than you," he said.

Bob pouted and leaned back in his chair with his arms across his chest. He didn't leave.

Frank frowned.

"You know you can't sit here all day, right?"

Bob shrugged. "I was thinking maybe we could go bowling."

"I'm at work, Bob. I'm an actual working sheriff. At *work*."

Bob leaned forward. "Aw, come on. Nothing ever happens around here."

"If that's true, then it's thanks to the fact that I *do my job* instead of bowling."

Bob lifted his chin.

"What do you have to do today?"

Frank stood and put his hat on.

"As a matter of fact, before you showed up to waste my time, I was on my way to talk to a farmer about a stolen peacock."

Bob hooted. "*Ooh*, stolen peacocks. That *is* a serious crime. I stand corrected."

"It's serious to the farmer. It's his guard peacock."

"His guard peacock?"

"It watches over his chickens."

Bob stood. "I want to come, too."

"You can't come."

"Come *on*. You've promised me a ride-along for years."

Frank groaned. He'd hoped Bob had forgotten his moment of stupidity. He'd promised to take Bob on a ride-along one night after a few too many bourbons.

Guess not.

He shook his head.

"Well, now isn't—"

Like a coyote with a chicken carcass, Bob wasn't letting go.

"Why not? Wouldn't you rather take me on this peacock call *now* or some robbery or murder in the future?"

Frank frowned. "I'm pretty sure those aren't my only two options."

Bob bounced in his seat like a petulant child.

"*Come on.* What can go wrong during a stolen peacock case? Don't you want to get this off your list so I stop bugging you?"

Frank considered this. Bob had a point. It *did* seem like a good way to get him to stop nagging about the ride-along.

He sighed.

"Fine. Come on."

Bob pumped his fists in the air.

"Whoo hoo!"

With a nod goodbye to his receptionist, Ruby, the two men took Frank's human-sized cruiser to a small family chicken farm fifteen miles inland.

They weren't far away from the property when Frank looked at Bob.

Something had been bothering him.

"What's Mariska doing today?" he asked.

"I dunno. *Hanging* with the sloth, I guess."

Bob waggled his eyebrows to let Frank know he'd meant the pun.

Frank grunted. "Good one. Is she with Darla?"

"I don't know. Why?"

Frank clucked his tongue. "I don't know. I've got this weird feeling Darla's up to something. It's a survival skill I've developed over the years. Like a sixth sense. Do you ever get that?"

"Do I ever get a weird feeling that your wife is up to something?"

"No, do you ever feel like *your* wife is up to something?"

Bob sniffed. "Every morning. I've learned to ignore it."

Frank nodded.

"You might be on to something there."

He shook away his suspicions and pulled down a dirt road leading to the Eggcellent Chicken Farm, nestled on the outskirts of Charity.

A rustic wooden fence painted red maybe ten years earlier encircled the property, the sun-bleached slats weathered by the Florida sun and salty coastal air.

As Frank rolled to a stop in a large dirt parking lot, a scattering of puffy chickens hustled out of his way, their white feathers flashing bright against a small but well-kept lawn.

"Those chickens are wearing little fur coats," said Bob, motioning to them as he reached for his door handle.

Frank scowled.

"Where are you going?"

"I'm coming with you."

Frank shook his head. "Nope. No way. You wait here."

Bob gaped. "How is that fair? It's not a ride-along unless I get out of the car."

"That is *literally* the opposite of the term."

"You know what I mean."

Frank gathered his hat and sat for a moment, glaring at his friend. Bob made puppy-dog eyes at him, and he relented.

"Oh, for crying out loud. Fine. You can come but don't say a *word*."

Bob pantomimed locking his mouth shut with the twist of an invisible key.

"My lips are sealed."

Frank exited the cruiser and walked through the little crowd of fancy chickens as they pecked at the ground, clucking softly to themselves.

A square-built man exited the farm's ranch-style home to greet them, pulling a trucker-style cap onto his balding head as he moved. He wore a faded plaid shirt, sleeves rolled to his elbows, and baggy jeans that hung to the center of his shins. Sturdy work boots, scuffed and well-worn, completed the outfit.

"Hey, Frank. Thanks for coming out," said the farmer.

"Hey, Dale."

The men shook hands.

Dale's focus shifted to Bob, and Frank took the opportunity to introduce his temporary sidekick.

"This is Bob. He's a friend of mine. He, uh, was with me when I got the call, so he came along. Hope you don't mind."

"No problem. Nice to meet you," said Dale.

Bob sang as he shook Dale's hand.

"*The farmer's name is Dale, the farmer's name is Dale, hi ho the derry oh the farmer—*"

"*Okay*," snapped Frank with a gruff throat clearing.

Bob glanced at him and twisted the imaginary key at his lips again.

Frank turned to Dale, who stood stroking his impressive salt-and-paper mustache as he eyed Bob. The action made Frank touch his own lip curtain.

Dale's seemed *fuller*.

He considered asking him if he did anything special to it to keep it so lush and then decided against it.

"Show me where you kept the peacock if you would," he said.

Dale led them around the side of the house.

"I keep most of the chickens and the little petting zoo back here."

Chicken wire sectioned off a large dirt area behind the home. A wooden coop, painted red more recently than the outlying fence, occupied one corner, its roof adorned with a rooster weather vane.

A collection of average-looking white chickens milled inside, picking through the dust, watched over by a large rooster.

Dale ran a calloused hand through his gray-streaked hair.

"The peacock lived in there with the chickens. If anything got near them, he'd make an awful racket. I saw him run at a coyote once with those tail feathers fanned—that jackal couldn't run away fast enough."

"And this peacock just went missing?" asked Frank. "Can it fly—?"

Before Dale could answer, Bob crossed his arms against his chest.

"Did you find any of those pretty feathers—you know—sort of piled up in there? Maybe the coyote came back with some friends—"

Dale scowled.

"He wasn't *eaten*. He was *taken*. I've got it on video."

He pointed to a camera above the house's back door and pulled his phone from his pocket to show Frank the footage.

"See here? This guy walks right in there with a net and grabs him."

Frank watched as a figure in a long sleeve, hooded sweatshirt walked into the pen and threw what looked like a fishing net over the peacock. Frank heard the frightened peacock squawking.

"He is loud," he said.

"We were out to dinner when it happened," said Dale.

"This guy—does it seem to you he knows what he's doing? He doesn't look scared of that big thing."

Dale shrugged. "I don't know. He gave it some thought, though, for him to show up with a net like that."

"Agreed. Doesn't look like a random, spur-of-the-moment drunken prank."

Frank looked up to realize Bob had disappeared. Scanning the yard, he spotted him outside a fenced area adjacent to the chicken pen, taunting goats by making horns against his own skull with his fingers. A white goat with a patchwork of brown bleated at him, and Bob bleated back.

Frank gritted his teeth and focused on Dale.

"What time did this happen?" he asked.

Dale waited for Bob to finish bleating a second time to answer.

"Last night around eleven."

Frank pulled his notepad from his pocket.

"Did you see any vehicles?"

Two other goats decided they wanted in on the bleating contest. Bob and the three goats had a barbershop quartet.

"No," answered Dale over the racket.

Frank watched an alpaca wander over to the goats as if it were jealous of the attention. It leaned over the fence with its long neck and nibbled at Bob's sleeve. Bob didn't notice.

He was too busy waving at Frank.

With his other hand, he pointed at the alpaca like a kid who'd spotted Santa Claus.

"Doesn't it look like an alien?" he called over.

Frank growled and turned back to Dale.

"Anything else taken?"

"No, just Pickle."

"Pickle?"

"That's the peacock's name. My granddaughter named him."

Frank nodded and let his gaze roam over the expanse of the farm. He saw a small barn, a tractor, fencing, animals, and land. What he didn't see were neighbors.

"Is there any place within walking distance from here?"

Dale shrugged. "I have a few neighbors, but nobody who'd ever do this. I think this fella parked on the road, ran out to grab Pickle, and then walked right back to his truck."

"Do you have a camera on the front?"

"Yeah, but it didn't catch anything. I checked. He must have parked down the road."

Frank looked up from his notepad to see Bob sticking his leg through the fence, attempting to join the animals on their side.

He'd had enough.

"Bob! Let's go!" he barked.

Bob looked back and frowned. He pulled his leg out of the fence and said goodbye to the animals.

Frank sighed.

"I guess I have what I need, Dale, except can you send me a picture of Pickle? That video clip, too?"

Dale spat into the dust, his eyes still locked on Bob.

"Sure."

Bob strode up, wiping the sweat from his forehead.

"Those llamas are crazy-looking," he said.

"It's an alpaca," said Dale.

Bob shrugged. "Same thing."

"*Not* the same thing," said Dale.

"I'll let you know as soon as I know something," said Frank.

He nodded to Dale, glared at Bob, and headed toward his cruiser.

"You think you got a bead on it?" asked Bob on his heels.
"The peacock? No. Someone took it, though. He's got a video. Looks like a young man."
"How'd he catch it? The kid?"
"Net."
"Hm. I never thought about a net. Good idea."
Frank grunted.
"Let's get you back—"
The radio on his shoulder squawked, and Ruby's voice crackled through.
"Frank, I need you to swing by the zoo. Someone stole their lemurs."
"Their lemurs?" Frank squinted, trying to picture what a lemur looked like before he answered. He couldn't think of it.
"Will do. On my way."
He got in the car and looked at Bob as his friend joined him.
"I guess I'm going to have to take you with me," said Frank.
Bob raised his hands.
"*Whoo hoo!*"

CHAPTER FIFTEEN

Della put the castle's oversized kitchen island between herself and bleeding Jarrett.

"She did something to my *brother!*" Jarrett roared from his side of the island. "Look what she did to my arm. She *stabbed* me."

"He's *insane*," said Della, waggling her knife. "I didn't do anything to his stupid brother, and I can't find Timmy."

Charlotte thought Della had to be genuinely upset to deign to call her partner *Timmy*.

"Everyone calm down," said Declan, holding his palms in the universal symbol of *take it easy*.

He focused on Jarrett.

"One thing at a time. What's happened to your brother?"

The man huffed. "I can't find him. He went to the first floor to look for his cufflink while I was working on a puzzle in the guest bath, and he never came back."

"Why would you think Della has something to do with him disappearing?" asked Charlotte.

Jarrett sneered.

"Because I found her hovering outside the bathroom with that *knife*. Plus, Timmy is missing. It only makes sense she did something to him, too."

Della huffed. "Why would I kill someone on my own team?"

Jarrett's eyes widened.

"*Kill?* Who said anything about *killing* anyone?"

Della held up the knife.

"Isn't that what you're implying?"

"You tell *me*," snapped Jarrett, poking a finger at her.

Della took a deep breath.

"Look, this is getting stupid. Timmy already paid me more than enough to run through this unbearable evening. If I wanted to do him wrong,

I'd just leave. The money's already in my account."

Jarrett shook his head.

"You can't get out of the castle."

"So I decided to kill him? Come on. And there's a bonus for me if we win. Timmy can't pay me if he's *dead*. I can't claim any part of an inheri*tor*."

"Then why do you have a knife? Why did you *stab* me?"

Jarrett motioned to the blood on his sleeve. Charlotte could see he'd already stopped bleeding. It couldn't have been much of a wound.

Della glanced at his arm, and her anger seemed to dissipate a little more.

"I had the knife because Timmy went missing. It was handy, I guess, and something didn't feel right. I *used it* because you ran up and *grabbed* me. What was I supposed to do?"

Her reasoning made some sense to the remaining twin. Jarrett ran his hand over his reddish hair, glowering at the floor.

"I don't have time for this. I have to find Barrett," he said before spinning on his heel and storming off.

Charlotte watched him go and turned her attention to Della.

"That was exciting," she said.

Della lowered her knife.

"What do you two want?" she asked, but she didn't sound half as sure of herself as earlier in the evening. Her smooth golden ringlets had started to escape from her partially upswept hairdo, and a smear of blood—presumably Jarrett's—marred the hip of her peach gown.

"We don't want anything. This is our next room," said Charlotte. "You still haven't found Timmy?"

She sighed. "No. Granted, I didn't spend any real time looking for him. At first, it was nice not to have him hovering, trying to be helpful, but then it got weird that he'd disappeared."

Declan and Charlotte exchanged a look.

Della scowled.

"What? Do you know where he is?"

"No," said Charlotte.

"Then why are you looking at each other like that?"

Declan leaned to Charlotte's ear to whisper.

"We could go with a *keeping your enemies closer* plan?"

Charlotte nodded and whispered back.

"She had a good point about needing Timmy to get paid."

"Stop *whispering*," snapped Della. "What's going on? You want to work together again, and you're afraid to ask?"

Charlotte smirked. She guessed Timmy's disappearance had rattled her. Della feigned a tough demeanor, but it sounded like she'd warmed to working together.

"It's a little more complicated than working together," said Declan.

"Then *what*?"

"We think there's a murderer in the house," said Charlotte.

Della laughed. "Come *on*. You're trying to scare me out of the competition."

Charlotte motioned to her. "Said the girl holding a knife. *You* know something's off. We don't need to tell you."

Della glanced at the blade in her hand.

"*Off*, but—why would you say there's a *murderer* loose?"

"Because we found Tristan. He's been stabbed."

"*Stabbed*? As in, *stabbed to death*?"

Charlotte nodded.

Della dropped her knife to the counter with a clatter.

"You don't think I did it—?"

"No. Not now," said Charlotte. "But there's more. Xander's also dead and has been for maybe a day."

Della pointed up. "But we saw him on the landing?"

"Wasn't him."

Della's attention wandered as she processed this new information.

"We were all accounted for in the foyer," she said.

"Right. Which means the person on the landing dressed like Xander wasn't one of *us*."

"Which means we're not alone in the house." Della looked at her. "Do you think *Timmy's* dead?" She pointed at the doorway through which Jarrett had disappeared. "Do you think that's what *he* was up to? He was going to kill *me*?"

She picked up the knife again.

"We don't know," said Charlotte. "We don't even know if we trust *you*, but as Timmy's ringer, you're our best bet as an ally. Have you seen any of the others?"

Della thought for a moment. "No, now that you mention it, I haven't. I bumped into you, and Jarrett tried to kill me, but other than that—" Her eyes bounced in their direction. "Mildred was all alone."

Charlotte nodded. "Yes. If I was killing us one-by-one, I would start with Mildred and move on to Tristan. They were the loners."

"Comforting to hear you've thought about it," muttered Della. "Where did you find Tristan?"

"In a hidden passageway in the billiards room."

"A hidden passageway? So if Mildred is dead—"

"There's no guarantee we'd find her if we wanted to," said Declan, finishing her thought.

Della put her hand on her head. "I need to get out of here. I didn't sign up for this."

"There's no way out. The castle is sealed until dawn or until one of us figures out the final clue."

Charlotte looked through the window over the sink. A large pool, tennis court, giant hedge maze, and expanse of gardens glowed beneath the backyard landscape lighting.

She shook her head.

Of course, he has a hedge maze. What crazy castle guy doesn't have a hedge maze?

Declan tapped the window with his knuckle. "The windows are all hurricane glass, and even if we could break them, crawling out only lands us in the alligator moat."

The air seemed to be leaking from Della.

"I should have told Timmy to turn the car around the second I saw the castle. How was this *not* going to turn into a freak show?" She squinted at them. "Do you think we should stick together? Bang this out and trigger the doors?"

Charlotte nodded. "Seems like our best option to me."

"What about the others?"

"Probably best not to trust more people than we have to," said Declan. "None of the contestants was the person on the landing, but any one of them could be helping him."

"How do you know I'm not helping him?" asked Della.

Charlotte snorted a laugh. "You made a good point about Timmy. You don't get paid without him, so killing off the competition doesn't make sense for you. Plus, you just called him *Timmy*—the name you refused to call him earlier—which makes me think you aren't faking how upset you are."

"I *would* have to be half out of my mind to call a grown man Timmy," Della agreed.

She pointed the knife at them.

"And how do I know you two aren't the killer?"

"Because I'm not Hollie," admitted Charlotte. "She hired me. Pulling something like this would only focus more scrutiny on me as the winner at the end, and, like you, I have no real power."

"It doesn't make any more sense for you than it does for me," said Della, quietly.

"Right."

She thrust a chin at them.

"What are your real names?"

"I'm Charlotte Morgan, and this is Declan Bingham. We're detectives."

Della straightened. "Oh. That makes me feel a little safer." She held up the knife. "But maybe I'll hang on to this little longer."

She pulled a white card from the front of her gown. "Your clue or mine? I think every room has more than one way to skin a cat, so to speak."

Charlotte nodded.

"Our kitchen clue was *what food never spoils*?"

"Honey," said Della without delay.

"Yep. How about yours?"

"What type of food is a peanut?"

"A legume," answered Charlotte.

Declan chuckled. "You ladies can have your nerd-off later. We'll go with whatever answer we find first. Let's look for honey *and* nuts."

"*Legumes*," corrected Charlotte. "Like beans."

The three of them rustled through the pantry. Della found carrying a knife cumbersome, and her slinky dress left nowhere to secure it. She left it on the counter while she searched.

Declan found the honey.

"Got it. There's a sticker on the bottom. *I have a neck, but no head, even though the metal man wore me on his.*"

Charlotte and Della both lipped the words *metal man* in silence.

"You're both thinking so hard I can smell the smoke," said Declan.

"A metal man? A robot?" asked Della.

"What do robots wear on their heads?" Charlotte pictured a silver robot's head, and the idea gave her a thought.

"The *tin man*," she said. "From the *Wizard of Oz*. He had a hat."

"A *funnel*," said Della opening drawers. She found a red plastic funnel and peered into it.

"Another clue." She turned the funnel over and puffed air through the small end. A small scrolled piece of paper shot out, and she picked it up to read the next clue.

"*What island food do the Tampa Bay Rays famously sell to their fans?*"

The girls looked at each other.

"Not a baseball fan," said Charlotte.

Della shook her head. "Me neither."

They turned to Declan, who stood smirking.

"I suddenly feel so *important*."

Charlotte rolled her eyes.

"You can feel smug after we escape the castle alive."

"Fair enough. They sell Cuban sandwiches."

"Sandwiches? Should we look for bread?" asked Della.

Declan opened the bread box on the counter. "I'll look through here," he said, pulling out a loaf of white bread.

"What else is in a Cuban sandwich?" mumbled Charlotte, ticking off the ingredients on her fingers. "Ham, pork, mustard, cheese—"

"What kind of cheese?" asked Della, opening the refrigerator's lunchmeat drawer.

"Swiss, I think." Charlotte scowled. "I'm forgetting something."

"Nothing in the bread," reported Declan. Slices of bread and crumbs littered the counter.

Della tore a pile of Swiss cheese into bits and started dumping the mustard into the sink to be sure nothing was in the plastic squeeze bottle.

"*Pickles*," said Charlotte, remembering the last ingredient. She jogged to the pantry and found a jar of dill pickles.

"Got it," she called to the others, finding an orange sticker on the bottom of the jar.

"Please tell me it's orange," said Della.

Charlotte nodded. "It is. *What food was Casey Becker, played by Drew Barrymore, making in the opening sequence of the movie 'Scream'?*"

"Popcorn," said Della.

Charlotte nodded. "Yep."

Declan agreed. "I knew that one, too." He took a beat to straighten his jacket. "I don't know how to tell you ladies this, but I *might* be a genius. Don't be jealous."

Della looked at Charlotte.

"Is he always like this?"

She nodded. "Pretty much."

Declan chuckled.

Della frowned.

"It's another food question. Are you sure we're leaving the kitchen?"

Charlotte reexamined the sticker on the pickle jar.

"It's orange—but it's about popcorn. Is there a theatre room?"

Declan pulled the map from his pocket and nodded.

"Down on the first floor. Let's go, but everybody keep your eyes peeled."

Della grabbed her knife, and the three left the kitchen to creep down the stairs, heads on swivels as they moved through the house. They walked past the library on the first floor, where their puzzling evening had begun.

"The theatre room is down here," said Declan, motioning down the hall.

"Wait." Charlotte stopped and turned to face a door with a *DO NOT ENTER* sign identical to the one they'd found on Xander's bedroom door.

Della looked annoyed.

"What? We need to hurry."

Charlotte drew Declan's attention to the door.

"Like upstairs," he said.

"Yep." She turned to Della. "The same sign was on Xander's bedroom door where we found him dead."

Della's head tilted to the right. "You think the killer put up these signs to hide what he didn't want us to see?"

Charlotte nodded. "Makes sense, right? Maybe we should check for Timmy and Barrett?"

Della grunted. "I don't know. Is it smart to *actively* look in the most dangerous places on *purpose*? And what if Timmy or the idiot's brother is in there, all chopped up or something? Do we want to see that?"

Charlotte looked at Declan. She could tell they were on the same page.

Yes.

"Could be they don't want us to find the room with the controls to open the drawbridge," she suggested.

Della nodded. "Ah. Now *that* doesn't sound bad."

"Stand back," said Declan.

He kicked the door the same way he'd broken the lock on Xander's bedroom, but the door didn't swing very far after breaking.

"It's stuck on something," he said, shoving it with his shoulder. This time it gave way, and the smell of gasoline accosted their nostrils.

"Don't hit the light," warned Declan, throwing out his arm to keep them back. He pulled out his phone and shone his flashlight into the darkness.

The room was smaller than most they'd visited, though it had the same stone floors and walls. From the random junk and tools piled inside, Charlotte guessed it served as a storage area. A large mound of towels and bed linens sat piled behind the door.

Not a body.

Old rags, broken lawn ornaments, discarded newspapers, and items taken from the old *Tiki Trivia* set littered the floor and piled on metal shelving units. A hanging beach towel on the back wall blocked light from the only small window.

A dozen plastic red gasoline containers sat lined against one wall.

Unless Xander was paranoid about running out of gas, there were too many containers for the collection to be innocent.

"Why would he keep so much gasoline down here?" asked Della, covering her nose as the fumes snaked into the hall.

"I don't think he had any idea these were here. This is someone else's plan," said Charlotte.

Declan nodded.

"Someone's plan to burn the place down."

CHAPTER SIXTEEN

Darla walked to the front of Rose's house, where Mariska and Rose stood waiting for her return. Her legs and lungs were killing her after chasing Rose's grandson. She puffed like a post-race greyhound and felt like a squeezed sponge. Sweat leaked from pores she didn't even know she had.

"I lost him," she said, bending over and pinching her waist as a stitch tightened in her side. "And I think I'm going to die."

Mariska clucked her tongue. "What are you thinking running after that kid? You're going to give yourself a heart attack."

Darla nodded, still winded. "Yep. I did. I think I did. Four or five."

Rose bit her lip. "I am *so* sorry. I should've *never* agreed to take Owen in. If he's too much for my daughters, what made me think *we'd* be able to handle him?"

"The thing I don't understand is why would he take my sloth? What's he going to do with it?" asked Mariska.

Rose shook her head. "I have no idea. I can tell you he's been spending a lot of time outside the house, though. Who knows what he's up to? I think he fell in with a bad crowd. *Again.*"

She touched Mariska's arm.

"Honestly, I think he *is* the bad crowd," she whispered.

"I guess he wants ransom," suggested Mariska.

Rose nodded. "Maybe, or they're going to sell it for drugs."

Darla winced as she straightened.

"There has *got* to be easier ways to get drugs than selling sloths."

Rose shrugged. "I don't understand the world anymore."

Darla squinted at the house.

"Any chance Sir Sleepsalot is in there?"

Mariska and Rose turned and then looked at each other.

"Oh my goodness," said Rose, raising a hand to her mouth. "We didn't even look."

"I was so worried about you I didn't think to check," said Mariska to Darla.

The three entered the house and hurried to the guest bedroom, where Owen's music still blared. Darla realized the boy's phone was playing tunes through a small WIFI speaker, which she disabled.

The three of them sighed as silence fell.

"I hear that song in my sleep," muttered Rose.

"No sloth, but he left this behind," said Darla holding up the boy's phone. "He probably used it to send us the ransom note, so we can maybe use it to prove he's the thief. Do you know the password?"

Rose shook her head. "Try *juvenile delinquent.*"

Darla snickered. "Is that a capital J?"

Mariska remained silent, staring at the chalkboard-paint black walls. Sketches covered almost every inch—images of skulls, snakes writhing around the bodies of scantily clad cartoon women, flowers, tigers, alien laser battles, and various words ranging from *Dope!* to *Tiger Lily.*

"Look what he's done to your beautiful guestroom," she said.

Rose sighed. "I told him to make himself at home."

Darla nodded. "He did."

Rose sat on the edge of the unmade single bed.

"I never dreamed he'd do something like this."

"What's his full name?" asked Mariska.

"Owen Palmer. Our daughter and his father got divorced last year, and I don't think he's taking it well."

"No?" said Darla, eyeing a sketch of a clown holding a skull. "What gave you that idea?"

"How old is he?" asked Mariska.

"Eighteen."

Darla tilted back her head, still out of breath.

"He runs like a track star."

Rose nodded. "He *was* a track star in high school. Four hundred meter dash. He *was* a good kid..."

"Does he know anyone around here? He has to have stashed Sir Sleepsalot at someone else's house?"

Rose frowned. "I have no idea. My other daughter, Iris, had already kicked him out, and we found him living in our camper. Pete moved it so he couldn't find it again and told him to set up here."

"Why did Iris kick him out?" asked Mariska.

"I don't know. We don't talk very often. She keeps to herself." She sighed. "And it hasn't been too bad—like I said, he's been spending time *somewhere*, but I don't know who with. He came home on the back of a motorcycle the other day, but the driver was wearing a helmet painted with tiger stripes, so I couldn't see much."

"That's something," said Darla, though she had no idea if Frank had a database of helmets worn by criminals in the area.

She also didn't want to have to ask him.

Rose sniffed and stood to step away from the bed.

Her lip curled.

"I need to wash these sheets," she said before turning her attention back to the ladies. "I'll try and reach him, and if he comes back, I'll certainly let you know."

"I'm going to take his phone," said Darla, holding it aloft.

"By all means."

"Thank you, Rose. We appreciate your help with everything," said Mariska, patting the woman on the shoulder. "I'm sorry about your room. I'm sure it will be easy to paint over."

She said the words but didn't believe them for a second.

Rose looked as though she might cry.

"I'm sorry about your sloth."

Mariska and Darla said their goodbyes and headed back to Mariska's house.

"Poor Rose," said Mariska as she made herself and Darla a cup of tea for dunking the cookies they'd been waiting to eat.

Darla nodded. "That grandson of hers seems like a nightmare."

Mariska clucked her tongue. "He's just a kid. He's angry. He's acting out."

"I'd like to act my foot up his butt," muttered Darla.

Mariska set the steaming mug before Darla and held her friend's gaze as she sat.

Darla squinted. "Why are you looking at me like that?"

"*Now,* can we get Frank involved?" she asked.

Darla shook her head.

"Seamus said he'd help."

"That's great, but Seamus isn't a sheriff. He doesn't have the same resources—"

Darla held up a finger.

"One day. Give me *one* day. If we can't find Owen by the end of today, I promise I'll get Frank on it tomorrow. Okay?"

Mariska huffed. "Fine. By then, Sir Sleepsalot will be living in *Ohio* with his new weirdo parents."

Darla looked at her. "Why Ohio?"

"*I don't know.* Whatever."

They sighed in stereo and jumped when someone knocked loudly on the door. Miss Izzy and her twin buddy flew from the back bedroom, barking the alarm.

"Get back, get back," said Mariska, pushing them with her foot as she opened the door.

Seamus stood on her step, grinning with his arms wide.

"Have no fear—Seamus is here," he announced.

"You're just in time," said Darla, hustling to the foyer to greet him.

"I'm guessing you're still missing your sloth?" he asked, entering.

Darla nodded and led him into the kitchen.

"Yes, but we know who took him."

"Yeah? That's half the battle. Who?"

"His name is Owen Palmer. He's the visiting grandson of a couple in the neighborhood, but he ran away when he saw us coming after him. Sir Sleepsalot wasn't at the house, so he must be keeping him somewhere else."

Seamus nodded slowly. "Or he already sold the thing."

Mariska moaned and stuffed a cookie in her mouth.

He patted her hand. "We'll find him, lass, we'll find him. Tell me, how'd you track him down?"

"The sweatshirt he was wearing in the video. It says *Ocean State Surf*, and their family is from Rhode Island," said Darla.

Seamus put his hands on his hips.

"Nice job, ladies. I'm impressed."

Mariska smiled. "Thank you. We help Charlotte with her cases sometimes."

Darla nodded. She eyed the dwindling cookie supply and dragged the package away from Mariska's reach before taking one.

Seamus squinted at the mugs of tea steaming on the table.

"Do you have any whiskey?"

Mariska's eyes narrowed.

"No."

Darla knew she did but didn't rat her out. She needed Seamus sharp, or she'd need Frank's help.

Seamus grunted his disappointment.

"How old's the lad?" he asked.

"Eighteen."

Seamus grunted. "Old enough to know better. You said he ran?"

Darla nodded. "I ran after him, but he was so fast. He wove in and out between the houses until I lost him."

"When was this?"

"Fifteen, twenty minutes ago."

Seamus straightened. "He can't go back to his grandmother's house. Unless you think she's in on it?"

"Definitely not, and she'll call us if he comes back," said Mariska.

"Hm. I think the chances of the boy stowing the beast in one of the neighbors' houses are slim...and he's on foot?"

"Yes. I didn't get the idea he had a car?" said Mariska, looking at Darla for confirmation.

Darla shook her head. "Rose said he's been getting rides home from someone on a motorcycle. Someone with a tiger helmet."

Seamus glanced at her and then took a beat staring at the floor. He nodded as if he'd had a silent conversation with himself.

"He's got to be out on the main road right now, waiting for his partner to pick him up or headed for somewhere on foot."

"You think we can catch up to him?" asked Darla.

Seamus nodded. "I do. Let's go. I'll drive."

The three of them hustled to Seamus's faded blue car.

"*Shotgun*," called Darla, jumping in the passenger seat.

Mariska grumbled and clambered into the back, pushing away old mail and soda cans.

Seamus hit the gas with a screech of balding tires.

Pineapple Port only had two exits, and both dumped onto the main road traveling north and south through Charity. After weaving through the neighborhood, Seamus made a hard right and headed south.

"Keep an eye out," he barked as Mariska and Darla gripped what they could to keep from jostling around the car.

"Slow down!" scolded Mariska as she slid from one side of the car to the other, sweeping old bar napkins and towels with her.

Darla scanned sidewalks and sideroads as they cruised.

"Maybe we should turn around. I don't think he could have gotten this far," said Mariska after a few minutes of speeding south.

Seamus slowed as if he'd had the same idea. As he drifted toward a U-Turn, Darla spotted a lone figure standing on one of the sidestreets as they passed.

"I see him!" she yipped, poking her finger into the window. "I think I saw him down there."

"Hold on," said Seamus, speeding up to make the U-turn as planned.

He traveled back an eighth of a mile and made a second U-turn. Ahead of them, a motorcycle turned onto the road where Darla thought she'd spotted Owen.

"Turn where that bike turned," directed Darla. She squinted. "Wait. Is that a tiger helmet?"

"Where?" asked Mariska, poking her head between the two front seats for a better look.

Darla bounced in her seat. "That's his *friend*. He must have found a way to call him. Rose said he had a friend with a tiger motorcycle helmet."

Seamus looked at her.

"Like that? Are you sure?"

Darla slapped the dashboard.

"Yes. *Yes*. Hurry!"

Seamus turned hard. The ladies braced themselves again.

"Uh-oh," said Mariska as her grip on Darla's seat gave way, and she rolled against the side door.

"There he is!" yelled Darla.

Up ahead, Owen swung his leg over the back of the motorcycle, which had pulled beside him at the side of the road. The boy glanced over his shoulder and slapped the back of the person driving as if urging them on.

Seamus stomped on the gas.

"Oh *no*," said Mariska.

They roared toward the pair. They were fifteen feet away when the motorcycle took off.

Seamus drove faster.

"We're going to *die*," moaned Mariska, who'd managed to right herself in the backseat.

Darla watched the motorcycle kick up dust as it cut down a narrow dirt road winding through a clump of pines.

Seamus hit the brakes, and the car skidded to a stop.

"What are you doing? They're getting away!" said Darla.

Seamus slapped his steering wheel and swore.

"I can't fit down there."

He stared after the motorcycle as it disappeared into a cloud of dust.

"He *does* have a partner," said Darla.

Mariska flopped back against the seat.

"We'll never find him now."

"Oh, we will," said Seamus.

"How can you say that?" asked Darla. "I mean, I guess he'll have to return to his grandmother eventually, but by then, the sloth will be dead or long gone—"

Darla heard Seamus's last words in her head again and stopped. Something about his calm, confident tone struck her as odd.

"Wait. Why do you sound so sure?" she asked.

He looked at her.

"Because I know who was on the motorcycle."

"Who?" asked Mariska as Seamus made another U-turn to head back the way they'd come.

"Tiger Lily."

Darla gasped. "He had *Tiger Lily* written on his wall at Rose's house."

"Tiger Lily's a person?" asked Mariska.

Seamus nodded.

"We used to date a million years ago."

Darla blinked at him.

"Is there anyone around here you haven't dated?"

Seamus grinned. "What can I do? It would be selfish of me not to share."

Both ladies rolled their eyes.

"Why would your ex-girlfriend be involved with an eighteen-year-old boy?" asked Mariska.

He shrugged and pulled back onto the main road, heading for Pineapple Port.

"She's an opportunist in every sense of the word," he said.

"You mean she's a *thief*," said Mariska.

"Tomato, *tomahto*. She's got a thing for exotic animals, though. I'll tell you that much. It's half the reason we broke up."

"She had too many animals?" asked Mariska.

He frowned. "*One* too many. Long story."

"You broke up with her because she had *one* too many pets?" asked Mariska.

He snapped his lips. "Not exactly. I'm pretty sure she broke up with me."

"Why?"

"I may have had a small indiscretion with her cousin, Iris."

Mariska grunted with disapproval.

"Her cousin? Oh, Seamus, that's *terrible*."

"Aye. Iris had a wee crush on me. It wasn't my fault—"

"It never is," muttered Darla. "But the important part is you know where to find her?"

He nodded. "Yes, if she hasn't moved. I don't think she will have. Her place is a compound—her pride and joy. But, getting in won't be easy."

"We'll send Frank," said Mariska.

Darla snapped her attention to her.

"*No*, we won't. You're missing the whole part where Seamus has us *covered*."

"Calling the sheriff is a terrible idea," agreed Seamus. "If Tiger Lily sees the sheriff knocking at her gate, I can't say what she'll do. By the time he gets a warrant, the sloth and Lily will be long gone."

Darla looked at him, pleased he'd backed her up for his own reasons.

Seamus turned into Pineapple Port as he continued to muse over their options.

"No, we'll have to sneak in, find the sloth, and get out without Lily knowing. That's our best bet."

"See?" asked Darla, twisting to look at Mariska. "Seamus says *no Frank.*"

"Of course he does," said Mariska, flopping back in her seat.

CHAPTER SEVENTEEN

"This is the missing piece of the puzzle," said Charlotte, glaring at the gas cans in the castle storage room as if she could intimidate them into being less dangerous.

"Don't say *puzzle*. I never want to hear anything about trivia or puzzles again," muttered Della.

Declan motioned toward the hall. "We've got to close this door before the fumes fill the whole house."

They backed into the hall as he shut the door and turned to Charlotte.

"What were you saying? We've found the missing part of *what* puzzle? The part where we all die in a fiery inferno?"

Charlotte nodded. "*Yes*. I couldn't figure out why the killer thought he could knock us off and walk away with the money. How would he explain *seven* missing people?"

Della raised her hand like a student eager to answer.

"I'll take *they burned to ashes* for a thousand, Alex."

Charlotte poked a finger at her. "Wrong show, but yes. He'll say it was a tragic accident in a sealed castle. The fire hides the murders."

Declan grunted. "Xander *would* get slapped with a fine by the fire marshal for having no exits, but he'll be too busy being dead."

Charlotte nodded. "And the only reason the place didn't light up the second the doors locked is that this guy needs us to solve the puzzle to get proof he won fair and square."

Della scoffed. "*Fair and square*—like me, the ringer, and you, the impostor. There's nothing fair or square about any of us. The old guy really didn't think this out."

"Once we find the final clue, we'll be bumped off, too," said Declan.

"There'll be poison in the celebratory champagne," suggested Della.

Charlotte side-eyed her. "That seems like a pretty specific guess. Do you know something we don't?"

Della smirked. "Maybe. Think about it. You said Tristan was *stabbed*. After the flesh melts off his bones in the big fire, no one can tell how he died unless they nicked a bone—and why even look for nicked bones after a massive fire?"

She turned to Charlotte.

"How was Xander killed?"

Charlotte's mouth hooked. "I don't know exactly. We didn't spend a lot of time investigating—"

"I can tell you his hand's broken in several places," mumbled Declan.

Della's brow knitted. "What?"

"*Nothing.*" Charlotte shot him a look. "I didn't see any marks on him. Maybe strangulation. Suffocation?"

Della raised her hand. "See? There you go. After the huge fire, the authorities will write off everything as an accident, short of a bullet dropping out of a corpse."

"So we won't be shot to death. We've got that going for us," said Declan. "*Yay.*"

"Guns are noisy, too," said Charlotte. "They want us blissfully solving the puzzle, not running for our lives."

Della nodded. "I suppose they waited to see which of us were the best puzzle solvers and then started killing the others."

Charlotte gasped. "They *know* we're the best."

"That's a *good* thing, isn't it? It means we're safe," said Della.

"Yes, but how would they know we're the best unless they were *watching* us?"

Declan straightened, looking alarmed.

"*Cameras.* They've been watching us the whole time."

Della looked up and down the hall.

"*Where?*"

"I don't know. Maybe not everywhere, but enough. If I had to guess, every room with a puzzle in it." Declan sighed. "They've heard every word we've said."

"It's how they knew where to find Tristan and when Barrett left his brother behind."

"And when Timmy wandered off," said Della.

Charlotte nodded. "We have to assume whoever's watching us knows what we've figured out—"

"*Help me,*" called a woman's voice.

The three looked at each other and then turned toward the direction of the voice, somewhere near the bottom of the stairs.

"Who was that?" whispered Della.

Declan took the lead and headed down the hall.

"Stay behind me. It could be a trap."

"Don't have to ask me twice," said Della, urging Charlotte in front of her.

They crept toward the stairs until Declan stopped to peer around the corner.

"It's Mildred," he said, rushing out.

Charlotte and Bella followed. Mildred sat slumped on the bottom step, her back against the banister. She gripped the left side of her abdomen with her right hand.

"What happened?" asked Charlotte.

"Someone stabbed me," she said, moaning. "I don't know where they came from. It was like the wall opened, and there they were."

"That pile of towels in the storage room. Someone get me one," said Declan.

"I've got it," said Della, jogging back the way they'd come.

"Can I see?" asked Declan.

Mildred squinted at him, her expression twisted with pain.

"Are you a doctor?"

"No, but I've had training," he said.

Mildred looked at Charlotte as if she needed confirmation.

"He was a soldier. He knows wounds," said Charlotte.

Mildred closed her eyes and nodded her consent.

Declan gingerly lifted the woman's spangled top to examine the wound in her side. Charlotte leaned forward to take a peek. The incision was small, and there wasn't much blood. She guessed it wasn't deep but imagined being stabbed might have sent the woman into shock.

"It's not too bad. You're lucky," said Declan. "Did you see who it was? How did you get away?"

Mildred shook her head. "I didn't see. It all happened so fast. I just swung my arm at him and ran. Why would someone do this?"

"It was a man?" asked Charlotte.

She nodded. "I'm pretty sure. He seemed big."

Charlotte tapped Declan's arm and grinned.

She'd been right about it being a man doing all the stabbing.

He rolled his eyes.

Charlotte turned her attention back to Mildred but decided not to tell her about Tristan and the other missing players. The last thing they needed was a hysterical, wounded woman on their hands.

Della returned with a few towels. Declan picked the cleanest of the bunch and tore it into strips. He tied them together and wrapped them around Mildred's waist.

"That should keep it safe until we can get help."

"Tell Xander to call an ambulance and the police," said Mildred.

Charlotte and Declan exchanged a look.

"Xander, uh, *left*," said Charlotte.

Mildred's eyes ringed with white. "*Left?*"

"Yes. He's coming back at dawn or when we solve the puzzle."

"*Ridiculous*," she muttered. She seemed tired.

"We're close to finishing. We're going to the theatre room around the corner."

Mildred's eyes bulged again. "You can't leave me here with a maniac in the house."

Declan took her hand. "No, of course not. We'll take you with us. Let's get you on your feet. The theatre room is just down here."

Moving at Mildred's speed, the group walked to the back of the first floor. They pushed through grand, gilded double doors and entered a room lit by glowing conch-shaped sconces. Rich, dark turquoise drapes dripped from the ceiling to the plush carpeted floor.

A massive projection screen hung at the front of the room.

Declan helped Mildred into one of the dozen leather armchairs arranged in the center of the room. Each chair had a cup holder and a small side table for snacks—a stocked candy bar stood nearby against one wall. An antique popcorn machine and a smattering of movie posters encased in ornate frames finished the theme.

"We're looking for popcorn, right?" said Della, heading to the antique popcorn machine. She opened the door and felt inside. She grimaced as grease slicked her arm.

"Not there?" asked Mildred.

Della offered her a withering glance.

"So nice to have you back," she said.

She looked at Charlotte.

"It has to be in here. This popcorn is fairly fresh, and the rest of the place looks like no one has used it since *Gone With the Wind* took home the Oscar."

She scooped the kernels to the floor until the bottom of the machine appeared.

"Ah *ha*."

She held up a small key for everyone to see.

"Hey."

All eyes turned to the entrance.

Jarrett stood in the doorway. He'd removed his jacket and bow tie and rolled up his sleeves.

"Has anyone seen Barrett?" he asked, sounding defeated.

They shook their heads.

"Someone tried to stab me," said Mildred.

Jarrett looked at Della.

"Her?" he asked, pointing.

"No, not *me*," said Della.

He scowled and walked down the aisle, shaking his head.

"I've looked everywhere. I don't understand. He wouldn't leave me like this..."

He flopped into one of the leather chairs and looked at Charlotte.

"Do you think he fell through one of those trapdoors? Maybe he's stuck in a puzzle room?"

"Maybe. That would make sense," said Charlotte.

I doubt it.

"You could maybe help us get out of here," suggested Della.

Jarrett dropped his redheaded skull into his hands.

"*Or*, you could just sit there like a useless clown," muttered Della before dipping behind the candy counter.

"Nothing opens with a key back here," she reported. "There's a cabinet with a combination lock, though."

She stood and pulled out her phone to use the flashlight on the key.

"Hold on. It says something on it. I couldn't see it in this crappy light. R-E-E-L."

"Reel?" Charlotte looked to the back of the room. "It must open the projection booth."

Della, Charlotte, and Declan headed to the booth. Jarrett watched them, looking sad and out of energy.

"Jarrett looks wrecked," said Declan quietly when they were far enough away from the others.

"Could be a trick," said Della.

"Could be. We should keep an eye on him," agreed Charlotte.

"Key lock," said Declan, motioning to the knob.

Della unlocked it, and they entered the booth. Charlotte flipped on the light and moved to the projector.

"I bet we have to turn it on," she said, finding and flipping a switch while the others searched the desk and closet.

The garbled sound of music and talking burbled until the film rolled smoothly, and an old episode of *Tiki Trivia* glowed on the giant screen.

Della groaned. "I hope we don't have to watch a whole episode of this to find the next clue."

As she finished, the screen went dark for several seconds before returning to the show. Charlotte scowled at the projector, which hadn't stalled.

"Hold on," she said, stopping the film. By hand, she rolled it back until she reached the dead spot.

"Someone put masking tape over the film here," she said, seeing why the screen had gone blank.

She pulled the film out to get a better look.

"There's a clue written on the tape. It says, *posters in order*."

"*Posters in order*? That's it?" asked Declan.

She nodded, and all three peered down at the classic movie posters on the wall of the theatre.

"Gotta be them," said Della, leading the way from the booth.

There were four posters—each picked one of the first three to investigate.

"This has a number eight on it," said Declan about a poster for *The Godfather*.

"I've got a number two here," said Charlotte for *Jaws*.

"*Wizard of Oz* is six," reported Della.

"The clue said *in order*—I'm guessing in order of release? *Oz, Godfather,* and *Jaws*, right?" Charlotte asked as she walked to a poster for *Alien*. It had four written on the poster case glass.

"I think so," said Della. "*Jaws* and *Godfather* are pretty close, the late seventies, but I'd say *Godfather* first. *Alien* last, of course."

"I think so, too," said Declan. "We can always swap them."

"Assuming something doesn't blow up if you do it wrong," said Della, moving behind the candy counter again. "What are the numbers?"

"Six-Eight-Two-Four if we're using *Godfather* in front of *Jaws*."

There was a pause, and Della reappeared with an orange card.

"Here's our ticket out of here," she said, holding it aloft. "It's another damn riddle."

Charlotte groaned as Della began to read.

"With each step, you'll trip with doubt,
Like a drunkard, you'll turn about,
A challenge of choice, no end in sight,
You'll wind through my arms both day
and night."

The three of them blinked at each other. Declan pulled out the map and laid it on the candy booth countertop.

"None of these room names are jumping out at me as the answer."

Della turned the clue over.

"There's more on the back. It says *Tell the Puzzlemaster*."

"Who's the Puzzlemaster? Xander?" She glanced over her shoulder at Mildred and Jarrett and lowered her voice. "That's not going to do us much good."

Della scowled. "The clue maybe isn't about one of the rooms? We never had to tell anyone the answer before."

Charlotte remained staring at the card, reading the riddle over and over.

"What about the hedge maze?" she asked.

Della looked at her. "What hedge maze?"

"I saw one in the back yard from the kitchen."

"Oh." Della threw a pointed look at Jarrett. "Right. I was sort of busy trying not to be murdered in the kitchen," she added louder.

Jarrett scowled and held up his scratched arm.

"I'm the one who got *stabbed*."

"Me too," peeped Mildred before closing her eyes again.

Della rolled her eyes and looked at the clue again.

"It fits a maze."

"Great, but we have no way of getting outside," said Charlotte. "That's probably why we had to talk to the *Puzzle Master*—he'd open the drawbridge for us to get into the back yard."

"And now, if we *did* get outside, I'd go right to my car, hop inside, and drive far, far away," said Della.

"You can take me to the hospital," mumbled Mildred.

Della nodded. "I'll get right on that."

She caught Charlotte's eye, shook her head, and mouthed, *nope*.

Declan headed for the exit. "That's it then. Let's figure out how to get out of the castle."

Charlotte started toward Mildred to help her to her feet and then paused.

"We should find a camera. If the killer is watching us and wants us to finish the puzzle, then they should want us to get outside, right?"

Declan stopped and turned to look at her. "That's a thought. There must be a camera in the library. That's where they would have watched to see which of us was best."

Declan tapped Jarrett on his slouching shoulder as he passed him. It didn't look like the remaining brother intended to rise from his seat.

"We need to stick together. Let's go," he urged.

"Just leave me here," muttered Jarrett.

Declan shook his head. "We're not leaving anyone alone. Let's go—"

"*Wait*," said Mildred, loud enough to stop Della and the others in their tracks.

The beehived woman wobbled to her feet, holding her side and wincing in pain.

"I just remembered. Xander and his buddies would often lock themselves in the wine room to play poker and smoke cigars. I'd find them there all the time. I'm pretty sure he could open the drawbridge from there."

"You're saying you think there's a mechanism in the wine room?" asked Charlotte.

"I didn't see a wine room on the map?" said Declan, double-checking his paper. "No. It's not on here."

"*Like a drunkard, you'll stumble about*," said Della quoting the riddle. "Maybe it had something to do with the wine room? Maybe we had to stop there on our way to the maze?"

"It's right next door," said Mildred, pointing.

Charlotte and Della walked to the hall to investigate the door to the wine room.

"Another combination lock," Charlotte reported when Declan appeared with his arm around Mildred. Jarrett schlumped along behind them, showing no interest.

"Wait, wait, I know the combination. I just need to think a minute," said Mildred.

She leaned against the stone wall and tapped Declan's hand away when he attempted to steady her.

"I'm okay. Let me think," she said.

She screwed her eyelids tight.

"He had me grab a bottle of wine once, and I remember the numbers were funny..."

"Funny *numbers*?" asked Charlotte.

Mildred ignored her and chanted.

"Xander! Xander!"

"Loss of blood," muttered Della, making a corkscrew motion near her head for Charlotte to see. "She's losing it."

Mildred heard her and opened her eyes to glare. "My mind is working just fine. I remember it was the chant. *Two-four-six-eight, who do we appreciate? Xander! Xander!*"

"Two, four, six, eight are the same numbers from the posters, in a different order," said Charlotte.

"I would have guessed he preferred *odd* numbers," drawled Della. "*Freak.*"

Charlotte punched the numbers into the lock, and the door sprang open an inch.

"It worked," she said, pushing open the door.

The room was dark, but she heard a voice.

"Here..."

Something moved at the back of the room. She flipped on the light and hustled around a large round poker table to find two men on the ground.

Barrett, still in his black tuxedo, held his arm in the air. He looked weak but alive.

Timmy, lying beside him, looked very, very dead.

CHAPTER EIGHTEEN

Frank pulled into the zoo parking lot to look into the missing lemur report and put his cruiser into park. He didn't bother to tell Bob to stay in the car. He couldn't bear the idea of arguing with him.

He wiped his forehead. The end of the day always felt the hottest, and the heat bouncing off the parking lot asphalt didn't help.

"Do you have any idea what a lemur looks like?" he asked as they headed toward the entrance.

Bob shook his head. "No. I want to say like a monkey. No—like a *monkeycat*."

"A *monkeycat*?"

"A cross between a monkey and a cat."

"I figured that's what you meant, but I don't think that's a thing."

"I know it's not a *thing*—I'm saying that's what they *look* like." He straightened. "Wait, don't they call them *ring-tailed* lemurs?"

Frank had to admit that sounded familiar.

"I think they do," he said.

Bob scowled. "Does that mean their tails are shaped like a ring?"

"That doesn't seem right. I think it's rings around their tails. Black and white, maybe?"

"Oh, well, hopefully, they didn't steal *all* of them, so we can see."

Several people milled around the ticket area, but Frank spotted a heavy-set, dark-haired woman wearing a zoo uniform among them.

She noticed him and waved.

"You must be the sheriff," she said as he neared. "I'm Marcy."

"Frank. This is Bob."

She nodded hello.

"Someone took your lemurs?" he asked.

She nodded. "I'll take you to the enclosure."

They followed her through the crowds to a section of the zoo cordoned off with a *Closed* sign hanging on a chain.

Bob pointed to an informational stand featuring a photo of a creature with wide yellow eyes and a sharp nose. Its long tail had rings of alternating black and white.

"Ring-tailed. I get it," he said. He leaned toward Marcy. "I thought maybe their tails were shaped like a ring."

Her brow knitted, and she turned her focus to Frank.

"They were locked in here last night. The door was open this morning, and they were gone."

Frank nodded.

"This the only way in?" he asked as they passed through a plexiglass door into the enclosure off the zoo's main path.

"Yes," said Marcy.

Bob looked over Frank's shoulder as he stopped to inspect the door for damage.

"No sign of forced entry," said Bob.

Frank scowled at him, and he grinned.

"I always wanted to say that."

Frank ignored him and scanned the tall, leafy trees stretching toward the sky, branches interweaving to form a natural canopy. A series of wooden platforms and ropes hung interspersed among the trees. Glass enclosed one side of the pen, allowing visitors to get an up-close view. A high, sturdy mesh covered the rest, stretching over the top to prevent breakouts by the more adventurous *monkeycats*.

The little man-made forest was still. Nothing like the creature in the photo moved through the trees.

"How many did you have?" asked Frank.

"All four, *gone*," said Marcy, motioning to the aerial platforms above. "This time of day, they'd be there with their fruit."

Frank pulled out his notepad. "Any idea why someone would take them?"

"No idea."

"Has it happened before? Do you have any cameras?"

"No, and we do have cameras. We have a partial view of who did it."

Marcy pulled out her phone and logged into the zoo's security system. She played Frank the video, and he suffered a flash of déjà vu.

What looked like a young man entered the frame of the camera trained on the front of the lemur enclosure. He wore a hoody sweatshirt with the hood pulled up to cover his face and carried a large dog shipping crate. He approached the door, set down the crate, tapped a code into the lock's keyboard, and let himself inside.

He disappeared into the greenery of the enclosure and then reappeared an hour later with the crate.

The crate seemed less easy to manage on the way out. He lugged it beside him this time, stopping once to rest before disappearing from the frame.

It made Frank's back hurt just watching him lug the box.

One thing stood out to Frank.

The young man on the zoo's security system was dressed exactly like the man in Dale's peacock video.

He took a moment to send the clip to himself and then returned the phone to Marcy.

"Do you recognize him? It looks like he knows the code. Who knows that code?"

"I'm the only one with last night's code because I was due in this morning. He must have watched me open the door. We change the code, but apparently, not often enough."

Bob wandered deeper into the enclosure to tug on some ropes hanging there, and Frank let him go, happy he had something to distract him.

A radio hanging on the zookeeper's hip came alive.

"Marcy, we need you at the monkey cages."

Marcy sighed and focused on Frank.

"Is there anything else you need from me? This might take a while if it's what I think it is. We've been having trouble with one of the spider monkeys."

"No, that's fine. I'll have a quick look around and let you know if I find anything."

She nodded and left.

"Not a bad place to live," said Bob, rejoining Frank near the exit.

"I'm sure Mariska wouldn't mind if you came here and lived with the lemurs for a while."

"Ha. I don't think *I'd* mind if I could get a TV in here. So, what do you think we got?"

Frank frowned at him. "*We* don't got anything. But...I think it's the same guy."

Frank's bushy eyebrows popped high on his forehead.

"Same guy as the peacock?"

"Yep. I'm wondering if we don't have some black market animal dealer rolling through town."

"Hm. Wow. My first ride-along and we're already hot on the heels of a black-market dealer."

"Not your first ride-along, your *only* ride-along."

Bob grunted and wandered toward a tiny rope ladder near the glass.

Frank took the opportunity to loop around the enclosure but found nothing useful. He returned to the exit.

Seeing Frank's attention return to him, Bob swung on the rope ladder, imitating a monkey.

"Bob, get off that thing before you break—"

The ladder snapped at the top, sending swaying Bob stumbling. His back slammed into the glass wall, shaking the structure. Hinges jostled, and the door began to swing shut.

"Grab the door!" screamed Frank, lunging forward.

Bob couldn't push himself off the glass fast enough.

Frank dove for the door but was too late.

He heard the lock *click*.

"You *idiot*," he said, stopping his momentum against the glass.

Frank shook the door, but it remained secure.

He whirled to face Bob, who'd managed to right himself. The two men stared at each other, a moment of silence hanging between them.

"Whoops," said Bob.

CHAPTER NINETEEN

"Barrett!"

Jarrett pushed past the others into the room to reach his brother.

"What happened?" he said, sliding to his knees beside his twin.

"Taser, I think," said Barrett. His breathing sounded labored.

"Who did it?"

Barrett tried to sit up with his brother's help. "I didn't see. My heart... I woke up here. I think they thought I was dead." He looked at Timmy. "*He's* dead."

"Why? How?" asked Jarrett.

Barrett shook his head.

Jarrett helped his brother to his feet.

"What is going on?" he asked no one in particular.

Charlotte inspected Timmy, searching for signs of life, but it was clear he'd been dead for some time. A burn mark encircled his neck. It looked as though someone had strangled him with a coarse rope.

"How do you feel?" she asked Barrett.

"He's got a bad heart," explained his brother.

"It might have saved his life," said Charlotte. "They thought he was dead and piled him in here with Timmy instead of finishing him off."

Della walked over to stare down at Timmy. She didn't say anything— just shook her head and wandered away.

Charlotte straightened and scanned the wine and cigar room. Custom-built wooden wine racks covered the walls, showcasing more bottles than she wanted to count. Above one rack, a row of glass shelves held crystal decanters and wine glasses.

What she didn't see was a way to open the drawbridge.

Declan stood near what looked like a panel on the wall beside the door, but he didn't look as excited about it as she hoped he would.

"This is for temperature control. Not the door," he explained when she looked at him, hopeful.

She nodded. It did feel cooler in the wine room than in the rest of the castle. She noticed Della rubbing her bare arms.

In the center of the room sat a large, circular poker table. It looked as though it had arrived as a set with the pool table upstairs—the same tropical animal carvings snaked around the legs.

High-backed leather chairs surrounded the table, but Jarrett and Declan opted to help Barrett to the cozier seating area in the corner.

Charlotte didn't know how sick Barrett was, but she imagined getting him away from poor dead Timmy would improve anyone's mood.

Poor Timmy.

He stared with wide glassy eyes.

She closed them.

"How did you find me?" asked Barrett, his voice weak.

"We think the next clue is outside, and Mildred thinks there's a way to open the drawbridge from here," said Jarrett, grunting as he lifted his brother to the padded leather chair. "How are you feeling?"

He looked at his brother.

"It feels like my heart is working for every other beat. I think the taser knocked me into arrhythmia."

Charlotte frowned. "All the more reason we have to get out of here. We need to find that controller. Mildred, do you have any idea where—"

She turned to find Mildred standing at the doorway, the only member of the group who hadn't entered the wine room.

She had a gun in her hand.

Della saw Charlotte's eyes widen and followed her gaze to Mildred.

"*You?*" she said.

Mildred glowered at her.

"Yes, *me*, Della. Thank you for solving the puzzles. Xander wouldn't let me enter the contest. He said I was too stupid."

Della let a beat pass and then cocked an eyebrow. "I hope you're not waiting for me to argue."

Mildred sneered. "You're so *smart*. Let me ask you a trivia question, Della Dear—which of us is standing on the wrong end of this gun?"

Della crossed her arms against her chest.

There wasn't much she could say.

Mildred had a point.

"You stabbed yourself?" asked Charlotte, hoping to distract Mildred and diffuse the situation.

Before Mildred could respond, there was a *boom!* so loud it felt as if it shook the castle.

Charlotte thought it could only be one thing.

"The drawbridge," she said.

Mildred nodded. "Now that we know where the prize is, we'll be leaving."

Charlotte straightened.

"*We*? Who's *we*?"

Mildred clucked her tongue. "Don't worry about it. You'll be staying here."

"Think about what you're doing," said Declan. "You're not a murderer."

She chuckled again. "Ask Tristan if that's true."

Mildred's eyes narrowed, and her nose wrinkled as if she were auditioning for the part of Cruella de Vil in an on-Broadway remake of *101 Dalmatians*.

For her cartoonish response and many other reasons, Charlotte doubted she'd killed Tristan. She suspected her partner was the killer. She felt her conjecture was solid—but not solid enough to risk rushing an armed woman.

Mildred huffed.

"You try working with Xander for forty years. That *pig*. You'd murder a few people to get what you deserved, too."

That part felt true.

Jarrett took a step forward as if he were thinking of leaping at her.

"Stay back," she warned, swinging the gun in his direction.

Charlotte's mind raced. She felt desperate to find an angle she could use to change Mildred's mind.

"You didn't kill Tristan," she said.

Mildred's eyes widened.

"Yes, I did."

Charlotte shook her head.

"How?"

Mildred glanced at the gun in her hand.

"I shot him, of course."

Charlotte nodded and gave Declan a meaningful glance.

Unfortunately, something about that look startled Mildred.

"*No*," she barked.

Without a second of hesitation, she pulled the trigger.

CHAPTER TWENTY

Trapped in the lemur enclosure, Frank clenched a fist and shook it at Bob.

"Why? Why?"

Bob chuckled. "You think people will be disappointed when they come to see the lemurs, and we're in here?"

Frank spoke through gritted teeth. "That's the problem, isn't it, *Bob*. No one will be here to *find* us because they've closed this section."

Bob shrugged. "Just call the zoo."

Frank slapped his pockets and realized he'd left his phone in the car.

"Do you have your phone?"

Bob shook his head.

"Nope. I hate that thing. Nothing but spam calls and Mariska telling me to come home when I don't want to come home."

He motioned to Frank's shoulder.

"Radio."

It took Frank a moment to realize what he was saying. He reached up and felt his shoulder mic.

"Oh, right. *Ruby*. Good idea."

He pulled the handheld from his shoulder.

"Ruby?"

He waited for an answer.

None came.

"Ruby?"

Nothing.

He looked at his watch.

"Oh no. She's gone *home*. That woman wouldn't be late for dinner if you paid her. I've tried."

Bob rubbed his stomach.

"Speaking of dinner, I hope Marcy comes back for feeding time. I'm *starving*."

Frank peered through the glass. Beyond the closed sign, he saw people in the main section of the zoo walking back and forth.

He banged on the plexiglass.

"Hey! *Hey!*" he screamed, trying to get their attention.

No one's head turned his way. Worse, now his knuckles ached.

"They can't hear me. This isn't going to work," he grumbled.

Bob picked up the little rope ladder that had dropped to the ground beneath his weight.

"We can't crawl out the top. The ladder's broken."

Frank rubbed his face.

"Also, thanks to *you*. That ladder wasn't made to support the weight of a *moron*."

He knew he sounded irritable.

He *felt* irritable.

Even beneath the lemurs' tree canopy and so close to sunset, he felt hot beneath his uniform.

"Someone will let us out eventually," said Bob, unaffected by his cranky enclosure buddy.

Frank couldn't understand his optimism.

"*Why?* Why would someone check on us? *There are no lemurs.* There's no reason for anyone to come back here. Marcy will finish up with her monkeys and think we're long gone."

Frank paced the cage looking for another way out. He knew there was only one door, but a tiny part of him hoped walking might create his own personal breeze.

It didn't.

He wiped his sleeve across his sweaty brow and eyed the ropes and nets above him.

He shook his head.

Nope. Not an option.

Young Frank would have found a way to scale the walls.

He wasn't young Frank anymore.

There was no way they could climb out of the pen. Even if they managed to get high enough, once over the perimeter, it was a straight drop to the ground on the other side. They were old enough to know that move had *broken hip* written all over it.

Or broken arm.

Or broken *head.*

He glared at his friend until he thought Bob might burst into flames.

Breaking Bob's head might improve his brain...

He spotted the camera mounted on a post across from the cage and jogged toward it as far as he could go before the plexiglass stopped him.

He jumped up and down, waving his arms.

Bob stared at him, looking bemused.

He found himself getting annoyed again.

"What? Why are you staring at me? *Do something*," he said.

Bob leaned his back against a tree.

"They don't check the cameras very often, or they wouldn't have lost their lemurs in the first place," he said.

Frank stopped jumping and leaned forward with his hands on his knees, panting.

Bob had a pretty good point.

Frank threw his back against the glass and slid to the ground to sit in the dirt.

"What time does Ruby get back?" asked Bob.

"Tomorrow morning. I am *not* sitting here until tomorrow. That much I know."

The sun was going down. Frank felt torn. He wanted it cooler, but he also wanted people to be able to *see* them.

He turned his head and noticed a bucket sitting in the corner with flies buzzing around it.

He moved to it and peered inside.

"Gotta pee?" asked Bob.

Frank side-eyed him.

"You think this bucket is here as a toilet? For who?"

"The lemurs."

"Why would they train the lemurs to go to the bathroom in a bucket?"

Bob shrugged. "Less work cleaning up if it's already all in a bucket."

Frank sighed and plucked a round, green-purple fruit from the pail. He held it up for Bob to see.

"What are these things?" he asked.

Bob wandered over to squint at it.

"Figs, I'd say," said Bob.

Frank looked to the top of the plexiglass wall of the enclosure and then across at the people walking through the zoo. Soon, those people would go home, and the zoo would close.

Their window for escape was closing.

What *wasn't* closed was a gap above the door uncovered by netting. It was too far away from any of the trees for the lemurs to escape over it.

He looked at the fig in his hand.

He had an idea.

"We need to toss these at the zoo people," he said.

"The *zoo people*?" asked Bob.

"The people walking out there. They can't hear us but might notice figs falling from the sky."

Bob moved beside him to study the figs' potential path over the glass to the crowd.

"You could be on to something," he muttered.

Frank waited until a small family strolled by and tossed a fig at them. His first attempt hit the glass. He'd tried too hard to muscle it over and lost the required arc.

"Shoot."

Bob clucked his tongue. "You're terrible at throwing."

Frank rolled his eyes.

"I *kill* you at darts."

"You do not. And even if you did, I kill you at bowling."

Frank scoffed. "No, you don't. And you don't *throw* bowling balls."

"Yes, you do."

"You *bowl* them."

"That's a type of throw."

Frank considered this. "Okay, maybe technically, but this is totally different."

Bob selected a fig.

"I'm still better at it."

He threw the fruit through the opening, and it rolled onto the walking path. Unfortunately, no one was there to see it.

Frank grunted. "I'll give it to you; that was pretty good, but you have to wait until there's someone there. Don't waste them."

He retrieved his failed toss and waited for people to wander by. When a group of pre-teens appeared, he tried again.

This time, he made it over the glass.

The fig landed near the group and rolled away. No one seemed to notice.

"Dammit," he muttered.

"Good throw, though."

Frank nodded.

"We need to hit them, though."

Bob put his hands on his hips and stared at the bucket.

"What are you thinking?" asked Frank. "And *stop* it. Nothing good ever comes from you *thinking*."

"Hold on—I'm thinking we can't do this one at a time. We should grab a handful—throw a ton all at once. Even if we don't hit anyone, someone has to notice them *raining* all over the place."

Bob nodded. "I like it. This might be more of a shotgun situation than rifle."

He scooped up an armful of figs, and Frank did the same. They tossed as fast as they could—some hitting the glass, some going wildly astray, but many landing in the splash zone.

One bounced and hit a woman's leg.

She looked down, annoyed, just as another dropped from the sky in front of her.

Frank paused as she looked directly at him.

"She sees us, she—"

She scowled and walked on.

"No, no, *no*—" He jumped up and down, waving his arms, but it was too late. The woman walked out of view.

Frank dropped his head back to stare at the netting above them.

"I thought she saw us," said Bob.

"She *did*. She thinks we're a couple of weirdos throwing fruit at passersby."

Frank tapped the bucket with his toe. They were running out of figs.

"One last shot," he said, grabbing the rest. He handed half to Bob. "Wait for the next group."

They stood cocked and ready for a minute before people appeared.

"Go!" barked Frank, letting his first fig fly.

A man in a security guard uniform appeared. A fig bounced off his shoulder.

"Score!" screamed Bob. "That was mine."

"No, it wasn't. That was *definitely* mine," said Frank.

"Hey!" screamed the guard, spotting them. He marched toward them.

Frank dropped his last fig.

"We're locked in here," he called back at the man, cupping his mouth with his hands.

The guard's angry expression relaxed a notch. He'd heard them.

"What?" He pulled at the door.

"We're *trapped* in here," repeated Frank.

The guard tugged the door a few more times.

"You're going to have to unlock it," said Bob before rolling his eyes at Frank. "Finally get someone, and it's *this* genius," he muttered.

"Do you know the combination?" asked the guard.

"Why would we know the combination?" asked Frank.

"Marcy knows it. You have to find Marcy," said Bob.

The guard nodded. "I'll get her."

He jogged off.

"Think we'll ever see him again?" asked Bob.

"I wouldn't put a *ton* of money on it," grumbled Frank.

A few minutes later, Marcy appeared to punch in the code.

"How did this happen?" she asked as she opened the door.

Frank glared at Bob.

"Things happen when he's involved."

Bob slapped him on the back.

"That's the nicest thing you've ever said to me."

Once they were freed from their cage, Marcy stood staring at them. Frank could tell any hope she'd had of him finding her lemurs had dissipated.

"I'll, uh, I'll call you when I know more," he said.

She grunted and walked them to the main path, where she scowled at the collection of figs littering the cement.

"Bye," said Frank, grabbing Bob's arm and hustling toward the front gate.

"You think she's mad about the figs?" asked Bob.

"Just keep walking," said Frank.

He drove them back to Pineapple Port and pulled up to Mariska's house to let Bob out.

"Thanks for a fun day," said Bob.

Frank grunted.

Bob exited and shut the door of the cruiser.

That's when Frank had a thought.

He slid open the passenger side window.

"Hey, Bob?"

Bob turned. "Hm?"

"Tell *no one* this happened."

"Hm?" Bob shuffled back to lean in the window. "What's that, now?"

Frank scowled. "You heard me. I'm serious, Bob. Don't tell Mariska. If this gets back to Darla that I was locked in a monkey cage—"

"Lemur."

"*Whatever*. I'll never hear the end of it."

Bob grinned. "No problem. So, when do you want to do this again?"

Frank scoffed.

"We are *not* doing this again."

Bob smiled. "I think we aaaare..."

Frank hit the window button, and Bob headed toward his house, chuckling.

CHAPTER TWENTY-ONE

Mariska and Darla stood in Mariska's kitchen, waiting for Seamus to pick them up. Both had dressed in thin dark sweatpants, dark long-sleeve tee shirts—Mariska's was turned inside-out to hide the cat design on the front—and black gloves.

They felt pretty sneaky.

Mariska's husband, Bob, entered the front door. He glanced into the kitchen, met their gazes, eyed their outfits, and continued to the bedroom without a word.

"I thought for sure he'd say something about the outfits. You have him trained so well," said Darla.

Mariska snorted a laugh. "No, we got lucky. He couldn't think of a joke."

She sniffed. "What's that smell? It smells like a *zoo*."

Darla sniffed her shirt.

"Not me. Probably leftover sloth."

She motioned to the window as Seamus's headlights appeared outside. "He's here."

She headed to the door, checking the security of her black fanny pack as they left the house to walk to Seamus's car.

Mariska found herself assigned to the back seat again. She stepped in and was about to close the door when her bedroom window shot open. Bob stuck his head out.

"*That ninja certification board sure has gone to hell!*" he called out to them.

"There it is," said Mariska as she shut her door. "He thought of something."

Seamus paused to eyeball Darla's outfit and oversized fanny pack. He wore khakis and a blue long-sleeve tee shirt—dark but not as ninja-like as their outfits.

"You've come prepared, I see," he said, pulling away from the curb.

Darla nodded. "You have no idea. I've got my lock picks, a flashlight, a pen knife, some tissues—"

Seamus chuckled. "I'm surprised you managed to lift yourself into the car." He looked at Mariska in his rearview mirror. "What do you bring?" he asked.

She pulled a granola bar from her bra.

"Snacks."

He nodded. "We should be good, then."

"Give us the breakdown," said Darla.

Seamus licked his lips. "I don't know if her place is the same as it was twenty years ago, but it's a good-sized property in the middle of nowhere surrounded by a tall metal fence to keep people from snooping around."

"Sounds terrifying," muttered Mariska.

"Do you have a plan?" asked Darla.

Seamus nodded.

"I'm going to climb the fence and get a lay of the land inside. See if it's like I remember. If I see the sloth, I'll grab him. If I don't, I'll lock down the location of Tiger Lily, the kid, and whoever else is there. If they don't look like a problem, I'll come back for you two, let you in, and we'll find the critter together."

"Can't you just talk to this Tiger Lily person? Ask her to give us back Sir Sleepsalot?" asked Mariska.

Seamus winced. "Me talking to her might make things worse. If you remember, we didn't end things on the best terms."

"Oh, right. She caught you with her cousin, Iris," said Mariska recalling his story.

He glanced in the rearview.

"Not exactly. *She* didn't catch us."

"Iris confessed?" guessed Darla.

"No..." Seamus sighed. "It was the parrot. That little bastard was the one animal too many."

Mariska scrooched forward in her chair. She didn't want to miss any of this story.

"The *parrot*?"

He nodded grimly. "Her African Grey. It told on me."

Darla laughed. "You're pulling our legs."

"Nope. I wish. It's a tragic tale. Which is good because I'm Irish, and, as an Irishman, I'm required by law to have an endless supply of tragic tales for sharing at the pub."

Darla shook her head. "I'm not buying it. How could a parrot tell on you? They can't talk. They just imitate—"

"Exactly."

Darla scowled. "*No.*"

"What?" asked Mariska.

Darla gaped. "Are you saying—"

"*What?*" repeated Mariska, moving forward on her seat another inch.

Seamus nodded. "The parrot imitated us at our most intimate moment."

Darla squealed with laughter and covered her mouth with her hand.

"You're *kidding.*"

"I'm not."

"Oh, for crying out loud." Mariska shook her head. "I think I can speak for both of us when I say we're sorry we asked."

"You might have to speak for yourself on that one," said Darla, tittering.

Seamus drove west until they reached a network of paved but small roads running through a rural area. Houses appeared every half a mile, most rancher-style and set far off the road.

After a lengthy drive past a cow field, Seamus pulled to the side of the road and pointed to the property ahead of them, evidenced by little more than a rusting mailbox.

"This is it. Back behind that clump of trees," he said, cutting the engine. "The driveway is a wee up the road, but she might have a camera there. Better to start from here and approach from the side."

Mariska peered into the darkness. She saw lights and the edge of a structure far off the road. Trees obscured the rest of the home, but she noticed the large metal fence Seamus had mentioned lining the property.

"It doesn't look like she wants visitors," said Mariska.

"She doesn't," said Seamus, grabbing a small bag he'd had sitting at Darla's feet.

They exited the car and walked down a grassy area lining the property. Seamus led the way over the lumpy terrain to a section of fence on the side of the property.

"Why do they call her Tiger Lily?" asked Mariska as she tromped through a grassy patch and felt mole-ridden ground sink beneath her feet.

"Her given name's Lily, and she's as mean as a tiger," said Seamus.

Mariska nodded.

She'd been afraid of that.

As they reached the edge of the property, Seamus motioned to the top of the wire fencing.

"There are trees inside the fence line here. No one will see me. Wait here."

Without waiting for a response, he climbed the fence, his thick, muscular body moving slowly and steadily until he reached the top and swung his leg over to the opposite side.

"Pretty impressive," whispered Darla.

Mariska had to agree.

"You could give Bob four weeks and a ladder, and he couldn't get himself over that fence."

Seamus climbed halfway down the opposite side and then dropped to the ground to peer at them through the wire.

"Let me look around. I'll be right back."

He put his finger to his lips and then disappeared into the trees.

The ladies waited.

Sitting with her back against the fence, Darla tapped her knee. Mariska watched her fidget, knowing nothing good could come of a bored Darla.

"I don't like that Lily is as mean as a tiger," said Mariska.

Darla shrugged. "The woman owns a *compound*, organized a sloth theft, and used to date Seamus. Did you think she'd be Suzy Sunshine?"

"*No*. I just think it's best not to mess with people with nicknames like *Tiger Lily*."

"I agree, but we don't have a choice."

Mariska clenched a fist.

"We *do* have a choice. We should tell *Frank*."

Darla scowled but didn't answer. She pulled back her sleeve to look at her watch.

"It's been ten minutes. How many minutes do you think we should wait?"

"How many minutes?" Mariska looked at her. "*All of them*. He said to wait until he gets back."

"But what if something happens to him?"

"If he doesn't come back in half an hour, we'll go get Frank."

Darla scoffed. "Half an hour? I'm not waiting here for half an hour."

She unzipped her fanny pack.

Mariska felt a wave of panic rise in her throat.

"What are you doing?"

"I'm getting my wire clippers."

"You have wire clippers? *Why*? What are we going to do with those?"

Darla stood. "Can you climb this fence?"

"You know darn well I can't climb a fence."

"So we'll cut a hole in it."

"Cut a—*Why*?"

"Because we can't climb it."

Mariska huffed. "You're missing the point. Seamus will let us in if he wants us in there at all. He said to *wait*."

Darla wasn't listening. She already had her clippers in hand. She started talking as if she'd been halfway through a conversation with someone else.

"—plus, what if Seamus comes running with Sir Sleepsalot? He can't climb the fence with that thing."

Mariska looked at the top of the fence. "He probably can."

"I don't think so. We'll clip a hole in the fence so *he* can slip out."

"Not us slipping in?"

Darla snipped the fencing.

"Or that," she muttered. "It's kind of a chicken and egg thing."

Mariska groaned.

Darla snipped away the fencing until she could peel it wide enough to crawl through.

Which, to Mariska's horror, she did.

"What are you doing *now*?"

Darla stood up on the other side of the fence and clapped her hands together.

"I'm looking around."

"You said you'd cut the fence for *him*."

"Or us. Whatever."

She took a few steps into the trees beyond the fence.

"*Darla!*" Mariska hissed. "Don't leave me."

She waited for an answer, but none came. Darla had disappeared into the trees.

Mariska grumbled under her breath.

"You are so *pigheaded*."

Something white on the opposite side of the fence caught her eye, bobbing to the right of where Darla disappeared.

It flashed, vanished, and flashed again.

Mariska froze.

"Darla?"

Multiple white things bobbed in the dark now—all headed her way. They were on the opposite side of the fence, which made Mariska feel a little better, but of course, now the fence had *a big hole in it*.

She took a small step forward to peer into the darkness.

Large yellow eyes blinked back at her.

She gasped and stumbled back.

"*Darla...*"

The creature attached to the eyes stepped into the moonlight as it approached the fence.

She could see it now.

She still had no idea what it was.

It was furry, about as big as Miss Izzy, and had a white face with a small black mask around the eyes. Something behind it whipped, and she realized the creature had a long tail of black and white stripes.

It was the strangest raccoon she'd ever seen.

She swallowed.

Maybe it's sick?

Oh no.

Maybe it has *rabies*.

The thing approached the hole in the fence as Mariska tried not to breathe. It sniffed the clippers Darla had left on the ground inside the fence line.

"Leave that alone," scolded Mariska.

It glanced at her and then grabbed the clippers in its furry little hands.

She shook a finger at it.

"*No*. Drop it. *Leave* it."

The weird raccoon didn't listen to her commands any better than Miss Izzy did back home. It took the clippers and loped off, tail flipping back and forth as it disappeared into the underbrush.

Mariska let out the long breath she'd been holding. A moment later, Darla reappeared.

"It looks safe. Come on," she said.

"It didn't bite you?" asked Mariska.

"What? The tiger? I told you there's no tiger—"

"No. The freaky raccoon."

"The freaky raccoon?" Darla scowled. "What's wrong? You look like you saw a ghost."

"Not a ghost—*a freaky raccoon*. It stole your clippers."

"What?" Darla's attention dropped to the ground. "Where are they?"

"I just told you. The freaky raccoon took it."

Darla stomped. "What is a *freaky raccoon?*"

Mariska took a moment to think how best to describe it.

"It had a smaller face than a normal raccoon, big yellow eyes, and a long striped tail. It trotted over, looked me straight in the eye, and stole your clippers."

Darla squinted. "Either you're trying to keep me from cutting more fences, or you're losing your mind."

"I *swear*. It went that way." Mariska pointed into the bushes.

Darla sighed. "Whatever. Just get in here."

Mariska eyed the hole in the fence. "Through that? I can't fit through there."

Darla pointed at her.

"Ah ha! You hid the clippers to keep me from making the hole big enough for you."

"*No, I didn't*. I just don't think it's big enough."

Darla put her hands on her hips.

"Well, it's going to have to be because a *freaky raccoon stole my clippers*."

Growling to herself, Mariska approached the fence and lowered herself to the ground. Once on her hands and knees, she saw Darla's gap was bigger than she'd realized.

Bigger than she'd *hoped*.

It was clear she'd fit through.

Dammit.

With some grunting, she worked her way through, careful not to hook her shirt on the wires.

"See? You made it just fine," said Darla.

"Shut up."

Mariska brushed the grass off her creeper outfit as she eyed the trees and bushes, looking for freaky raccoons and tigers.

"We shouldn't be in here," she muttered. She didn't need to say it louder. She could scream it over the hillside, and Darla would still ignore her.

When she didn't think it could get any worse, Darla turned to look the way she'd come.

"We can cover more ground if we split up," she said.

Mariska gasped.

"You want me to walk around this crazy place alone?"

"Not *you and me*, us and Seamus. He goes one way, and we go the other."

"But what happens when he comes back and we're not there?"

"I imagine he'll wait for us. We won't be long. It's a big property. We can have a quick look around." She pointed to her left. "He went that way, so we'll go this way."

With a quiet whimper, Mariska followed Darla as she marched into the trees.

"I hate this. This place is crawling with who-knows-what. There *could* be tigers."

Darla snickered. "Ah, but if she had tigers roaming the property, they would have eaten the freaky raccoons, so I think we're safe."

"Haha. Maybe the little monkeys climb the trees when the tigers come."

"Tigers can climb trees," said Darla.

Mariska looked up into the branches.

"Why did you have to tell me that?"

She ducked as something overhead rustled.

"You know, there are a few rules in Florida, and one of them is *you don't walk around jungles at night.*"

"This is hardly a jungle. It's a few trees. Look—"

They broke through the treeline to an open stretch of freshly mowed grass. A breeze blew through the thick, humid air, carrying the sweet scent of flowers and the faint, wild musk of things Mariska wanted to avoid.

It was nice to be out of the trees. The extensive landscaping felt like a vacation after the jungle.

Mariska had four full seconds of relief before something moved in the darkness.

Something *taller* than a freaky raccoon.

Much taller.

Something was getting *bigger*.

"What's that?" she whispered, pointing.

"Where?" Darla shifted to stare at where Mariska was pointing.

"There. See it? Something's *moving*," whispered Mariska.

Darla grunted. "Oh. I see. What *is* that? Is that your raccoon thing?"

"No. It's *bigger*."

The creature moved again. It made a low growling noise.

"Oh no," said Mariska as pins and needles fired in her cheeks and forehead.

"That's not good," agreed Darla.

The growl turned into a sort of honk.

Darla grabbed Mariska's arm.

"It's coming this way."

The creature moved closer and tripled in size. It honked again.

"Run!" said Darla.

The ladies sprinted in the opposite direction of the monster toward a landscaped garden sitting area. They passed under an overhead light, and Darla glanced over her shoulder.

She slowed but didn't stop.

"What are you doing?" asked Mariska.

"I can see it. It's a *bird*."

The bird screeched as if confirming her observation.

"A really *angry* bird," added Darla.

Mariska dared to look. She saw the bird's vibrant feathers quivering with each powerful stride of its sturdy legs as it passed beneath the light.

This animal, she recognized.

"It's a *peacock*," she said.

"An *attack peacock*," agreed Darla.

The enraged bird closed in and fanned its plumage—a dazzling mix of shimmering blues and greens.

"It would be pretty if I wasn't terrified," said Mariska.

The bird closed in.

"We better get a move on," said Darla.

As Mariska turned to run again, a short, manicured hedge popped out from the darkness. She tried to stop, but it was too late. She crashed into the greenery.

The peacock, sensing weakness, let out a piercing shriek and lunged forward, closing the distance between them.

Mariska floundered, fighting to escape the bush almost as hard as her pounding heart fought to leap from her chest.

The bird's beady eyes locked on hers.

"What did I ever do to you?" she screamed at it.

Driven by adrenaline, she found her feet and ran after Darla, who'd dodged the bush and kept running. Mariska saw her pause to *consider* helping, but the second she found her feet, Darla sprinted.

Emboldened by Mariska's entanglement, the crazy bird found a new gear in speed and volume.

It screeched like a banshee.

The ladies ducked under a collection of low-hanging branches and snaked through a row of animal topiaries. Relentless, the peacock expanded its wings, its long iridescent train undulating like a shimmering cape behind it as it ran.

Darla pointed toward box hedges lining a stucco wall.

"Get behind those!"

Mariska gasped for breath. She appreciated the idea of *not running* but wasn't sure she *loved* Darla's solution.

"What if it can climb over the bushes? We'll be stuck. It'll peck out our eyes. We'll be stuck and eyeless."

Darla headed for the bushes.

"*Just do it.*"

They scrambled behind the hedges and held their breaths as the creature slowed. It paced in front of them, honking with agitation.

"Go. *Git*," said Darla, waving it on.

Wedged behind the hedges, the women leaned heavily against a garden wall, chests heaving.

"What is his *problem*?" asked Mariska.

"The good-looking ones are always jerks," said Darla.

Mariska looked at her.

"This is all your fault."

Darla put her hand on her chest.

"*Me*?"

"Yes, *you*. We wouldn't even be here if it wasn't for you."

Darla chuckled. "Oh, come on. This is exciting."

Mariska glared.

The peacock offered a final honk before strutting away, its ruffled feathers settling into place as it moved.

Darla sighed. "I think we're safe now. We can—"

She cut short as a strange hissing sound grew louder around them.

"What is *that*?" asked Mariska as the crackling around them reached a crescendo too fast to do anything. She could only think one thing.

"We're going to die!"

The sharp sputtering eased into a steady hiss as cold water blasted their bodies from every angle.

Mariska screamed.

"Sprinklers!" yipped Darla.

They scrambled out of the bushes and jogged to a small square English garden, gravitating toward a white stone bench to sit.

"I'm soaked," said Darla.

Mariska glowered at her, wet curls dripping down her forehead.

"Did I mention I'm going to kill you?" she asked.

CHAPTER TWENTY-TWO

Everyone in the wine room yipped and ducked at the sound of Mildred's gun firing. The bullet passed over their heads to break a bottle of racked wine, which splattered the group and splashed all over poor dead Timmy, adding insult to injury.

The shock of the gunshot gave Mildred the time she needed to escape. She slammed shut the wine room door with her free hand even as Declan and Jarrett leaped forward to stop her.

Charlotte heard the latch click, her heart thumping in her chest.

"Why would she do that?" roared Jarrett, his expression alive with rage. "What is going on? Is she crazy?"

"I didn't see any of that coming," said Della, her chest heaving.

"Me neither," said Charlotte. She'd never dreamed her questions would spur Mildred to *shoot* at them. She'd only been trying to buy them time.

The door had a keypad lock on the inside. Declan punched in the code they'd used to get into the room, but before he could finish, they heard a beep.

"What was that?" asked Della.

Declan entered the last number of the code, and his first attempt to unlock the door failed to the tune of a buzzer. His second died a similar death.

"I think that beep was the sound of her resetting the code," he said.

"Assuming the code from the inside was *ever* the same," said Charlotte. "Why would Xander ever lock this room from the *inside*?"

Della scoffed. "If there's anything I've figured out this evening, it's that Xander was a deeply strange dude. Who knows what he was trying to hide when he was in here."

"*Was* a strange dude?" asked Jarrett.

Della glanced at Charlotte as they both realized she'd used the past tense. Before Charlotte could decide if they should share the news of Xander's death with the brothers, Della sniffed.

"*Is* a deeply strange dude. *Whatever*. He's like a thousand years old." She played her insider knowledge off well. Jarrett turned his attention back to his brother.

Charlotte looked at Della and realized something else about the woman.

She was an excellent liar.

Declan tried a few more combinations. Nothing worked.

Jarrett moved to the door.

"Back off," he snapped at Declan.

Declan stepped away from the keypad, and Jarrett slammed his shoulder into the door.

It didn't budge.

He kicked at it until he became winded and bent, supporting his body with hands planted on his knees.

"It's reinforced. There's no way we're pounding our way through that," he said between pants.

Charlotte stepped up and traced the door's edges with her fingertips, looking for gaps or hidden latches.

She found nothing. She put her hands on her hips to stare at the door.

"Maybe there's a puzzle to open it?"

Declan leaned in to whisper in her ear.

"Maybe *Mildred* and her partner added the lock to prepare a jail, just in case."

Jarrett slammed his fist against his opposite open palm. "I need to get Barrett to the hospital. We *have* to get out of here."

Barrett raised a hand. "I'm good as long as I take it easy, I think."

"You're *not*," insisted Jarrett. "This isn't funny anymore. We have to get out of here."

"I'm not sure it was ever funny," said Barrett, attempting to defuse his brother's temper. "Like I said. I'm good."

"I'm so *glad*," said Della, turning to him. "Mind if the rest of us work on getting out, though? Or should we all sit here and see how long we can live on nothing but expensive wine?"

Charlotte eyed the extensive wine collection.

"Sugar content, lots of bottles...pretty long time, I imagine."

Della wrapped her arms around herself. "Maybe we'll just freeze to death."

"We can turn up the temperature," said Declan, adjusting the climate panel.

Della nodded. "Thanks. Starvation it is."

Jarrett pointed at his brother. "I'm going to kill whoever did this to you."

Barrett held up a hand, and they high-fived.

Della rolled her eyes.

Charlotte's focus rose to the ceiling. She pointed to a large grate high on the wall.

"What about the ventilation? We could see if it leads anywhere."

Della followed her gaze and tilted her head. "I could fit through there."

"You'd never come back for us now that you know where the prize is," said Jarrett.

Della glared back at him. "You think I'd let you all die in a fire? What kind of monster do you think I am?"

Jarrett blinked at her.

"What fire?"

Della looked at Charlotte again, but it seemed she'd reached the end of her ability to hide the truth. Furious, she pointed toward the storage room down the hall.

"They've got enough gasoline stocked down there to burn the whole place down."

Jarrett's jaw fell open. "Why would they do that?"

"Because this whole thing is rigged, and we're going to die if we don't get out of here," said Della.

Jarrett and his brother searched the faces of the others.

"*Seriously?*" asked Barrett.

"Did you think Timmy dying and you getting zapped was an accident?" asked Della.

"No, I—"

Della didn't give him any time to answer. She was on a roll now.

"Mildred and some other jackass have a whole plan for winning that requires the rest of us dying."

Jarrett looked at Charlotte and Declan for confirmation.

They nodded.

"It's true," said Charlotte.

"How long have you known? Did you know when we were in the kitchen?"

They nodded again.

"Tristan and Xander are both dead," said Declan.

Jarrett's face flushed red.

"And you didn't tell me?"

"We didn't know if you were involved," said Declan, stepping forward. "Look. You're going to have to calm down. We need to get out of here, and we're not going to do that fighting each other."

Jarrett spun away and swore under his breath. His brother touched his leg, and he sat on the arm of the chair beside him.

After a moment, he huffed a sigh.

"This keeps getting worse and worse. Mom always said nothing good could come from getting involved with Dad."

Barrett nodded. "She was right. As usual."

The room sat quiet for a moment. Peace restored, Declan retrieved his phone, took a picture of the ventilation shaft's grate, and then zoomed in on the photo.

"Looks like it's got Philips-head screws."

"We don't have a screwdriver," said Charlotte, looking around the room. "We don't have anything except wine."

The group riffled through the few cabinets, finding nothing but wine glasses, ashtrays, coasters, and a cigar cutter.

"Maybe the edge of the coasters?" asked Charlotte as Della held one up to inspect it.

"Not strong enough. It's cork," she said, snapping the coaster in half.

Suddenly, she gasped and reached for her head.

"*Bobbypin*," she exclaimed, pulling one from her hair. "Finally, being dressed to the nines for this stupid contest will pay off."

Charlotte perked.

"That could work."

Declan and Jarrett arranged wine crates into a makeshift set of stairs leading to the grate.

"See if it's tall enough for you," said Declan, stepping back to examine their work.

Della climbed to the top but found the height too low to work on the grate's upper screws. Charlotte could tell even taller Declan wouldn't be able to reach them.

The stairs needed rebuilding.

"Come back down," said Declan, motioning to Della.

She did, and he climbed the stairs with a final crate in his arms, grunting as he hefted it on top of the highest.

He returned to the ground and frowned at the new, more wobbly version of their stairs.

"You'll have to hoist yourself up those last two boxes. We're out of crates to do it any other way."

Della set her jaw and climbed again. Jarrett and Declan placed themselves at the bottom of the pyramid to catch her if she fell. At the top, she kicked off her heels, and the men dodged as the stilettos clattered to the ground beside them.

"Grab them for me. They were expensive," she said.

Scowling, Jarrett kicked them aside.

Charlotte couldn't believe it had taken Della so long to rid herself of the four-inch heels. She would have abandoned them *hours* ago. She was suffering enough in her two-and-a-half-inchers.

Della adjusted the top box by a few inches to balance her naked toes on the edge of the first. Using the wall for support, she climbed to the top. The double-stacked boxes beneath her trembled as she turned the screws with her bobby pin.

"It's working," she reported.

She unscrewed the four fasteners at the corners of the grate and removed it, tossing it behind her. Declan ducked, and Charlotte dodged to the left to avoid being brained.

"*There are people down here*," said Charlotte.

Della looked over her shoulder.

"Sorry. It slipped. I'll be back."

She hoisted herself up and disappeared into the vent.

Declan looked at Charlotte.

"Maybe you should go with her."

She nodded. She'd been thinking the same thing. Half because Della might need help, half because she didn't trust the woman.

Charlotte left her shoes behind and started up the crate stairs. Climbing the last two boxes was not easy. Pulling herself atop the highest box, she paused to appreciate Della's athleticism. The southern belle didn't look like a tomboy, but she had *skills*.

She peered into the narrow vent passage. Della was nowhere to be seen.

She took a steeling breath.

Here goes nothing.

She crawled into the tight, dusty space with a final wave to the others.

"Della?" she called, dragging herself along by her elbows.

"This way," Della called back.

"Do you see anything promising?"

"There's light up ahead. You're just in time. I could use some help."

"I'm coming. Make noise so I know where you are."

Della hummed *Happy Birthday* as Charlotte navigated the twists and turns of the ductwork. She found Della on her back with her feet toward a grate leading to another room.

"I backed down this way to kick out the grate," she explained. "If you wedge yourself there, I can leverage my shoulders against you and get more power."

Charlotte nodded. "Sounds good."

Della scrambled forward like an upside-down bug until her feet reached the grate. Charlotte followed and wedged herself sideways to offer Della's head and shoulders support.

Della kicked as best she could with the vent's height restricting the movement of her knees.

"This is where a decent pair of shoes would have come in handy," she said, grunting.

She pounded on the right side of the grate until it popped loose. After another two kicks, the whole side gave way. She turned her attention to the opposite side until the grate swung down, attached by only one lower screw.

Out in the room, something crashed to the ground.

Della looked back at Charlotte.

"Now I have to drop out of this vent. This is the part I wasn't looking forward to."

Charlotte nodded. This *would* be tricky, with no wine crate stairs on the other side.

Della stared at the exit with pensive consideration. "I'd rather go feet-first, but then I can't see where I'm landing. If there's something awkward below me, I'll snap a leg."

"Do you want to turn around and take a peek?"

Della frowned. "Hold on. I have an idea."

She scrootched down the vent until her knees bent and her legs below her shins hung through. She lifted her head and peered past her legs.

"I see shelves on the other side. It's the library." She paused and then added, "I can feel books on my heels. We're above a shelf."

"So it should be a straight shot down?"

"I think so. I don't think any furniture was in front of the bookshelves."

She took a deep breath.

"I hope I'm right. Here goes nothing."

Charlotte reached for her. "Give me your hands. I'll try to ease you down."

Della seemed to like this idea.

"Okay. I might be able to get my heels on the shelves as I go."

She wiggled her arms back over her head so Charlotte could clasp her hands. Together they inched forward, Della's body disappearing over the edge an inch at a time. Once her tush moved past the opening, Charlotte strained to hold her.

"I was going to twist, but I can't now. This isn't working," said Della. "Abort, abort."

Charlotte helped her back into the vent a few inches.

"I'm breaking my back going this way, and I'll snap my neck if I fall too fast," said Della. "I need to roll on my stomach."

Together they worked her onto her stomach.

"Much better," said Della, pushing through the exit until she bent at the waist, her lower half dangling into the library. Charlotte heard her kick books off the shelves.

"I've got my toes on the shelf. This is much better."

Charlotte lowered her as far as they could go until it became too awkward for Della to keep her arms in the vent.

"Okay. I'm going to jump clear now. Let go on three."

"Got it."

"One, two, *three!*"

Charlotte released Della's hands, and she disappeared. She heard a single *thump*.

"Are you okay?" called Charlotte.

There was no response.

"Della?" she tried again.

Nothing.

Charlotte scrambled to the edge of the vent and peered down.

Della was gone.

Charlotte gritted her teeth.

She's making a break for the maze.

CHAPTER TWENTY-THREE

Seamus left the ladies behind at the fence and worked through a clump of trees and underbrush toward Tiger Lily's home. Emerging from the woods a minute later, he spotted a dirt path with shells lining the outer edge.

He recognized it.

That leads to the house.

So far, not much had changed at Tiger Lily's. The compound remained a mishmash of wild nature and manicured gardens.

Somewhere not far away, an angry bird screeched and squawked. He searched the skies for a swooping pterodactyl ready to snatch him up to feed its nest of hungry babies. He knew the place was crawling with unusual animals—Lily had a thing for critters of any sort—the weirder, the better.

He marched on, following the shell-lined path until he spotted the lights of Lily's stucco rancher in the distance.

Decision time.

He paused to consider his options.

He guessed the stolen sloth slept near the house—probably in one of Lily's guest animal pens. She stored a collection of such pens in her back yard. He remembered one particularly large cage with a monkey in it during his time with her. The pen had a tree *perfect* for sloth hanging.

That has to be it.

He glanced back the way he came, wondering if he should fetch Darla and Mariska for backup.

Nah.

It made sense to go alone. He knew the place and could, hopefully, find the sloth.

Get in and get out.

There was no reason to endanger the ladies if he didn't have to.

And, judging by the experiences he'd had with them since arriving back in Charity and the stories he'd heard from Charlotte and Declan, he knew those ladies could be a handful.

The path continued to the house, with a branch breaking toward the right. If memory served him, he thought the right fork took a more meandering path to the same place—around an herb garden and over a small stream running through the property on its way to Tiger Lily's home.

One thing that *had* changed since his time at the compound was the advent of cheap and easy-to-use home security. A camera might be watching over the main path. She probably didn't monitor the more indirect trail over the stream.

He glanced down both paths and made his decision.

He took the right path.

The proverbial path less traveled led him to the small wooden bridge arching over the stream. He walked to the top of the bridge and used its height to peer at the house. A little farther, and he'd be at the monkey cage. Fingers crossed, the sloth would be—

He heard a loud *crack!* and the ground collapsed beneath one leg.

"Gaah!"

He grabbed for the railing to catch himself, but he'd been standing in the perfect center of the bridge and couldn't reach it.

He plunged downward, stifling his scream by gritting his teeth. One leg crashed through a hole in the bridge, the meat of his thigh wedging between the slats. He felt the splintered wood dig into his flesh through his thin khakis.

His opposite leg bent at an odd angle on the bridge, skinning his knee.

He braced himself with his palms to ease the pressure on this thigh, steadying himself on the bridge—every wobble inspiring another stab of agony.

He hung there, muttering under his breath, inventing compound swear words the world had never heard. Under the bridge, the stream wove around his ankle, filling his shoe with water.

He'd remembered the bridge but forgotten to take into consideration the thing was older than he was. Twenty years hadn't been any kinder to the little bridge than it had been to him.

Once Seamus came to terms with both his situation and the pain, he pushed against the planks beside him, attempting to lift his body from the hole.

He struggled, the broken wood tearing at his flesh, but he couldn't get high enough to make real progress. He needed something to grab—something he could use to hoist himself out.

He closed his eyes and relaxed again.

Not working.

He strained for the side rail, hoping to use it to pull himself upward, but couldn't reach it.

He glared at it.

Probably pull right out of the damn bridge anyway.

He sighed.

He'd fought drug dealers in Miami and guerrillas in South America, only to be taken out by a decorative bridge.

Seamus glanced in the direction of the house. The crack of the wood breaking had sounded like a shotgun blast. He was lucky Tiger Lily hadn't come running.

Of course, now he was stuck in a bridge with no help in sight, so how lucky was he?

He considered breaking the slat next to the one he'd fallen through to give his leg more space, but that one felt solid.

Just my luck to step on the only rotted board.

He heard a scratching noise to his right and turned to see a possum waddling along the river bank. It moved to cross the bridge, distracted by something behind it.

"*Get away*," said Seamus.

Two feet from him, the animal snapped its pointed noise in Seamus's direction and froze.

It hadn't counted on a man sticking out of the bridge.

It made a half-hearted attempt to turn and run but didn't get an inch before toppling on its side.

It lay there, still.

Playing possum.

Seamus's lip curled.

Fake dead or alive, the thing smelled *awful*.

He shook his head.

As usual, the *luck of the Irish* was no luck at all.

Now, he was stuck in a bridge, bleeding, *and* staring at a stinky possum butt.

He heard people talking in low voices and bent low, wincing as the movement pained his leg. The sound came from the direction of the same path on which he'd traveled.

He pursed his lips.

Someone *had* heard the wood crack.

"We shouldn't get so close to the house," said a voice.

"But we've looked everywhere else," said another. This one was louder, female, and *familiar*.

Seamus perked.

"Darla? Mariska?" he stage-whispered in their direction.

The talking stopped.

"It's Seamus," he added.

"Seamus?" came a voice. He wasn't sure which one spoke.

Darla and Mariska's heads popped from behind a tree on the bank from which he'd come.

He waved at them, and their focuses lowered to him.

"What are you doing down there?" asked Darla.

"Oh, you know. Just hanging out," he said.

"Why are you so short?" asked Mariska as the ladies left the forest's edge and walked toward him.

"I'm stuck. The bridge gave way."

Mariska's hand covered her mouth.

"Oh, you poor—*aaah*!"

She'd been about to step on the bridge and instead jumped back and knocked into Darla. Darla only managed to stay upright by grabbing her frightened friend's shirt.

"There's a thing next to you," said Mariska, pointing.

Seamus glanced at the critter lying beside him, its mouth open, pointed teeth hanging out like a snaggletoothed rat.

"It's a possum. He's playing dead."

"It's *alive*?" asked Mariska.

Seamus realized he'd made things worse by admitting the animal still breathed.

Darla crept forward to peer at the critter.

"Why would it do that right next to you?"

"I startled it. It didn't expect to see me here." He snorted a laugh. "Come to think of it—*I* didn't expect to see me here, either."

"How are we supposed to get to you with that thing there?" asked Mariska.

Seamus sighed. "Just drag him out of the way. It won't know."

He saw Mariska's eyes pop wide and white in the moonlight.

"Are you insane? It'll wake up and bite us."

"No, it won't. Fun fact—it isn't faking. When possums do this, it's involuntary. It won't wake up for hours."

Seamus had read something to that effect a long time ago. He wasn't sure how much of it was true, but it sounded good.

"You don't think me touching it will wake it up?" asked Darla. She didn't sound happy, but she moved closer.

"Just push it off the side of the bridge with your foot," suggested

Mariska.

Darla looked at her.

"Won't it drown?" She turned back to Seamus. "Will it drown if I push it off the bridge?"

He shrugged. "Probably?"

Darla shook her head. "I don't feel good about that."

"It's a possum. It's a giant *rat*," said Mariska.

Darla frowned. "I know, but how'd you like it if someone pushed *you* in the water when you were sound asleep and frozen still?"

Mariska grunted. "If I was a possum, I'd figure I deserved it for being a disease-ridden Rat King."

Darla stepped onto the bridge.

"I'll pull it off to the bank."

"Careful where you step—stick to the sides of the bridge," said Seamus.

Darla treaded along the edge of the bridge until she parallelled the possum. Grimacing, she leaned forward and pinched the end of the animal's long pink tail.

"*Ew, ew, ew,*" said Mariska, looking away.

"This is so disgusting," said Darla, dragging the creature's lifeless body down the small bridge and onto the dirt. She left it by the side of the stream.

It didn't move.

Mariska pointed at her friend.

"You need to wash your hands. Do you have any hand sanitizer in your fanny pack?"

Darla shook her head and squatted at the stream's edge—far away from the possum—to rinse her hands.

"That'll have to do for now," she said, drying them on her pants before returning her focus to Seamus.

"Okay, now, what's the best way to help you?" she asked.

He sighed. "That's a good question. Some of the broken wood is stuck in my thigh—"

Mariska waved both her hands and squeezed her eyes tight.

"Ooh, ooh, ooh, *no*."

Darla side-eyed her and then turned back to Seamus.

"Looks like it's me and you, Irish."

"I don't like blood," said Mariska.

"I'm not a big fan of it myself," said Seamus. "Particularly when it's mine."

He motioned to Darla.

"Come here beside me, but, *again*, be careful to keep your weight toward the outer edge of the bridge."

Darla did as instructed, sliding along the bridge's railing until she reached him.

Seamus held up his arm.

"Give me your hand, hold the rail, and maybe I can use you to pull myself out before I bleed to death."

"Oh no," moaned Mariska from the bank.

Darla held out her arm. Seamus reached up to grasp her wrist and arm.

"Ready?" he asked.

She braced herself and nodded.

Seamus pulled himself from the hole with a slow and steady tug, gritting his teeth as the splintered board tore from his leg.

"My arm is going to pull out of the socket," Darla grunted as she supported his weight.

"Almost there," he assured her, secretly terrified she'd let go and he'd impale himself on the bridge a second time.

A few seconds later, he was free. He shifted back on his butt to inspect his wound.

"Do you have any first aid in there?" he asked, motioning at Darla's pack.

"No." She looked at Mariska. "I'm going to have to get a bigger fanny pack."

Seamus grimaced. He needed something to stop the bleeding.

"Anything sharp?"

"Ooh, *yes*. Swiss Army Knife?"

She unzipped the pack and handed the familiar red tool to him.

Seamus used the knife to cut his pants below the knee and shred the fabric into a bandage, which he tied around his thigh. When it felt tight and secure, he used the railing to pull himself to his feet.

"That'll work," he said, leaning to return the knife to Darla. "Let's get off this bridge."

The two shuffled to the opposite bank, avoiding the bridge's center.

"Don't leave me over here with the possum," said Mariska, creeping along the bridge's edge to join them.

"Are you going to be okay?" asked Darla.

Seamus nodded. "I'm fine, but why are you two here?"

"It's a good thing we were," said Mariska.

He frowned. "Maybe, but that's not the point. I told you to stay put where I knew you were safe."

"You went to the left, so we went to the right. We thought we could cover more ground that way," said Darla.

"We didn't find anything," admitted Mariska. "Except the world's meanest peacock."

He cocked his head. "Why are you all wet?"

Darla shook her head. "Long story."

Seamus sighed. There was no point scolding them now.

He peered around a line of bushes at Tiger Lily's rancher.

He motioned to the ladies to take a peek.

"The house is right there. I'm going to see if the sloth is in the back. She used to have some cages there. I need you two to head back to the car. When you see me come running, start it up."

"But we're your *backup*," said Mariska, a little pouty.

"You're my *getaway driver*," he reiterated.

Mariska frowned. "Does that mean we have to go back over the bridge?"

"Yes. Go. *Now*."

He pointed the way.

"Fine," said Darla.

Seamus watched them shuffle over the bridge and disappear into the trees.

Satisfied they'd listened to his direction, he rounded the bushes to head for Tiger Lily's, pushing aside the pain in his leg.

Cutting across an expanse of lawn, he slipped into the back yard and circled it, checking the cages there.

No sloth.

He cursed his luck again and approached the all-season porch attached to the back of the house.

The door was locked.

He glanced down at a chipped ceramic snail with a ladybug on its back. It smiled at him with wide eyes and a peeling green face.

Good to see you again, Mr. Snail.

He lifted the statue to reveal a hole in the bottom and a hollow center. The key hidden inside rattled as he turned it over.

Some things never change.

He used the key to open the door to the sunroom and slip inside.

Bird cages lined the room.

Again, no sloth.

Feathers and seeds crunched beneath his feet with each step as he crept to the back door. Inside, he heard a television playing.

He passed a large silver cage with what looked like fifty finches inside. They fluttered and chirped at the sight of him.

Seamus pressed his eye to the back door's glass. Curtains on the other side blocked most of his view, but he saw a television flickering in the living room. The kitchen, the room directly on the opposite side of the door, appeared empty.

He pulled the sliding bottom from a small parakeet cage hanging nearby.

There sat the second key.

He couldn't help but smile at his luck.

He eased the key in the lock and was about to turn the knob when a loud voice to his left squawked.

"Oh, *Oirus*."

He whirled and spotted an African Gray parrot gripping the side of its cage, staring at him.

"Oirus, oh, Oirus," it taunted.

He recognized his own Irish accent from twenty years ago, saying *Oh, Iris*.

The name of Lily's cousin.

The damn bird was ratting him out.

Again.

"Shut *up*, Pollywood," he hissed at it. He'd never forget the name of that stupid bird.

The parrot became more agitated.

"Oh, *Oirus*! Seamus. I love you. Oh aye, oh aye, *sqaaawk*!"

"Shut up, you stupid bird!"

Seamus stepped toward the cage.

He heard a rattle behind him.

He glanced over his shoulder as the back door of the home flung open.

Tiger Lily stood in the doorway with a shotgun pointed at him, glaring.

"Hello, *Seamus*," she said.

Swallowing, he turned to face her.

"Hello, Lily."

He offered her a sheepish grin.

"Fancy meeting you here."

CHAPTER TWENTY-FOUR

Still grumbling over Della's betrayal, Charlotte slithered back down the vent until she found a spot where she could make a sort of K-turn and head back down the shaft to the library feet-first and on her stomach. She eased out her legs until she was hanging.

"Keep your feet toward the outside of the shelves. They're flimsier than you think in the center," said Della's voice below her.

Charlotte gasped.

"You're there!"

"Of course, I'm here. Did you think I broke my neck?"

"No, you *disappeared*."

"Oh. I thought I heard something out in the hall. I wanted to make sure Mildred wasn't creeping around, ready to shoot us."

Charlotte huffed a relieved sigh.

Maybe I can trust her after all.

She worked down a few shelves until it seemed safe to jump and landed on her bare feet. Della steadied her.

Charlotte sneezed and took a second to brush the dust off her hands and dress.

She looked at Della.

"Now, we have to get through that wine room door."

They jogged to the wine room to find a heavy dresser tilted against the door.

"How the heck did they get that there? No way *Mildred* did that," said Della.

"Her partner must be strong," said Charlotte.

They shifted the dresser upright, away from the door, so it sat against the wall. It wasn't as heavy as it looked.

"We're here," she called to the people inside the wine room.

She punched in the door lock code they used the first time, but it didn't work. It seemed Mildred had reset the code.

"I was afraid of that," she muttered.

"God forbid it be *easy*," agreed Della.

Charlotte glanced down the hall.

"The storage room down there—maybe there's a hammer or something we can use to break the lock."

She yelled at the door.

"We'll be right back. We're going to get some tools!"

The women ran to the storage room. The moment the door swung open, Charlotte stopped.

Uh oh.

"What's wrong?" asked Della.

"The gasoline canisters are *gone*."

Della peered around her to stare at the floor.

"Oh. That's not good." She looked up. "If they're upstairs getting ready to burn down the house, shouldn't we go stop them *now*?"

Charlotte considered this option and shook her head.

"They've got at least one gun and who knows how many helpers. If something goes wrong and we end up dead, the others will die trapped in that wine room. I think I feel a lot better about letting them out first."

Della nodded. "Then we can send the men upstairs to stop the fire, and we can stay safe down here."

Charlotte scowled at her, and Della rolled her eyes.

"Oh, sorry. I forgot you're engaged to one of them," she said.

They searched through the storage room junk until Charlotte found a hammer and held it up as if she'd won it.

"*Hammer.*"

They returned to the wine room and wailed on the lock until it cracked and broke away. Charlotte used the hammer handle to poke through the hole left in the door. She heard the inside knob clatter to the ground.

Peering through the circular opening, she saw Declan staring back at her.

"Hello there," she said.

"Now we have a locked door with no knob," he said.

She grimaced. "It must be *weaker*. She had a bureau tilted against the door. That might have been half the problem. Try and barrel through again?"

His eye bobbed, and she assumed he was nodding. He moved away from the peephole.

"Stand back," she heard him say a moment later.

There was a thud, and the door shuddered.

"I think I felt it move," said Declan.

Two more thuds and the door gave way. Declan and Jarrett stumbled through and slammed into the bureau. It had taken both of them to crack the last bits of the locking mechanism.

"Good job," said Charlotte. "But we have a new problem. The gasoline is gone."

Declan looked up the way Della had.

"They took it upstairs," he said.

She nodded. "I assume so. Now, we *really* need to get out of here. We're going to have to carry Barrett—"

"Uh, *guys*," said Della from somewhere down the hall.

Alarmed by her tone, Charlotte and Declan jogged around the corner to the lower landing where Della stood, staring up the stairs.

Charlotte smelled smoke.

"We really, *really* need to get out of here," she said.

Declan touched her shoulder.

"Hold on. I'm going to take a peek."

She grasped his arm to hold him in place for a beat.

"Be careful. Don't forget they have guns."

He nodded and crept up the stairs, disappearing into a cloud of smoke.

Della and Charlotte waited until he returned, jogging down the stairs, coughing.

"I don't see anyone, but they built a sort of bonfire in the foyer. There's no way to stop it at this point."

"Do they have a whole crew working for them? What about the drawbridge?" asked Charlotte.

Declan's focus drifted to a curtain at the far wall. He pulled it back to reveal a thick window with a view of the steep moat.

He tapped the glass with his knuckle.

"Impact resistant. We'll have to find a way to break it and take our chances with the moat before the place collapses on our heads."

Della closed her eyes. "Fantastic. Avoid the fire. Die in the mouth of an alligator."

Declan pointed toward the back of the castle.

"Della, go help Jarrett get his brother out here. Charlotte, come with me. We have to find something to break this hurricane glass."

"What about Timmy?" asked Della.

Charlotte and Declan exchanged a glance.

"I think we'll have to leave him and Tristan behind and worry about the living for now," said Declan.

Della nodded in agreement before running back to the wine room.

"Take this," said Charlotte, handing Declan the hammer she still held.

He took it and hit the glass with increasing force. On the fourth smack, the head of the hammer broke and shot toward him. He dodged in time to save his skull, and it flew through the air to bounce off the stairs.

The window hadn't cracked.

Charlotte and Declan looked at the broken hammer in his hand and grimaced at each other.

"Back to the storage room?" she suggested.

They strode there. Charlotte avoided concentrating on the big empty spot where the gas cans once sat. Part of her wanted to calculate how much time they had based on how much gas was used, but most of her worried the whole house would fall on their heads by the time she figured it out.

"Look at these," she said, pointing to long, thick bamboo poles. They looked like leftovers from Xander's bedroom decorations. "Maybe we could *ram* the glass with them?"

"I don't think that will cut it," said Declan, digging through piles of junk. "No pun intended."

Charlotte rummaged through a toolbox, but nothing inside seemed hefty enough to break the glass.

Declan hooted, and she spun to face him.

"Find something?"

He raised what looked like a fat axe above his head. It had a long orange handle and a solid wedge of metal *cheese* at the end.

"That looks perfect, but what is it?" she asked.

"Log splitter. For the fireplace in the foyer, I guess," said Declan.

They returned to the stairs as Jarrett and Barrett made slow progress down the hall toward them. Della waited at the window.

"Did you find something?" she asked.

She spotted the log splitter in Declan's hand. Her eyes widened.

"*Ooh.* I've never been so excited to see whatever the heck that is. It *looks* impressive..."

"It's a log splitter," said Charlotte as if she'd always known.

"Stand back," said Declan.

He swung the heavy cheese-wedge-on-a-stick at the glass.

The window *cracked.*

"Wow, that hurts my arms," said Declan, swinging a second time.

The glass cracked and chipped away until he'd made a small hole. By the time he'd swung four more times, they had a hole big enough for a small dog to escape.

Sadly, all of them were larger than a small dog.

Jarrett took a turn as Declan stepped away, rubbing his arms. The smoke snaked around them as the hole to the outside world sucked it down the stairs.

Finally, they had a space big enough to get everyone through.

Declan crawled through onto the bank and peered over the edge.
"Any gators?" asked Charlotte, joining him outside.
She peered over the edge.
The eyes of three half-submerged alligators stared back at her.

CHAPTER TWENTY-FIVE

Frank parked and walked into his Pineapple Port home. All he wanted was a shower to rid himself of the smell of lemurs and rotting figs.

"Darla?" he called as he hung his hat.

No answer.

Turbo, their miniature Dachshund, lay curled up on the sofa. He lifted his head, and the dog's tail wagged.

He smiled.

He'd lucked out.

Darla's out.

Now, he didn't have to explain to her why he smelled like a zoo.

He walked toward the bedroom, unbuttoning his uniform as he moved.

A minute later, he stood in hot water, covered in suds. The shower felt *amazing*. Five hours of barns, chickens, and lemurs washed down the drain.

Once clean, he put on his comfy clothes and padded into the living room.

"Darla?"

Still no answer.

Hm.

Turbo hopped off the sofa and trotted over to say hello, and Frank picked him up.

"Where's your mama?" he asked.

Turbo didn't know.

He sat and watched part of a baseball game before checking his watch.

Still no Darla.

It was past dinnertime. She wasn't always punctual, but she'd usually call if she was going to be late for dinner.

He reached for his phone and called her.

No answer.

He took a few minutes to rewatch the video from the peacock and the lemur robberies. He watched the young man appear on screen, gather the animals, and leave. The videos were very similar.

Same size, same look, same clothes.

Definitely the same kid.

He noticed words running down the kid's sleeve and, after a few tries, managed to pause the video in the right spot. He cocked his head to the side to read it.

Ocean State Surf.

Ocean State.

Hm.

He wanted to say the Ocean State was somewhere up north. He did a quick search and discovered it was Rhode Island.

He didn't know much about Rhode Island. He knew it was the smallest state, and they had a neighbor people affectionately called Rhode Island Rose because she hailed from there.

That was about it for his Rhode Island knowledge.

Turbo shoved a stuffed chipmunk into his leg to get his attention, and Frank patted his little head.

"You want to go for a walk?" he asked.

Hearing the word *walk*, Turbo made excited circles.

Frank found the dog's leash and went outside with his phone to call Bob as he walked.

"Yello," answered Bob.

"Is Darla over there?" asked Frank.

"Not anymore."

"She's on her way home?"

Frank glanced over his shoulder to see if he saw his wife walking down the street from Bob and Mariska's. He didn't.

"I don't think so," said Bob.

"You don't think she's on her way home?"

"No."

"But she's not there?"

"No."

"Did she say where she was going?"

"No."

"Is she with Mariska?"

"Yes."

"And Mariska didn't tell you where she was going?"

"Nope. I thought it best not to ask."

"Why?"

"Because they were dressed like ninjas."

Frank stopped his walk.

"*What?*" he asked.

"*What?*" echoed Bob.

"Did you say they were *dressed like ninjas?*"

"I did."

"What does that mean?"

"They were in all black."

"No, I *know* what ninjas wear, Bob. I mean, *why* were they dressed in black?"

"I don't know. I didn't ask."

Frank pinched the bridge of his nose while Turbo lifted his leg on a fern. He took a deep breath and tried again.

"Okay. Let's take this a little slower. Let me know if I have this right. Darla and Mariska, dressed all in black like ninjas, left together but didn't tell you where they were going?"

"Yep. That's it," said Bob after a pause.

Frank recalled seeing Darla's car in their driveway.

"On foot? Or they took Mariska's car?"

"Neither."

"Then how did they go?"

"Seamus picked them up."

"*Seamus?*" Frank's budding headache grew a little worse. He trusted Declan's uncle about as far as he could throw him.

"Are you telling me our wives drove off with Shifty Seamus dressed like ninjas, and you didn't think to tell me?"

"I just did." Bob chuckled. "*Shifty Seamus.* I like that."

Frank sighed. "I just tried to call Darla, and she didn't answer. Do me a favor and give Mariska a ring?"

"I just did."

"Ha—so you *are* worried?"

"No. I didn't know how long to microwave this burrito."

Frank gritted his teeth.

"I imagine it says on the package."

"That's the problem. I can't find my glasses either."

Frank lifted the phone. He knew throwing it across the street would feel good, but he resisted.

"Did she answer?" he asked.

"Who?"

He heard the infuriating sound of Bob chewing.

"*Mariska!*"

"Oh. No." Bob sighed. "I overcooked the burrito. It's too rubbery now."

"Look. If you hear from either of them, tell Darla to call me and find out where they are, what they're doing, and *why*."

"Aye aye, *el capitan*."

Bob hung up.

Frank lowered the phone and stood breathing heavily through his nose. He wished he had his blood pressure cuff. He bet he could break a record.

He slipped the phone into his pocket and looked up at the house where Turbo had grown bored and started rolling in the grass.

He recognized it.

Rhode Island Rose.

He walked up the path and knocked on the door.

Rose answered.

She had a smile on her face as the door opened, but her expression dropped the moment she saw him.

"Oh no." Her hand fluttered to her throat.

"What's wrong?" he asked.

"You caught him?"

"Caught who?"

"My grandson."

He blinked at her.

"I'm sorry. I don't know what you're talking about?"

The tightness in Rose's shoulders eased.

"You don't?"

"No."

"Oh. *Good.* I guess that's good." Her smile faded again as her brow creased with what looked like confusion.

"But, then, why are you here?" she asked.

"Oh, I know this is a little out there, but—" He fished his phone back out of his pocket and pulled up the lemur video, the better of the two. The one with the peacock had the thief too far away to read the words on his sleeve.

He held the video up for her to see, and Rose pulled her glasses down from on top of her head.

"I was wondering if you knew who this is?" asked Frank. "Probably not—I'm only asking because his sweatshirt says—"

"Ocean State Surf," said Rose, her expression falling again. He couldn't help but feel he kept disappointing her.

"Right."

"What is he stealing there?"

"Lemurs."

"*Lemurs?*"

She looked away, but he heard her mutter.

"*What is wrong with that boy?*"

She remained looking away for some time. It was as if she thought he couldn't see *her* if she couldn't see *him*.

"Rose?" he prompted.

She turned back to him and *stared*.

He found it unnerving.

"What is it?" he asked.

"You're kidding, right?"

"I'm sorry?"

She huffed. "Darla was here earlier about the sloth."

"Darla was here about the—?"

Frank straightened.

No.

Something had to be wrong.

Is it me?

To get into so many confusing conversations, at this point, it had to be *his* fault somehow, didn't it?

He decided to slow things down.

"Can we take this from the top?" he asked. "You said Darla was here about a *sloth?*"

Rose nodded. "Darla and Mariska. They said Owen—my grandson—stole their sloth. They had a video, too."

Frank nodded.

Okay. She did say sloth. Bob had mentioned the sloth. Go with it.

"Did they find him?"

"Owen or the sloth?"

"Either?"

She sighed. "No. Darla ran after him, but she couldn't catch him."

"The sloth?"

"Owen."

Frank nodded. "And, um, what happened to the sloth?"

Rose shrugged. "We don't know. Owen's probably keeping it wherever he's staying now."

"Which is?"

"I don't know. He *was* staying nearby with my other daughter, Lily, but she kicked him out. Then he was here, and now—honestly, I don't know where he'll go."

"Does he have friends in the area?"

"No. I don't think so. He's not good at making friends. There *was* someone with a—"

She stopped as if someone had pulled her plug, staring over Frank's shoulder. He turned, expecting to see someone approaching, but found no one.

"What is it?" he asked.

"I'm sorry. It just hit me. Someone on a motorcycle dropped him off wearing a tiger helmet yesterday."

"A tiger helmet? You mean striped like a tiger?"

She nodded. "I assumed it was some punk, but that's my daughter's nickname, *Tiger Lily*. Because her name is Lily—"

"Right, I get it. So, you think he might be back staying with his Aunt Lily?"

"Maybe. She didn't call me, but she wouldn't have known to, maybe." She sighed. "We don't always get along."

"Can you call her for me to confirm any of this?"

She nodded. "Just a second."

She slipped back into the house, and her husband, Peter, appeared at the door.

"Hey, Pete," said Frank.

Pete rubbed at his bald head.

"You here about Owen?" he asked, eyeing Frank's sweat shorts.

Frank looked down, suddenly feeling self-conscious. "Yeah, no uniform. Sorry. I didn't know I was looking for your grandson, but it looks like maybe I am."

Pete leaned in to talk low.

"Throw him in the clinker. Leave him there for a week. Bread and water. That's what he needs."

Frank chuckled. "I got the impression he's a bit of a troublemaker?"

Pete scoffed. "You have no idea."

Frank nodded. "Speaking of which—do you have any idea why he might be stealing exotic animals?"

"Like the sloth?"

"The sloth. Maybe a peacock? Tribe of lemurs?"

Pete stared at him and shook his head, muttering under his breath.

Rose appeared behind him.

"I can't reach her. Neither of them. I tried both."

"Okay. No problem, Rose, I appreciate it. Could you maybe give me Lily's address?"

She nodded. "Sure."

She rattled off her daughter's address, and Frank punched it into his phone.

"Thank you."

He paused, thinking about asking if either knew where Darla might be, but then decided against it.

He suspected he knew.

He said his goodbyes and headed down the stairs.

"Come on, Turbo." He said, pulling the little dog toward home. "Pa's got to go find your crazy mama."

CHAPTER TWENTY-SIX

With the fire in the castle behind them and alligators ahead, Declan stood on the muddy bank and studied the closed drawbridge to his left.

He grunted as he noticed the portcullis gate remained open.

Lucky us.

To his left, stone stairs led from the bank to a shallow landing outside the main entrance, where the drawbridge lowered.

"If the drawbridge was down, we could reach it from here," Charlotte noted, echoing his thoughts as she crawled through the window to join him.

Declan nodded. "There has to be a way to open it from the parking lot. Some kind of *garage door opener* situation."

One of the alligators swam closer to establish a holding pattern while it decided how hungry it was.

Charlotte frowned. "I hate taking our chances with these guys. I don't think Xander's been around to feed them."

Declan straightened.

"Hold on. I've got an idea."

Charlotte looked hopeful.

"I was hoping you'd say that."

He turned as the others crawled through the smashed window onto the bank.

Jarrett propped Barrett against the wall and helped hold him there. Della remained inside, peering through the window at the alligators below.

Declan pointed back into the castle. "Della, go to the storage room. There are long bamboo poles in there. Bring me one."

Della arched an eyebrow.

"Or, you know, we could just *die* here," Declan added.

She huffed and disappeared into the castle.

Charlotte looked at him.

"You're going to poke them with a stick? You're not supposed to poke them—or is that just bears?"

He chuckled. "I'm not going to *poke* them. Well, maybe. If I have to, but that's not the idea."

"Heads up," called Della as she threaded the long, thick bamboo pole through the window. Declan helped pull it clear.

"It's perfect," he said. He stabbed it into the center of the moat, where it hit bottom. One of the alligators paddled out of the way. It didn't seem happy.

Charlotte eyed the pole.

"Are you insane? You're going to pole-vault across?"

He shrugged. "You have a better idea?"

She shook her head.

"No, but that doesn't mean I have to like this idea."

He stepped back and took a deep breath.

Charlotte bit her lip. "If that doesn't go across, and you slide into the moat, they'll tear you to pieces."

"Good pep talk." He leaned in to kiss her. "Don't worry. It'll be a piece of cake."

"Good luck, buddy," said Jarrett.

Declan held up a hand to show he'd heard.

Charlotte took a step back, but she still didn't seem convinced.

"*Wait—*"

Declan took a few quick breaths, one long stride, and launched himself into the air.

The group gasped as he stalled in the center long enough for her to see his life flash before her eyes.

With his brain racing through the best ways to outswim an alligator, he lurched to push himself the extra inch needed to travel past the center. He arced through the air to land on the opposite bank.

The group whooped and applauded. He flashed Charlotte a grin as she stood with her hand on her chest, shaking her head.

"That was *so stupid*," she said, but she smiled.

He offered a humble bow and turned to look up the steep embankment behind him. His work was only half done. He'd reached the opposite bank, but the deep moat didn't offer any access to the parking lot.

Luckily, he still had his handy pole.

He shot the group a reassuring nod as he plucked the rod from the water. One of the alligators floated a one-eighty turn to eyeball him.

Declan stuck the pole in the mud beside him and leaned the other end against the wall, where it crested the top. He kicked off his shoes and pulled off his socks before tossing them up into the parking lot.

Using his hands and bare feet, he climbed the pole to the top like a live version of Xander's many decorative monkeys.

"How did you do that?" Charlotte called to him as he stood, triumphant.

He grinned.

"Now to get the drawbridge down."

"That would be nice," called Della, who'd deigned to step outside but remained on the stone window ledge, heels dangling in her hand.

Declan jogged to the area where the drawbridge would land. A keypad on a post marked the spot.

"There's a keypad here," he called back to them.

"Great. Another keypad," he heard Della quip.

"I'm going to try variations on two-four-six-eight."

As his first attempt failed, he spotted the bravest of the three alligators swimming closer to the far bank. Any closer, and it could make a running lunge for Charlotte or one of the others.

"Push back the pole," called Della.

"It won't work for Barrett," said Jarrett.

"I'd rather not have any of you try it," said Declan. "Give me a second."

He wiped the sweat from his forehead and punched in every combination of numbers they'd used in the other challenges. The next five attempts to guess the code failed.

The keypad wasn't working. He needed to find another solution.

He turned to survey the parking lot.

Maybe, if I can find a giant limb to—

He spotted an old VW Thing parked in the driveway. The strange old Volkswagen from the late 1960s had a unique boxy, quirky chassis. The foldable, flat windshield, roll-up canvas top, and removable doors made it perfect for open-air beach driving.

Declan had only ever seen VW Things driving around beach towns, but he didn't find it odd to find this one so far inland—especially since it had a mural of palms, monkeys, and toucans painted on the side.

There was no doubt about it.

The vehicle has to be Xander's.

Declan ran to the Thing to search the glove compartment. Inside, he found what looked like a garage door opener and gasped.

He hadn't been wrong.

The drawbridge garage door opener *did* exist.

He pointed it at the castle, said a little prayer, and pushed the button.

Clanking started as the drawbridge chains dropped the platform toward his side. Smoke billowed around the edges of the drawbridge. The glow of the fire raging inside lit the night.

The scene looked like an elaborate pyrotechnic display from one of the local theme parks. Declan wouldn't be surprised if a dragon stuck its head out to roar a hello.

A cheer erupted from the others. They started across the bank toward the stone stairs leading to safety. Declan waited for the drawbridge to land and then jogged across it to help them.

He offered Charlotte and Della a hand up. Jarrett steadied his brother on the lowest step, and once the girls were up, Declan walked halfway down the steps to grab Barrett's hand. Jarrett stayed behind to keep his brother from stumbling backward.

As Barrett reached the top and Charlotte and Della helped him across the drawbridge, Declan heard a low growl.

The water behind Jarrett rippled.

He pointed.

"Jarrett!"

One of the alligators had decided it didn't want to miss a meal. It lunged out of the water and ran toward Jarrett on its squat, powerful legs, its mouth open wide.

Perched on the first steep step, Jarrett turned fast and slipped back to the muddy bank. He scrambled to climb back onto the stairs, only to slip again, his hand slapping against the stone.

The alligator's ragged teeth shone in the fire's light against its dark, bumpy skin. It lunged with a sudden burst of speed, jaws snapping shut inches from Jarrett's foot.

Jarrett kicked at the alligator's snout.

"Get away from me," he roared.

The alligator hissed, teeth flashing as its tail thrashed. It lunged again.

"I'll get the *pole*," Charlotte called out, rushing to retrieve the bamboo in the parking lot.

Before she could reach the weapon, Jarrett found his feet and stood on the bank.

He raised his arms and *roared*.

He looked terrifying.

Even Declan, who'd been heading down the stairs to help, froze.

The alligator's mouth closed a few inches as it reconsidered its attack.

"*I have had it with this place*," raged Jarrett.

There was no doubt he meant it.

Instead of taking advantage of the reptile's confusion and running up the stairs, Jarrett stepped *forward*.

The alligator panicked and twisted, exposing its side. Jarrett kicked, shoving the beast toward the water with his foot.

The gator half-slipped and half-dove into the water, using its powerful tail to swim away.

Jarrett turned back to the stairs, panting. Thick mud covered the lower half of his body. Declan saw the castle fire's reflection in his eyes as he stomped up the stairs.

"Not today, *lizard*," he grumbled, storming past Declan and down the drawbridge.

Della, who'd moved in to help, skittered out of his way and stood with billowing smoke from the castle as a backdrop.

Jarrett took off his muddy shirt as he marched toward the parking lot and tossed it in the moat. Barechested, he reached his car, started it, and backed it as close to the drawbridge as possible.

Without a word, Declan and Charlotte flanked Barrett and helped him to his waiting brother's car.

As they lowered him into the passenger seat, Declan heard a *whoop!*

He spun in time to see a figure dragging a struggling Della into the castle.

The two disappeared into the smoke.

CHAPTER TWENTY-SEVEN

Mariska and Darla walked into the forest and out of Seamus's view. They had their marching orders—they'd return to the car while Seamus found and grabbed the sloth.

Two steps into the woods, they glanced over their shoulders like synchronized swimmers, stopped walking, and turned to each other.

"We're not *really* leaving him behind?" asked Mariska.

Darla scoffed. "Of course not."

Mariska smiled and headed back the way they'd come, but Darla saw her expression drop as they approached the bridge.

"What's wrong?" she asked.

Mariska grabbed the rail.

"The possum's missing."

"*What?*"

Darla turned as the possum's head popped up from the tall grasses lining the stream.

It *hissed* at her.

With stifled squeals, the ladies scooted over the bridge, careful to avoid the center, even in their panic.

The possum loped in the other direction.

"Is it coming?" asked Mariska.

Darla kept an eye on the bridge. "No. It ran off that way."

Mariska huffed. "Why does that thing *collapse* for Seamus but hiss at us?"

"Because it's a little jerk, like all the animals around this place."

Darla peeked around the hedges separating them from the house, searching for some sign of Seamus.

"Do you see him?" whispered Mariska.

Darla squinted into the darkness.

"No. Wait. He's on the porch, at the back door."

"He's going in the house?"

"It looks like it. He's—"

A squawking filled the air, and both ladies ducked.

"Oh, Oirus!"

"What is *that*?" asked Mariska.

Darla shook her head. "I don't know, but it's *loud*."

The squawking continued as Darla dared to take another peek. She saw Seamus's figure suddenly bathed in light spilling from the back door.

"Someone opened the door," she reported.

"Tiger Lily?"

"I can't see."

Darla thought she saw the end of a shotgun sticking from the door. She straightened.

That's not good.

Her fears were confirmed when Seamus's hands lifted into the air.

"She's got a gun on him," she reported.

Mariska gasped. "Tiger Lily?"

"I guess so. I can't see her, and even if I could, I wouldn't know her from Adam."

"What's happening now?"

"He's going inside."

"She *captured* him?"

"That's what it looks like."

"What are we going to do?"

The light streaming onto the porch disappeared as the door shut.

Darla turned and rested her back against the thick hedge.

"We're going to have to save him."

"How? She's got a gun. Now, we *have* to call Frank."

Darla shook her head. "It would take him half an hour to get here. Seamus could be dead by then."

"If we try to save him on our own, *we* could be dead by then."

Darla ignored her and walked around the hedge into the back yard, staying low.

"Where are you going?" she heard Mariska whisper.

"I'm taking a look."

She heard Mariska cluck her tongue a moment before her friend appeared beside her.

Mariska motioned to a collection of large cages lining the back yard.

"Do you think he checked all these cages for Sir Sleepsalot?" she asked.

"I'd think he'd do that before he went up on the porch, but let's make a quick pass."

The two of them circled the yard, peering into the empty cages. They ended up back at the door of the sun porch.

Mariska frowned. "Are you *sure* we should go in? I mean, her name is *Tiger Lily*, and if she's half as mean as her peacocks—"

Darla nodded and put her fingers over her lips to ask for quiet as she opened the outside door.

Mariska sighed as they stepped inside.

Darla ogled the bird cages filling the room.

"Wow," breathed Mariska.

Darla nodded.

Tiger Lily had a *lot* of birds for a lady named after a cat.

Darla eyed a crowd of finches in a large standing cage. In the corner, another enclosure held a gray parrot busy sharpening his beak on a cuttlebone.

"I bet he's the loudmouth we heard," noted Darla.

On the ground, in a large shipping crate, two growling cats wrestled. Darla moved closer for a better look. The cats were babies and seemed to be missing part of their tails.

Mariska peered over Darla's shoulder.

"Are those *bobcats*?" she asked.

Darla nodded. "I think so, but the place is full of birds. Making these guys watch birds all day *must* be against the Geneva Convention."

Mariska tugged her shirt.

"Forget them! What are we going to do about Seamus?"

Darla straightened and returned her focus to the door leading into the house. She ran a hand through her still-wet hair.

"Right. Right. I think I was trying to forget about that mess."

She crouched to put her eye against a glass section of the door *not* blocked by the yellowed interior curtains. Inside sat an outdated kitchen and, beyond that, a small living room.

In front of a floral sofa, a middle-aged woman stood facing Seamus.

"I see a woman talking to Seamus," reported Darla.

"Is it Tiger Lily?"

"I don't know. Again, I don't know what the woman looks like. I think we should *assume* it is since this is her house."

Mariska grunted.

"Is he shot?"

She glanced back at Mariska.

"Did you hear a gun?"

"No, but maybe it's a quiet gun."

Darla squinted at her.

"What's a *quiet* gun?"

"One with one of those thingies on it. Or a BB gun."

Darla rolled her eyes. "I don't think she's been pelting him with BBs."

"What are we going to do?"

Darla leaned her back against the wall beside the door and noticed a half-open window beside her.

She put out her hand so Mariska could steady her and stepped onto an old sofa to look through to the kitchen. From this angle, she couldn't see into the living room.

Beside her, the finches twittered in their cage. She studied them as the seed of an idea sprouted in her head.

Everything seems the right size...

She had an idea.

She grinned and turned to Mariska.

"I've got it."

Mariska shook her head.

"No. No. I hate it when you smile like that. That's exactly the smile I never want to see, and this is the worst place for you to have it."

"Shh."

Darla pushed on the half-open window. It glided upward and stuck in place.

Perfect.

Inside, Tiger Lily and Seamus shouted at each other, but Darla couldn't tell what they were saying, thanks to the noise coming from the television.

It didn't matter. She felt confident no one would hear what was coming.

She pulled out her Swiss Army Knife to cut the screen separating her from the kitchen.

"What are you *doing*?" whispered Mariska.

"Hand me the bobcats," she said.

"Hand you the *what*?"

"The baby bobcats. Their box."

Mariska looked at her as if she'd grown a snout.

"Are you *insane*?"

"*Just hand them to me.*"

Mariska grunted.

"I don't know if I can pick up that crate."

"It isn't big. Do it."

Mariska puffed and lifted the crate with the growling bobcats inside.

"They're not that heavy," she admitted.

"They're babies. Hand it to me."

Mariska hefted up the crate.

Darla shifted her feet on the sofa to be sure she had a secure footing.

"I'm going to dip the box so they slide to the back. Stand there and hold it in place so it doesn't slip."

Mariska held steady the back of the crate while Darla opened its door.

"You're opening it?" Mariska asked. Darla heard the horror in her tone.

"*Yes.* Everything will happen fast once I do, so get ready."

"For what?"

"You'll see."

"Oh, I hate this," moaned Mariska.

Darla opened the crate door and rested the front on the window sill.

"Okay, tilt your end up so they slide forward."

Though Darla heard Mariska grumbling, her buddy lifted the back of the crate to send the bobcats tumbling into the house's kitchen sink.

"Ok, put the crate back," said Darla.

Mariska whipped the box away, and Darla jumped off the sofa to grab the finch cage. With it in her arms, she climbed back on the sofa and opened the cage's door with the opening facing the window.

"Get them out," said Darla, shooing the birds to freedom.

One by one, the birds flew from the cage into the kitchen as Mariska poked at them with the handle of a small pooper-scooper she'd found on the ground.

Inside the house, the finches took to the air, darting around the room like a swarm of feathered bees.

Satisfied with the number of released finches, Darla put down the cage and closed the window before moving to the door.

She put her hand on the doorknob and looked at Mariska.

"Ready?"

Mariska shook her head.

"*No.*"

Darla peeked through the window. Inside, Tiger Lily noticed the chaos unleashed on her home. Her jaw dropped wide, her attention pulled from Seamus.

Darla grinned.

"It's working. One, two—"

Mariska shook her head and threw out her hands.

"Don't say it—"

"*Three!*"

Darla flung open the door and screamed.

"Run, Seamus!"

CHAPTER TWENTY-EIGHT

"They've got Della," said Declan.

"I *saw*." Charlotte stood with her hand over her mouth, still unsure if she'd *really* seen Della disappear into the smoke. It was like a monster had pulled her into the depths.

Della was there, and then she was gone.

"Why would they grab her *now*?" asked Declan.

Charlotte shrugged. "They must need help with the maze puzzle."

Jarrett leaned across his brother to peer up at them through the open passenger-side window.

"Get in. I'm taking him to the hospital. We'll get help for Della as soon as we're in cell range."

Declan and Charlotte exchanged a look as another cloud of smoke belched from the castle.

"We can't wait. We've got to help her," said Charlotte.

Declan agreed.

"Go," he told Jarrett. "Send help as soon as you can. We're going after Della."

Jarrett shook his head.

"Idiots," Charlotte heard him mutter.

She wasn't sure he was wrong.

They shut the door, and Jarrett tore down the driveway as soon as they were clear of the vehicle.

Charlotte put her hand on Declan's arm. "I don't think we should try going after her through the burning castle. I'd bet anything they took her to the maze in the back."

He nodded. "I think so too. Let's go."

They sprinted around the castle to the back yard, where they jogged past a large porch, a hardscaped patio area, and a massive pool.

The hedge maze rose beyond the pool. Della and her captors were nowhere in sight.

Charlotte paused to catch her breath.

"They're probably in the maze. I guess they got to the center and realized they couldn't answer some final clue."

"Which means they know the way to the center and are way ahead of us," said Declan.

Charlotte glanced at her watch.

"Twenty minutes until sunrise," she reported as they entered the maze.

She wasn't sure what happened then, but she imagined Mildred and her crew would push to have the contest finished by then.

Sunrise would seal Della's fate either way.

"I can't believe they grabbed her like that," she muttered as they rounded the maze's first turn.

She hit a dead end and made an about-face, huffing with frustration.

Declan chuckled. "You're miffed they took her and not you, aren't you?"

She gasped. "What? *No*. She was at the entrance. She was the easiest to grab. It had nothing to do with *skills*."

Her attempt at self-defense only seemed to amuse him as they crept forward, eyeing both ahead and behind them as they progressed through the maze.

By design, a multitude of turns complicated their progress, but that wasn't why Charlotte hated them.

Corners made great spots for ambushes.

Looking down, she squinted at the soft earth. Thanks to strings of party lighting lining the maze, she could see a series of thin deep holes in the grass beneath their feet.

She stopped and pointed to them.

"*Heel marks*. That has to be Della. She put her shoes back on when we hit the drawbridge," she whispered.

Declan turned on his phone flashlight so they could better follow the heel trail.

"Once again, dressing up is paying off," said Charlotte.

"You follow the prints, and I'll keep an eye out so we don't get ambushed," he whispered.

She nodded.

They continued through the maze. Charlotte thought she heard people talking and worked in that direction.

Turning a sharp corner, she found they'd reached the center more suddenly than she'd imagined.

The tight walls of the hornbeam hedge rows ended. Charlotte froze, but it was too late.

A woman pointed a gun at them.

"Hold it there," she said.

Overhead lighting played across the gunman's face.

Charlotte recognized her.

"*Hollie*," she said.

She touched the H necklace around her neck and realized what their client had done. She'd *thought* it was odd Hollie insisted she wear the H necklace.

Now, it made sense.

"My body in the fire would have been wearing your necklace," she said.

Hollie smiled and motioned with the gun. "Walk toward me."

She held the weapon steady as they approached.

Charlotte noted the surroundings as she and Declan walked with their hands above their heads.

The center of the maze was a whole world of its own.

A tiki hut stood against the far hedge wall, looking flimsier than it was. Charlotte could tell the basic structure was a solid wood cabin, but stapled bamboo and grasses hung on the sides and roof, giving it the appearance of a flimsier, thatched design. A row of tiki torches lined the entrance, and a huge tiki head totem guarded the two stairs leading to the front door. On the porch sat a pair of brightly painted Adirondack chairs and a makeshift tiki bar with a metal citrus squeezer sitting on top.

Beside the tiki hut stood a majestic banyan tree, its wide canopy of glossy leaves shading much of the clearing. The tree looked more like a sculpture or leftover prop from a fantastical movie than anything Charlotte had expected to find in the maze's center. Ropey aerial roots cascaded to the ground, anchoring the tree to the soil and creating a natural cage.

Though nothing they'd seen so far led her to believe Xander had been a man prone to meditation, the banyan and tiki hut together did make for a peaceful scene. She wouldn't think it a bad idea if someone were to open a spa there.

Assuming Hollie wasn't still standing in the center holding a gun.

The woman Charlotte knew as Hollie—but who she now suspected was *not*—motioned them to the center where Della and Mildred stood.

Mildred looked both nervous and annoyed.

Hollie motioned from Charlotte to Della.

"Help her figure out the last clue."

Declan and Charlotte stepped to Della's side.

"Are you okay?" whispered Charlotte.

Della side-eyed her. "Oh, I'm *peachy*. You?"

"*Solve it*," snapped Hollie.

Charlotte looked from Hollie to Mildred and back again. Mildred hadn't taken her eyes off Hollie since they entered the center. At first, Charlotte thought she looked to the younger woman as the leader of their nefarious little group. Now, she wasn't so sure.

Hollie had auburn hair and blue eyes.

Just like the twins...

Just like Xander.

"Mildred is your *mother*," said Charlotte as fast as the thought gelled in her head.

Hollie and Mildred looked at her but didn't answer.

"*Shut up* and help her solve it," said Hollie, shaking the gun.

Charlotte recalled Mildred's bitterness when discussing Xander's sexual escapades as a younger man. She suspected Mildred, too, had fallen for his rogueish charms.

"Xander is your father," said Charlotte. "You're not *niece Hollie* at all."

Mildred's chin raised.

"She's *Hayley*. Yes, she's my daughter. She's the best thing that ever happened to me."

Hayley winced like an embarrassed teenager.

"*Mom.*"

"It doesn't matter now," said Mildred, dismissing her daughter's complaints.

She glared at Charlotte, defiant.

"He wouldn't give us a place in the competition. Hollie—his niece—turned down his invite, but I didn't tell him. Instead, I hired Hayley to be his nurse."

"You never told him about your daughter?" asked Charlotte, finding it hard to believe.

"Oh, I told him," said Mildred. "He refused to admit she was his. Back then, there weren't paternity tests. You didn't just *mail off* some spit and find your family tree."

Charlotte nodded. "And he never saw her."

"No. Not since she was a child."

Behind them, something collapsed in the burning castle, sending a plume of sparks into the night. Somewhere, a window exploded.

"We can stop the family drama now, Mom," said Hayley. She turned her focus to Charlotte and pointed the gun at Declan. "Now solve the stupid puzzle, or I'll kill the other two."

Charlotte grimaced.

"Do we have the clue?"

"We do," said Della, handing Charlotte a red card.

Charlotte looked at Hayley.

"Why should I solve it? You're going to kill us all anyway."

Hayley shrugged. "You can die slow or fast. You can die *first* or after watching me shoot holes in your friends. It's up to you."

Charlotte scowled and read the card.

"In legend, Buddha found enlightenment sitting here."

She looked at Della, who looked away. She suspected her puzzle buddy knew the answer but had refused to say. They'd let her live because she'd been their only option.

Now, they had leverage.

She had to think of a way out. Nothing about the last twenty-four hours implied Mildred and Hayley would let them go. They'd had no problem killing Timmy and Tristan.

"I don't know the answer," said Charlotte.

Hayley gritted her teeth and turned her weapon toward Della. "*You* know it."

"No, I don't," said Della. "I already told you."

Hayley licked her lips, a strange calm settling over her expression.

"Then what good are you?" she asked.

The muscles in her hand flexed around the gun. Sensing Hayley was about to shoot, Della lunged for a gap in the hedges.

Hayley fired.

Declan took the opportunity to leap, but Hayley swung the gun at him before he could reach her. She fired again, grazing his side as he spun away and then pointed the weapon at Charlotte.

Declan winced, put a hand against his side, and nodded at Charlotte to let her know he was okay.

"Should we go after her?" asked Mildred, looking where Della had disappeared into the greenery.

Hayley shook her head. "We can't. We have these two. But we have to *hurry.*"

Charlotte looked where Della had disappeared. She felt confident the bullet had missed the girl and traveled somewhere into the hedges, but everything had happened so fast.

Hayley was a terrible shot but wasn't shy about firing.

Maybe three times was the charm.

She didn't want to find out.

Charlotte didn't feel good about her chances of tackling Hayley before taking a bullet—

Movement at the window of the tiki hut caught Charlotte's eye. A curtain fluttered.

Someone was inside.

The curtain moved again, and a round-faced middle-aged man appeared, staring back at her.

He looked scared.

Charlotte couldn't imagine who he might be.

Friend or foe? Do Hayley and Mildred know he's there?

Hayley swung her muzzle toward Declan.

"Do *you* know the answer?" she asked.

He shook his head.

Hayley glared at Charlotte.

"Tell me the answer, or I'll shoot him right now."

Charlotte put her hands up, hoping the man in the tiki hut would notice she was being held against her will and have some way of calling the police.

"What are you doing?" asked Hayley.

"You're holding a gun on us," said Charlotte.

"Put your hands down and answer the question, or I'm shooting him in *three*. One, two—"

"A banyan tree," blurted Charlotte.

Hayley and Mildred exchanged a look.

"What does that mean?" asked Mildred.

"Buddha sat under a banyan tree," said Charlotte, pointing to the tree beside the tiki hut.

"*That's* a banyan tree?"

Charlotte nodded.

Hayley motioned to it with the gun. "Go look. Both of you. There has to be something there."

At gunpoint, Declan and Charlotte slipped into the network of prop roots, searching for another clue.

"You know this will all end with us opening the door to that tiki hut," said Charlotte as she searched. "Just break the window and go in."

Hayley shook her head.

"We have to do it the right way. I'm not risking blowing it now."

"Somehow, I don't think killing the other contestants is the *right* way," said Declan.

Hayley sniffed. "There is nothing in the rules that said I can't."

"You should go," said Charlotte. "You know Jarrett and Barrett left. They'll send the police any second."

Mildred looked at her daughter, eyes squinted with worry.

"I thought Barrett was dead," she said. "Maybe we *should* go—"

Hayley grew agitated.

"Just shut up and figure out the clue," she roared at Charlotte.

Stepping behind the tree, hidden from Hayley's view, Declan leaned to Charlotte to whisper.

"She can't kill you. She needs you to pretend you're Hollie to claim the prize."

Charlotte grimaced. "I'm not sure. If no one knows what Hollie looks like, *she* could pose as Hollie. The real Hollie is probably dead."

Declan grunted. "With the brothers in the wind, this will never work the way she hoped. I think she's hoping there's a safe full of money at the end that she can take for her trouble before the cops show up."

She nodded. "There might be. Who knows?"

Declan squinted at one of the aerial roots.

"What is that?" he asked, pointing at something shiny sticking from the bark.

She leaned in to get a better look.

Her eyes widened.

"It's a *key*. The tree grew around it. That had to take years—" She looked at Declan. "He's been planning this for *years*."

"Only to end up murdered."

"What is it? What's all the whispering?" asked Hayley, moving around the tree with her weapon at the ready.

Charlotte motioned to the root. "It's a key. The tree grew around it. We need to dig it out."

"Do it," said Hayley.

"With what?"

"I don't know. Figure it out."

Charlotte looked at the hut and the makeshift bar on the porch.

"Let me look behind the bar?"

Hayley nodded, and Charlotte walked to the porch. She tried to get a glimpse through the window but couldn't see anything past the now-closed drapes. She found a flimsy grapefruit knife behind the bar and returned to the tree with it.

"Don't get any funny ideas with that," warned Mildred.

Charlotte cut away the bark holding the trapped key until it broke free.

"Toss it to my mother," said Hayley.

Charlotte did. Mildred let it land on the ground and then picked it up. She took it to the door of the cabin.

"This should be it," she said, sounding excited.

Charlotte leaned toward Declan.

"There's someone inside there," she whispered.

Declan glanced at her.

"What? Who?"

She shook her head.

"I don't know, but get ready to run."

CHAPTER TWENTY-NINE

Frank returned from his eventful walk with Turbo to find Darla still not home.

The evidence had piled up past his ability to ignore it.

Someone had stolen Mariska's sloth. He still didn't understand *why* Mariska had a sloth, but it hurt his head to think about it, so he'd let that go.

Darla liked to be in the middle of everything, so she would have helped Mariska look for the sloth.

Like him, they'd followed video clues to Rhode Island Rose, where they discovered her grandson was probably the thief.

His last known address was out west at his aunt Lily's place. A woman known as *Tiger Lily*, which didn't bode well.

Bob had seen his wife get into Seamus's car with Mariska, both dressed like ninjas.

He didn't want to admit to himself how unsurprising that felt.

He wasn't sure how Seamus fit into the mix, but Declan's wild uncle had given the ladies a ride somewhere, so he was probably involved.

If he were a betting man, he'd wager his wife was at Tiger Lily's house looking for the sloth, and Seamus had agreed to help them infiltrate the place. Charlotte and Declan were out of town, so Darla had gone to him for help to avoid telling *her disapproving husband* what she was up to.

Frank looked down at Turbo.

"I'm sorry, little fella, but it looks like I'm going out."

Turbo hopped on the sofa to start a new nap as soon as he saw Frank redonning his uniform. Between the uniform and Mama not being home, the mini-Dach knew dinner wasn't on the way.

At least not the good one—the one Darla sneaked him under the table.

The one she didn't think Frank knew about.

Frank drove his cruiser to the address Rose had given him for Lily. He slowed as he passed a car parked on the roadside near the property.

The car looked familiar.

He pulled over and walked back to the vehicle to point his flashlight's beam through the window.

The car was messy with change, crumpled fast food bags, and clothing strewn around the floor.

Yep. Has to be Seamus's.

He spotted a wadded-up napkin with Seamus's bar logo on it.

Bingo.

He turned back to his cruiser, eyeing Lily's property as he walked. A patch of trees obscured the house and appeared to be grown expressly for that purpose. Unlike Seamus and the ladies, who, he suspected, had sneaked down the side of the property to search for the sloth under cover of darkness, he'd go in through the front, down the dirt—

A loud *bang!* echoed through the night, and Frank spun his attention to Lily's house.

That sounded like a shotgun.

Frank sprinted for his car.

CHAPTER THIRTY

Seamus walked into Tiger Lily's home as she backed into the kitchen to let him pass. She fell in behind him, shotgun still raised as he entered the living room.

"You've got a lot of nerve," she said.

He stopped and turned on the opposite side of a hideous floral sofa. She walked around to stand facing him, shotgun still raised.

"Can you lower the gun, lass?" he asked.

She scowled.

"Don't *lass* me. I'm way past *lass*."

He recognized the woman he'd known in this new, twenty-year-later version of Tiger Lily. She still had her long brown hair clipped back in a bun, loose wisps haloing her head. She'd maintained the same body shape with an inch or two of extra padding. She wore cutoff jeans shorts and a tee shirt from a ten-year-old music festival he could picture her enjoying.

"It's lovely to see you again," he said. He meant it.

She could tell. She lowered the gun.

"I'm serious, Seamus. Don't work your Irish charms on me. What are you doing here after all these years?"

"Would you believe I've missed you?"

She shook her head.

"No."

"Okay. Would you believe I'm looking for a missing sloth?"

She groaned. "A *sloth*? I don't believe that kid—" She took a deep breath. "Yes. *That*, I believe. What made you look here? Was that *you* chasing us when I picked Owen up on my bike?"

He nodded. "Aye. We know your young lover, Owen, took the sloth. We have it on video."

"My young *lover*?" Tiger Lily hooted. "He's a *child*."

"*Your* child?" Seamus did the math on his fingers before placing a hand on his chest. "He's not—?"

Lily laughed again. "Family, but not *my* kid."

He bit his lip. "Not your cousin Iris's? He's not, uh—"

She sighed. "No, Seamus. You didn't father a child with Iris or me. You're nobody's father."

He tucked in his chin.

"Well, now, you don't have to get *rude* about it." He let out a puff of air. "But enough of that. I just thought—since he seems a bit of a troublemaker—maybe..."

She chuckled. "He's a terror, so I could see why you'd think he's yours. He's my nephew. My sister's going through a hard time, so I took him in to give her a break, but he's more than I bargained for..." She shook her head. "I finally kicked him out. He crashed at my mother's."

"But you were with him this afternoon?"

She nodded. "I left early this morning for a landscaping job up north. By the time I got back, he'd stashed animals all over the property—a peacock, a pack of lemurs—" She pointed down the hall behind him. "There's a pot-bellied pig in my room as we speak. Owen stole them to win me over so I'd let him stay here again, but then he called me in a panic, begging me to pick him up. Said some crazy old lady was chasing him."

"Did he have the sloth?"

"No. I haven't seen a sloth, but I don't doubt he took it. It's probably here somewhere. I chewed him out so bad for the other animals he probably lost the guts to tell me about that one."

"Is the boy here?"

She nodded. "Down the hall on the left. Across from my room." She smirked. "You remember which room is mine, don't you, Seamus?"

He ran a hand over his close-cropped salt-and-pepper beard and smiled at her.

"I do. How have you been, Lily?"

She smiled. "Same as ever."

"Yeah? How's your family?"

Her smile dropped.

"You mean *Iris*?" she asked, raising the shotgun.

He held up his hands. "No, *no*—I meant in *general*."

"I think it's time for you to go."

"No, you're right. Of course. I just need the sloth, and we'll be out of your hair."

"We?"

"I've brought two ladies with me."

"Of course you have."

"No, not that sort of lady. They're the ladies who lost the sloth."

"Ah." Tiger Lily frowned.

"What is it?" asked Seamus.

"Giving you back the sloth might be complicated."

"Why? It isn't dead, is it?"

"No, but like I said, I don't know where it is, and Owen can get pigheaded about things."

Seamus waved her worries away.

"Do not worry about it. I'll work it out with him."

A tiny bird flew into the room, and they both stepped back to watch it land on the television.

"Looks like you've got one of your flock loose," said Seamus.

Her brow creased.

"How the heck did one of the finches get—"

Tiger Lily looked into her kitchen and gasped. The reaction pulled Seamus's focus, and his jaw dropped.

"Mother Mary," he muttered.

Finches filled the kitchen, flying everywhere. Below them, a pair of spotted cats jumped and swatted, trying to snatch them from the sky.

"Did you do this?" screamed Tiger Lily.

Seamus slapped his hand to his chest.

"Me? I didn't—"

The back door burst open, and Darla appeared.

"*Run, Seamus!*" she screamed.

"My finches!" yelled Tiger Lily as a bobcat knocked one out of the sky. She dove into the kitchen to tackle it before it could pounce on the stunned bird.

She scooped up the cat, holding it to her chest. It batted her in the face and fought to break free, but she held it tight.

"Get out of my way!" she said, knocking hard into Darla as she hustled the animal out the back door.

"What are you doing?" Seamus asked Darla.

"We're saving you."

Seamus shook his head.

"Hold it," said a voice.

Seamus turned to find a young man standing at the end of the hall.

"Owen?" he asked.

"Who the hell are you?" asked the kid.

Seamus held up a hand. "I'm an old friend of your aunt's."

A bird flew between them, and Owen glanced into the chaos of the kitchen.

Tiger Lily came rushing back inside to grab the other baby bobcat. This one scratched her arm before she managed to subdue it, and she howled.

Darla scooted out of her way as she ran it out to the porch. Seamus saw Owen's attention lock on her.

"That's the sloth lady," he said, pointing.

Seamus nodded. "We've come to gather him, son."

Owen's confused expression shifted into what looked like rage.

Seamus frowned.

Shite.

He knew that look. He'd made it a few times himself.

Owen pointed at him. "You're not taking anything, old man."

"Easy, son," said Seamus.

The wiry young man puffed his chest, his posture tense, his face locked in a sneer.

Seamus had seen it all before.

Here we go.

Owen lunged. Seamus sidestepped the charge. He used Owen's momentum against him, flinging him over a side table and onto the sofa. The boy didn't clear the furniture cleanly, and a leg snapped off the table as his lower half kicked it.

Seamus held up his hand. "Now, boy, there's no reason we need to—"

The kid was up in an instant—his face flushed with anger and embarrassment.

Seamus shook his head.

Damn kids.

He'd almost forgotten how hard it was to keep a young one down.

He didn't want to hurt Tiger Lily's nephew or her furniture, but he wasn't sure how to keep the boy down without a show of brute strength.

He faked a step forward as a distraction and then kicked a chunk of the broken table against Owen's legs.

It kept the boy from advancing for a moment.

"Listen to me, boyo. I don't want to fight you. Just give me—"

With a roar, Owen tossed the broken table out of the way and squared up.

Seamus rolled his eyes.

"Oh, come on..."

Owen leaped forward, all fists and headbobbing. Seamus found his opening and slapped him hard across the face, hoping one good openhanded smack would bring him to his senses.

As the boy's head snapped to the right, Seamus gave him a shove to clear some room between them. The boy stumbled until his head smacked into the corner of the room as if he'd been trying to plant himself in the wall. He dropped a hand to the floor to catch himself and stood back up with a scream of frustration.

Seamus grimaced. Making a fool of the young man was no way to calm him. His plan wasn't working in the least. Everything he did to avoid hurting the kid made him more determined to fight.

Owen ran at him again and swung. Seamus blocked the punch and gave him a short rabbit punch to the gut. The wind burst from Owen's lungs as he dropped to his hands and knees. Seamus moved quickly, striding over to him and pressing a knee into his back, pinning him to the ground.

He heard the sound of a shotgun blast and turned to find Tiger Lily in the kitchen. Plaster rained around her.

She'd blasted her own ceiling.

Everyone froze.

Lily lowered her weapon at Seamus and Owen as finches circled her head. She looked like a cartoon character who'd bonked her head.

"Cut it out!" she roared.

"He's trying to take your sloth," said Owen from his position on the ground beneath Seamus's knee.

Tiger Lily shook her head.

"It's not my peacock or my lemurs or my *sloth*. It's his. It's theirs," she said, flicking her head back to motion to Darla and Mariska, standing behind her. "You're going to end up killing one of my finches. Cut it out right now."

He scowled. "You're the one shooting—"

"Owen, I swear—"

"Fine," he grumbled as Seamus helped him up.

Once Owen was on his feet, Seamus held up his hands and stepped back.

"I've got no quarrel with the boy," he said.

"Where's the sloth?" asked Darla.

"Her husband's the sheriff," added Mariska.

Seamus glared at them.

"They're going to call the cops on me," said Owen, looking as if he were about to run.

"No, they're not. Not that you don't deserve it," said Tiger Lily. "You're out of control."

Seamus locked eyes with the boy.

"No one is getting the cops involved. We're going to take the sloth and leave."

Owen's shoulders slumped.

"Fine. It's stupid, anyway. It doesn't even *move*."

"Where is it?"

He motioned down the hall. "It's in my room."

Seamus strode down the hall and glanced into two rooms before finding the one with a sloth. Without a tree to hang from, the creature had balled up on an old torn beanbag chair with its long arms hanging over the side.

Seamus stared at it for a bit. It didn't seem very peppy, but he didn't know if it would go on a killing rampage the moment he tried to pick it up. He didn't like the look of the long claws.

"Don't tear my guts out," he said finally.

He hung his hands one way and then another, trying to figure out the best way to lift the creature when suddenly, the thing reached up and wrapped its arms around his neck.

"Okay, that works," he mumbled, lifting it and holding it against his chest like a baby.

He walked it down the hall.

Owen had taken a seat on the sofa. The boy glared at him as he walked into the kitchen.

"Sir Sleepsalot!" exclaimed Mariska at the sight of the sloth.

"Thank you," said Darla to Tiger Lily, who still held the shotgun pointed at the floor.

She nodded.

Mariska and Darla left, and Seamus followed to the threshold before turning.

"Can we go out the front?" he asked.

She nodded. "I'll open the gate for you."

He winked at her.

"Thank you for your help, lass."

She nodded.

"See you in another twenty."

CHAPTER THIRTY-ONE

Darla heard a loud pounding as they walked around Tiger Lily's house to take the proper path back out to the road.

"Open up! *Sheriff*!" called a gruff voice.

Darla stopped and looked at Mariska.

"Crap. It's *Frank.*"

Mariska giggled. "You're dead."

Walking behind them with the sloth in his arms, Seamus had to stop to keep from running into them.

"What are you doing?" he asked.

"Frank's here."

The door pounding started again.

"Open the door! *Sheriff*!"

"What should I do?" hissed Darla.

"You should tell him you're here and okay before he busts in there with a gun," said Seamus, but he didn't wait for her to do it.

"Frank!" he called, maneuvering around the ladies.

Darla bit her lip.

"Should we run?"

Mariska shook her head. "No. We're caught. And you couldn't pay me to run out into that crazy place again."

Darla's shoulders slumped. She'd come so far only to be captured in the end.

The ladies followed behind Seamus.

Frank had turned to scowl at the Irishman.

"*Seamus*—what the hell is on you?"

"A sloth. Want to know why? Talk to your wife."

Darla rounded the corner.

"Oh, hi, Frank. What brings you here?" she asked, smiling.

Frank's frown deepened.

The front door opened, and Tiger Lily stepped out.

"What's going on out here?"

Frank took his hand off his gun.

"Lily?"

She nodded. "Yes. What do you want?"

"Your mother said I might find you here. I thought I heard a shotgun," he said.

Lily sniffed. "Accidental discharge."

"You have a license for that gun?"

"Of course."

"Let me see it."

Lily sighed.

"You'll never take me alive!" Darla heard Owen scream inside.

Frank stiffened and returned his hand to his gun, but Lily flashed him her palms.

"Easy. He's an idiot. Ignore him. He's harmless," she said. "You'll take him. You'll take him and keep him for a few days."

"What for?" asked Frank.

Lily nodded at the sloth in Seamus's arms.

"That. A peacock. Some lemurs. A pot-bellied pig."

"A pig?" Frank hung his thumbs in his belt. "I didn't know about that one—"

"Owen, get your butt over here, or I swear they'll never find your body," screamed Tiger Lily.

She shook her head at Frank to be sure he knew she was kidding.

Darla wasn't sure if she was kidding.

Owen walked up beside his aunt, looking sullen.

"I made a deal with the sheriff. You return all the animals, and he won't take you before a judge."

"What animals?" asked Owen.

Lily scowled. "Don't *even*."

Frank squinted at Lily. "I don't remember saying—"

Lily continued. "The sheriff is going to keep you in the local jail for a night or two. Go make yourself up an overnight bag."

"But—"

"*Go.*"

The boy shuffled off.

Frank frowned.

"We didn't make any deal."

Lily seemed amused. "No? Sounds good, though, right? You get all the animals back to their rightful owners, and I get a couple of days' peace to plan how to send that kid back to my sister."

Frank huffed. "I'm not a babysitting service."

"You want the animals? They're out on my property. You want to catch them yourself?"

Frank chewed his lip for a second.

"You've got a point there. Fine. I think this'll work."

Lily nodded. "I thought so. I'll be back with the idiot in a second."

"*Don't forget to bring me that gun license*," Frank called after her.

Darla stepped up to her husband and gave him a light punch in the arm. She wanted to talk to him while things were looking up.

"See? Look at that. We got the sloth. You solved your case. This worked out for everyone."

Frank glowered at her.

"We'll talk later."

Darla frowned.

The boy arrived with a backpack hung over his arm and pointed at Seamus.

"He hit me," he said.

Frank looked at Seamus, and the Irishman shook his head.

"Nah. The boy's touched, Frank, but not by me."

He adjusted the sloth clinging to his chest and walked on.

CHAPTER THIRTY-TWO

Mildred bent in front of the tiki cabin's door as Hayley watched from the steps, glancing back and forth from her mother to Charlotte and Declan.

"Should I kill them?" she asked as Mildred fiddled with the key.

"Not yet. There might be one more clue inside."

She opened the door and then took a step back.

"Oh my," she said, nearly slipping down the stairs. She caught the porch railing in time to right herself.

A short, chubby man in a casual tan suit walked out with his hands over his head.

"Don't shoot me," he said.

Hayley backed up to keep Charlotte, Declan, and the little man in pistol range.

"Who are you?" she asked.

"I'm Mr. Flummox's lawyer, Greg Sandal," he said, lowering his arms.

"What are you doing here?"

"Did we win?" asked Mildred.

He shook his head. "I don't know."

Hayley stomped her foot.

"What do you mean you don't *know*?"

He offered her a little shrug. "I don't know. I'm just here to change the will to the winner."

"There's no safe? No cash?"

He shook his head.

"Well, we're the winners," said Mildred, lifting her chin. "Change the name to us."

"No, you're not," he said, wincing as if he were about to be slapped for speaking.

Hayley turned her gun on him, and he stepped back into the doorway.

"Don't shoot me," he said, his voice quaking. "I mean, you *might* be the winner. I have to wait for Xander."

As the first rays of morning sun rose over the hedge, Charlotte thought she saw Hayley pale.

"Think we should run now?" whispered Declan.

Charlotte bit her lip. She agreed running while Hayley was distracted seemed like the smart thing to do, but if they miscalculated, they could end up dead, and she was a little worried about poor Mr. Sandal's chances without them.

"Let's creep a little closer to the exit every chance we get," she said, shifting a foot to the left.

Declan sidestepped in her shadow.

"What do you mean we have to wait for Xander?" screeched Hayley at the lawyer.

Mr. Sandal swallowed.

"Mr. Flummox has to approve the change and sign."

"He has to *approve*—" Hayley's eyes widened. "*Mom?*"

Mildred's hand fluttered to her chest. "He never told me that part of it. He never said anything about having to sign something—"

Hayley's eyes bulged. "But you helped him plan *everything*. You *said* you did."

Mildred aped her daughter's shock.

"I *did*. A lot of it, anyway. I mean, he didn't tell me any of the clues or answers, and he had a lot of lawyers involved, of course, like he told you. But I know he said the first person to arrive got the prize—"

Mr. Sandal checked his watch. "The prize involves correcting his will, which he needs to do personally, but he hasn't arrived yet." He squinted at the sun. "He was supposed to be here by sunrise."

"*No!*" screamed Hayley, looking like she was about to throw the gun at the lawyer. "Who gets his money if he doesn't change his will?"

Mr. Sandal's arms began to lower.

"Oh. I'm not at liberty to say."

Hayley held the gun with two hands, poking it at the man, whose arms shot back into the air.

"*Say*, or I will shoot you dead right now," she growled.

His forehead grew shiny. At first, Charlotte thought it pained him to break his code of ethics, but once she heard his answer, she knew it wasn't ethics violations that worried him.

It was the answer.

His answer wasn't the one Hayley wanted to hear, and *she* had a gun.

"The parrots," he peeped.

"*What?*"

"His *parrots*. He has a whole collection in the aviary at the back of the property. Past the tennis courts. All his money goes to them for care, feeding, etc."

Hayley's screech hit a new high.

"*Parrots*? All his money goes to *parrots*?"

Mr. Sandal pushed his glasses up his sweaty nose as the sun started the world around them steaming.

"Largely. There's also, um, a toucan and, er, a monkey..."

He faded to silence as Hayley gawped at him.

The sound of sirens filled the air.

"The *twins* sent the cops," said Charlotte.

Hayley swung the gun at them as if she'd remembered they were there.

"Mom, we have to go," she said.

Mildred stood leaning against the porch railing. Her face had grown pale. Her skin shined with sweat.

"I can't run," she said.

Hayley stepped toward her, the gun still trained on Charlotte and Declan. It seemed she'd decided Mr. Sandal wasn't a threat.

Charlotte agreed with her assessment. The man was slowly melting into the shade of the cabin, arms still above his head.

"Mom. Come *on*," urged Hayley.

Mildred shook her head and lifted her glittering top to glimpse at her wound.

"It's too much. I can't. That stab. I think you did it a little too deep."

Hayley shook her head.

"No, I didn't. It had to look real—"

She backed toward the break in the maze where they'd entered.

"I'll come back for you," she said to her mother.

Before she could turn and run, Charlotte saw something thrust from the bushes and rise into the air behind her. It crashed on Hayley's head with a ferocious splintering of wood. The gun fired, but the bullet shot over the cabin as she crumpled to the ground.

Della stepped out from behind the hedge, holding the remains of a splintered branch in her hand. Wisps of blonde hair surrounded her head in a tangled nest. Panting, she looked at Charlotte with wild eyes.

"Did we win?" she asked.

CHAPTER THIRTY-THREE

The police found Timmy, Xander, and Tristan's bodies in the castle with Charlotte and Declan's help. The fire had raged as it burned Hayley's furniture bonfire but sputtered once it reached the castle's stone walls.

Hayley's plan had failed on too many levels to count. She'd left witnesses, failed to burn the bodies to ash, and killed the one man capable of crowning her the winner.

"No wonder she didn't think she could win. She didn't even know that stone doesn't burn," said Declan as they watched the police cart Hayley and Mildred away.

"Actually, castles *can* burn," said Charlotte. "As the things inside burn, the heat can weaken the mortar—"

"Okay, you can turn it off now, Trivia Queen," said Declan, putting an arm around her.

She chuckled and leaned against him. "Will you be my Trivia King?"

He hugged her to him.

"Of course, m'lady. But it looks like we won't be able to live the rest of the year off the treasure from this case."

Charlotte sighed.

"Nope. No bonus. But on the upside, Hayley paid us before she murdered everyone and got arrested."

"Thank goodness I cashed that check before we came." He leaned down. "And I think the real bonus is we didn't end up dead."

She nodded. "Excellent point."

"So, who won?" asked Della, approaching them after her interview with the police.

"The parrots," said Charlotte.

Della scowled. "*Parrots?*"

"Yep. Only Xander could approve the changes to his will. Without the changes, everything goes to his parrots."

Della shook her head. "Oh, well. I got a nice pair of shoes out of it," she said, holding aloft her heels. "And I fared better than Timmy."

Charlotte and Declan winced, and Della blinked at them.

"What? Too soon?"

🍍🍍🍍

Charlotte slept like the dead for a good part of the next day. She only forced herself awake so she'd have *some* chance of sleeping that evening.

The six missed calls on her phone suggested Mariska wanted to know about her time at Xander's castle. Once she'd woken up enough to function, showered, and eaten, she headed across the street.

"There you are!" called Mariska from her lanai as she walked up the driveway.

Charlotte waved to the people she saw inside staring back at her—Mariska, Darla, and Bob—and entered through the side door, unclipping Abby's leash so she and Miss Izzy could run around and collapse like they did every time they got together.

Miss Izzy stood, happy to see her friend, but Abby only had eyes for the sloth hanging in the living room. She refused to leave the lanai, and Miss Izzy was good with that.

"Did you win?" asked Mariska.

Charlotte shook her head. "No. No one did."

"We figured. We saw on the news Xander died," said Darla. "That happened while you were there?"

"That and a lot more," said Charlotte. "He's not the only one dead."

Mariska laughed. "I know. You poor thing. I was starting to think you would sleep all day."

Charlotte chuckled. "I don't mean me. Two other contestants died, and Declan and I were up all night trying not to join them."

"So were we," said Darla. She paused as Charlotte's words processed and then cocked her head. "Wait, are you serious? Xander didn't die of old age? It wasn't an accident?"

"The news didn't say anything about anyone else dying," said Mariska.

"Not so much dying as *murdered*," said Charlotte, making herself a drink at Bob's lanai bar.

She shared the story of their evening in Xander's castle. When she finished, even Bob seemed speechless.

"I can't believe—oh, *no*—" said Darla, her attention floating past Charlotte and through the glass door.

Charlotte twisted to see Frank storming up the driveway with a yellow flyer in his hand.

"*Incoming*," said Darla.

Frank opened the lanai door, entered, and nodded hello to everyone.

"Hey, Charlotte, did you win?" he asked.

She shook her head.

"You wouldn't believe the story she has," said Darla. "Tell him, Charlotte."

"I'd love to hear it again," added Mariska.

Frank shook his head. "I'll hear it, but first, what's this?" He held up the flyer, his eyes locked on his wife.

Darla and Mariska blinked at him like they'd never seen the flyer—or him—before.

"Hm?" asked Darla.

"Were you charging people to see the sloth? Selling them wine without a license?"

Darla shook her head. "Pfft. I think that's an old flyer."

Frank pointed at the sloth hanging on the stand in the living room.

"You've had a sloth for *one day*, and most of that time, it was in the possession of the juvenile delinquent currently residing in my jail, so the window for this event was pretty slim."

Darla opened her mouth, and Frank held up a hand.

"Don't tell me it must be someone else's sloth because Mariska's address is right here."

He poked at the flyer.

"Can I get you a drink, Frank?" asked Mariska, standing.

He looked at her. "No, Mariska, I—"

"What did you two get up to yesterday?" she asked.

Frank froze, but his eyes bounced in Bob's direction.

Bob didn't flinch.

Mariska turned to her husband.

"Bob? Didn't you go on a ride along with Frank? How'd that go?"

Bob smiled and looked at Frank.

"You want me to tell them, or should I?"

Frank sighed and lowered the flyer.

"Yeah, I'll take a beer, thanks," he said.

Mariska turned to get him his drink.

Charlotte saw her wink at Bob.

She didn't know what *that* was about, but she'd be sure to ask later.

After Frank left.

Keep reading for sneak-peek first chapters of other books by Amy Vansant.

Thank you—Please review on Amazon!

ABOUT THE AUTHOR

USA Today and *Wall Street Journal* bestselling author Amy Vansant has written over 30 books, including the fun, thrilling Shee McQueen series, the rollicking, twisty Pineapple Port Mysteries, and the action-packed Kilty urban fantasies. Throw in a couple of romances and a YA fantasy for her nieces...

Amy specializes in fun, exciting reads with plenty of laughs and action. She lives in Jupiter, Florida, with her muse/husband and a goony Bordoodle named Archer.

You can follow Amy on AMAZON or BOOKBUB.

BOOKS BY AMY VANSANT

<u>Pineapple Port Mysteries</u>
Funny, clean & full of unforgettable characters
<u>Shee McQueen Mystery-Thrillers</u>
Action-packed, fun romantic mystery-thrillers
<u>Kilty Urban Fantasy/Romantic Suspense</u>
Action-packed romantic suspense/urban fantasy
<u>Slightly Romantic Comedies</u>
Classic romantic romps
<u>The Magicatory</u>
Middle-grade fantasy

SNEAK PEEK
SHEE MCQUEEN MYSTERY THRILLERS #1
THE GIRL WHO WANTS

CHAPTER ONE

Three Weeks Ago, Nashua, New Hampshire.

Shee realized her mistake the moment her feet left the grass.

He's enormous.

She'd watched him drop from the side window of the house. He landed four feet from where she stood—still, her brain refused to register the warning signs. The nose, big and lumpy as breadfruit, the forehead some beach town could use as a jetty if they buried him to his neck...

His knees bent to absorb his weight, and *her* brain thought *got you.*

Her brain couldn't be bothered with simple math: *Giant, plus Shee, equals Pain.*

Instead, she jumped to tackle him, dangling airborne as his knees straightened and the *pet the rabbit* bastard stood to his full height.

Crap.

The math added up pretty quickly after that.

Hovering like Superman mid-flight, she couldn't do much to change her disastrous trajectory. She'd *felt* like a superhero when she left the ground. Now, she felt more like a Canada goose staring into the propellers of Captain Sully's Airbus A320.

She might take down the plane, but it was going to *hurt*.

Frankenjerk turned toward her at the exact moment she plowed into him. She clamped her arms around his waist like a little girl hugging a redwood. Lurch returned the embrace, twisting her to the ground. Her back hit the dirt, and air burst from her lungs like a double shotgun blast.

Ow.

Wheezing, she punched upward, striking Beardless Hagrid in the throat.

That didn't go over well.

Grabbing her shoulder with one hand, Dickasaurus flipped her on her stomach like a sausage link, slipped his hand under her chin, and pressed his forearm against her windpipe.

The only air she'd gulped before he cut her supply stank of damp armpit. He'd tucked her skull in his arm crotch, much like the famous noggin-less horseman once held his severed head. Fireworks exploded in the dark behind her eyes.

That's when a thought occurred to her.

I haven't been home in fifteen years.

What if she died in Gigantor's armpit? Would her father even know?

Has it been that long?

Flopping like a landed fish, she forced her assailant to adjust his hold and sucked a breath as she flipped on her back. Spittle glistened on his lips, and his brow furrowed as if she'd asked him to read a paragraph of big-boy words.

His nostrils flared like the Holland Tunnel.

There's an idea.

Making a V with her fingers, Shee thrust upward, stabbing into his nose, straining to reach his tiny brain.

Goliath roared. Jerking back, he grabbed her arm to unplug her fingers from his nose socket. She whipped away her limb before he had a good grip, fearing he'd snap her bones with his Godzilla paws.

Kneeling before her, he clamped both hands over his face, cursing as blood seeped from behind his fingers.

Shee's gaze didn't linger on that mess. Her focus fell to his crotch, hovering a foot above her feet, protected by nothing but a thin pair of oversized sweatpants.

Scrambled eggs, sir?

She kicked.

He howled.

Shee scuttled back like a crab, found her feet, and snatched her gun from her side. The gun she should have pulled *before* trying to tackle the

Empire State Building.

"Move a muscle, and I'll aerate you," she said. She always liked that line.

The golem growled but remained on the ground like a good dog, cradling his family jewels.

Shee's partner in this manhunt, a local cop easier on the eyes than he was useful, rounded the corner and drew his weapon.

She smiled and holstered the gun he'd lent her...without *knowing* he'd lent it.

"Glad you could make it."

Her portion of the operation accomplished, she headed toward the car as more officers swarmed the scene.

"Shee, where are you going?" called the cop.

She stopped and turned.

"Home, I think."

His gaze dropped to her hip.

"Is that my gun?"

SNEAK PEEK
PINEAPPLE PORT MYSTERIES #1
PINEAPPLE LIES

🍍🍍🍍

CHAPTER ONE

"Whachy'all doin'?"

Charlotte jumped, her paintbrush flinging a flurry of black paint droplets across her face. She shuddered and placed her free hand over her heart.

"Darla, you scared me to death."

"Sorry, Sweetpea, your door was open."

"*Sorry*," echoed Mariska, following close on Darla's heels.

Charlotte added another stroke of black to her wall and balanced her brush on the edge of the paint can. Her knees cracked a twenty-one-gun salute as she stood. She was only twenty-six years old but had always suffered from bad knees. She didn't mind. She grew up in a fifty-five-plus retirement community, and her creaky joints provided something to complain about when the locals swapped war stories about pacemakers and hip replacements.

Nobody liked to miss out on that kind of fun.

Charlotte wiped the paint from her forehead with the back of her hand.

"Unlocked and open are not the same thing, ladies. What if I had a gentleman caller?"

Darla burst into laughter, the gold chain swinging from her hot-pink-rimmed glasses. Another pair of plastic-rimmed glasses sat perched like a baby bird on her head, tucked into a nest of champagne-blonde curls. She sobered beneath the weight of Charlotte's unamused glare.

"Did you lose your other glasses again?" asked Charlotte.

"I did. They'll turn up."

Charlotte nodded and tapped the top of her noggin. "I'm sure."

Darla's hand shot to her head.

"Oh, there you go. See? I told you they'd show up."

Mariska moved closer, nudging Darla out of the way. She threw out her arms, her breezy cotton tunic draping like aqua butterfly wings.

"Morning *hug*," she demanded.

Charlotte rolled her eyes and relented. Mariska wrapped her in a bear hug, and she sank into the woman's snuggly, Polish grandmother's body. It was like sitting on a favorite old sofa, rife with missing springs...and then being eaten by it.

"Okay. Can't breathe," said Charlotte.

"I'm wearing the top you bought me for Christmas," Mariska mumbled in Charlotte's ear as she rocked her back and forth.

"I saw that."

"It's very comfortable."

"This *isn't*. I can't breathe. Did I mention that? We're good. Okay..."

Mariska released Charlotte and stepped back, her face flush with satisfaction. She turned and looked at the wall, scratching her cheek with flowered, enameled nails as she studied Charlotte's painting project.

"What are you doing? Painting your wall black? Are you depressed?"

Charlotte sighed. Darla and Mariska were inseparable; if one wasn't offering an opinion, the other was picking up the slack.

"You're not turning into one of those dopey Goth kids now, are you?" asked Darla.

"*No*, it has nothing to do with my mood. It's chalkboard paint. I'm making this strip of the wall into a giant chalkboard."

"Why?" Darla asked, her thick, Kentucky accent adding syllables to places the word *why* never considered having them. Her mouth twisted, and her brow lowered. Charlotte couldn't tell if she disapproved, was confused, or had suffered a sharp gas pain. Not one guess was more likely than any other.

"Because I think I figured out my problem," she said.

Darla cackled. "Oh, this oughta be good. You have any coffee left?"

"In the kitchen."

Darla and Mariska lined up and waddled toward the kitchen like baby ducks following their mama. Mariska inspected several mugs in the cabinet above the coffee machine and, finding one, put it aside. She handed Darla another. Mariska's mug of choice was the one she'd given Charlotte after her trip to Colorado's Pikes Peak. She'd bought the mug for herself, but after Charlotte laughed and explained the double entendre of the slogan emblazoned on the side, *I Got High on Pikes Peak*, she'd thrust it at her, horrified.

Nevertheless, Mariska remained proud of her fourteen thousand-foot spiraling drive to the peak, so she clandestinely drank from the offending mug whenever she visited.

Charlotte watched as she read the side of the mug, expelled a deep sigh, and poured her coffee. That heartbreaking look was why she hadn't broached the subject of Mariska's *I Got Baked in Florida* t-shirt.

The open-plan home allowed the two older women to watch Charlotte as she returned to painting the wall between her pantry and living area.

"So, are you pregnant?" Darla asked. "And after this, you're painting the nursery?"

"Ah, no. That's not even funny."

"You're the youngest woman in Pineapple Port. You're our only hope for a baby. How can you toss aside the hopes and dreams of three hundred enthusiastic, if rickety, babysitters?"

"I don't think I'm the youngest woman here anymore. I think Charlie Collins is taking his wife to the prom next week."

Darla cackled and then punctuated her amusement with a grunt of disapproval.

"Stupid men," she muttered.

Charlotte whisked away the last spot of neutral cream paint with her brush, completing her wall. She turned to find Mariska staring, her thin, over-plucked eyebrows sitting high on her forehead as she awaited the answer to the mystery of the chalkboard wall.

"So you're going to keep your grocery list on the wall?" asked Mariska. "That's very clever."

"Not exactly. Lately, I've been asking myself, *what's missing from my life?*"

Darla tilted her head. "A man. *Duh*."

Charlotte glowered at her. "*Anyway*, last week, it hit me."

Darla paused, mug nearly to her lips, waiting for Charlotte to continue.

"What hit you? A chalkboard wall?" asked Mariska.

Charlotte shook her head. "No, a *purpose*. I need to figure out what I want to *be*. My life is missing *purpose*."

Darla scoffed. "Oh, is that all? I think they had that on sale at Target last weekend. I'll pick it up for you."

Charlotte busied herself, resealing the paint can as Mariska inspected her handiwork.

"You're going to take up painting? I'll take a chalkboard wall. I can write Bob messages and make lists..."

"I'll paint your wall if you like, but starting a painting business isn't my *purpose*. The wall is so I can make a to-do list."

Darla sighed. "I have a to-do list, but it only has one thing on it: *Keep breathing*."

Mariska giggled.

"I'm going to make goals and write them here," said Charlotte, gesturing like a game show hostess to best display her wall. "When I accomplish something, I get to cross it off. See? I completed one project. I know it works."

A knock on the door, and Charlotte's gaze swiveled to the front of the house. Her soft-coated Wheaten terrier, Abby, burst out of the bedroom and stood behind the door, barking.

"You forgot to open your blinds this morning," said Mariska.

"Death Squad," mumbled Darla.

The Death Squad patrolled the Pineapple Port retirement community every morning. If the six-woman troop passed a home showing no activity by ten a.m., they knocked on the door and demanded proof of life. They pretended to visit other businesses, asking if the homeowner would attend this meeting or that bake sale, but everyone knew the Squad was there to check if someone *died* overnight. Odds were slim that young Charlotte wouldn't make it through the evening, but the Squad didn't make exceptions.

Charlotte held Abby's collar and opened the door.

"Oh, hi, Charlotte," said a small woman in a purple t-shirt. "We were just—"

"I'm alive, Ginny. Have a good walk."

Charlotte closed the door. She opened her blinds and peeked out, and several Death Squad ladies waved to her as they resumed their march. Abby stood on the sofa and thrust her head through the blinds, her nub of a tail waving at them at high speed.

Mariska turned and dumped her remaining coffee into the sink, rinsed the purple mug, and with one last longing glance at the Pikes Peak logo, put it in the dishwasher. She placed her hands on her ample hips and faced Charlotte.

"Do you have chalk?"

"No." Charlotte had been annoyed at herself all morning for forgetting chalk and resented having it brought to her attention. "I forgot it."

Darla motioned to the black wall. "Well, there's your first item. *Buy chalk.* Write that down."

"With what?"

"Oh. Good point."

"Anyhow, shopping lists don't count," said Charlotte.

Darla smirked. "Oh, there are *rules*. The chalkboard has *rules*, Mariska."

Mariska pursed her lips and nodded. "Very serious."

"Well, I may not have a chalkboard, but I have a wonderful sense of purpose," said Darla putting her mug in the dishwasher.

"Oh yes? What's that?" asked Mariska.

"I've got to pick up Frank's ED pills."

She stepped over the plastic drop cloth beneath the painted wall and headed for the door.

"ED?" Charlotte blushed. "You mean for—"

"Erectile Dysfunction. Pooped Peepee. Droopy D—"

"*Got it*," said Charlotte, cutting her short.

"Fine. But these pills are special. Want to know why?"

"Not in the least."

Mariska began to laugh, and Darla grinned.

"She's horrible," Mariska whispered as she walked by Charlotte.

Darla reached into her pocketbook and pulled out a small plastic bottle. She handed it to Charlotte.

"Read the label."

Charlotte looked at the side of the pill bottle. The label held the usual array of medical information, but the date was two years past due.

"He only gets them once every two years?"

"Nope. He only got them *once*. Since then, I've been refilling the bottle with little blue sleeping pills. Any time he gets the urge, he takes one, and an hour later, he's sound asleep. When he wakes up, I tell him everything was amazing."

Charlotte's jaw dropped. "That's *terrible*."

Darla dismissed her with a wave and put the bottle back in her purse.

"Nah," she said, opening the front door. "I don't have time for that nonsense. If I'm in the mood, I give him one from the original prescription."

Darla and Mariska patted Abby on the head, waved goodbye, and stepped into the Florida sun.

Charlotte shut the door behind them and balled her drop cloth of sliced trash bags. She rinsed her brush and carried the paint can back to the shed in her backyard. Returning to the house, she surveyed her neglected yard.

Ugh.

A large pile of broken concrete sat in the corner, awaiting pickup. As part of her new *life with purpose* policy, she'd hired a company to jackhammer away part of her concrete patio to provide room for a garden. The original paved yard left little room for plants. With the cement removed, Charlotte could add *grow a garden* to her chalkboard wall.

Maybe she was supposed to be a gardener or work with the earth? She didn't feel particularly *earthy*, but who knew?

Her rocky new patch of sand didn't inspire confidence. It didn't resemble the dark, healthy soil she saw in her neighbors' more successful gardens. She huffed and returned to the shed to grab a spade and cushion for her knees.

It was cool outside, the perfect time of day to pluck the stray bits of concrete from the ground before the Florida sun became unbearable. She knew she didn't like sweating, so gardening was probably *not* her calling. Still, she was determined to give everything a chance.

She needed to clean her new patch of land, shower, and buy topsoil, plants, and chalk.

"Tomatoes, cucumbers..." Charlotte mumbled, mentally making a list of plants she needed to buy.

Or seeds? Should I buy seeds or plants?

Less chance of failure starting with mature plants, though if *they* died, that would be even *more* embarrassing.

A scratching noise caught her attention, and she looked up to find her neighbor's Cairn terrier, Katie, furiously digging beside her. Part of the fence had been broken or chewed, and stocky little Katie visited whenever life in her backyard became too tedious. Charlotte's spade struck a large stone, and she removed it, tossing it toward a pile of broken concrete as Katie dug beside her.

Dirt cascaded through the air.

"Katie, you're making a mess. If you want to help, pick up stones and move them out of the garden."

Katie stopped digging long enough to stare with her large brown eyes. At least, she thought the dog was staring at her. Katie had a lazy eye that made it difficult to tell.

"Move the rocks," Charlotte repeated, demonstrating the process with her spade. "Stop making a mess, or I'll let Abby out, and then you'll be in trouble."

Katie ignored her and resumed digging. Sand arced behind her, piling against the fence.

"You better watch it, shortstack, or the next item on the list will be to *fix the fence*."

Katie eyeballed her again, her crooked bottom teeth jutting from her mouth. She looked like a furry can opener.

"Fix your face."

Katie snorted a spray of snot and returned to digging.

Charlotte removed several bits of concrete and then shifted her kneepad a few feet closer to Katie. She saw a flash of white and felt something settle against her hand. Katie sat beside her, tail wagging, tongue lolling from the left side of her mouth.

Between the dog and her hand sat the prize Katie wanted to share.

Charlotte froze.

One word repeated, picking up pace until it was an unintelligible crescendo of nonsense in her mind.

Skull. Skull skull skullskullskullskuuuuulllll...

She blinked, sure that the object would have taken its proper shape as a rock or pile of sand when she opened her eyes.

Nope.

Hollow eye sockets stared back at her.

Hi. Nice to meet you. I'm a human skull. What's up, girl?

The lower jaw was missing. The cranium was nearly as large as Katie's and shared a similar off-white coloring.

The skull had better teeth.

Charlotte realized the forehead of this boney intruder rested against her pinky. She whipped her hand away. The skull rocked toward her as if in pursuit, and she scrambled back as it rolled in her direction, slow and relentless as a movie mummy. Katie ran after the skull and pounced on it, stopping its progress.

Charlotte put her hand on her chest.

"Thank you."

Her brain raced to process the meaning of a human head in her backyard.

It has to be a joke... maybe some weird dog toy...

Charlotte gently tapped the skull with her shovel. It didn't feel like cloth or rawhide. It made a sharp-yet-thuddy noise, just the sound she suspected a human skull might make. If she had to compare the tone to something, it would be the sound of a girl about to freak out while tapping a metal shovel on a human skull.

"Oh, Katie. What did you find?"

The question increased Katie's rate of tail wag. She yipped and returned to the hole she'd dug, retrieving the lower jaw.

"Oh no... Stop that. You sick little—"

Katie stood, human jawbone clenched in her teeth, tail wagging so furiously that Charlotte thought she might lift off like a chubby little helicopter. The terrier spun and skittered through the fence back to her yard, dragging her prize in tow. The jawbone stuck in the slats, but Katie wrestled it through and disappeared into her yard.

"Katie, *no*," said Charlotte, reaching toward the retreating dog. "Katie—I'm pretty sure that has to stay with the head."

She leaned forward and nearly touched the jawless skull before yanking away her hand.

Whose head is in my garden?

She felt her eyes growing wider—like pancake batter poured into a pan.

Hold the phone.

Heads usually come attached to bodies.

Were there more *bones*?

What was worse? Finding a whole skeleton or finding *only* a head?

Charlotte hoped the rest of the body lay nearby and then shook her head at the oddity of her wish.

She glanced around her plot of dirt and realized she might be kneeling in a *whole graveyard*. More bones. More *heads*. She scrambled to her feet and dropped her shovel.

Charlotte glanced back at her house, where her chalkboard wall waited patiently.

She *really* needed some chalk.

Made in the USA
Las Vegas, NV
19 October 2023